NO WRITE WAY TO DIE

—A NOVEL—

NO WRITE WAY TO DIE

—A NOVEL—

NEAL LIPSCHUTZ

TUCKER
DS
PRESS

No Write Way To Die © 2025 Neal Lipschutz

All Rights Reserved.
Reproduction in whole or in part without the author's permission is strictly forbidden. This is a work of fiction. Names, characters, businesses, events, and places are products of the author's imagination or are used in a fictitious manner. Any resemblance to actual events, places, businesses, or persons, living or dead, is coincidental.

Cover design by Scott Ryan
Edited by David Bushman
Book designed by Scott Ryan

Published in the USA by Tucker DS Press
Columbus, Ohio

Contact Information
Email: TuckerDSPress@gmail.com
Website: TuckerDSPress.com
Twitter: @FMPBooks
Instagram: @Fayettevillemafiapress

For Jane,
with love and gratitude.

New York Police Department Detective Delmore Kerbich had offered to meet Scott Morgan where it was most convenient for him.
"You're an important man, a busy guy. You tell me."
Scott said he would come down to see Kerbich at the precinct.
"No lawyer? I'm surprised," Kerbich said by way of greeting.
"Let's get on with it," Scott said.
They sat across a chipped Formica table. Scott signed a piece of paper acknowledging the interview was being recorded and videotaped. Given the intense media and online scrutiny the case had generated, Scott worried that at some point the footage would make its way into the public arena, to be clipped for sharing on social media and featured on any number of true-crime programs, but there was nothing he could do about it. Scott was certain the camera would capture the most unflattering image of him, making him look guilty of something.
He chuckled gruffly.
"Funny?" Kerbich asked.
"Nothing, really," Scott said. "It's just you live your life a certain way, you never expect to wind up in one of these police interrogation rooms. The whole effort to achieve, to make something of yourself. The goal, if you want to look at it from a certain angle, is to make sure you're never on the wrong side of the table in a room like this."
"That's interesting. I try to see things from the vantage of people in the chair you're in. Some of them are surprisingly comfortable. Others, well, it's their worst nightmare come true. I'm thinking you're somewhere in between. But enough philosophizing. First question: you insisted on getting a lawyer to sit through the interviews with your daughter but you walk in here without one? You worried she's mixed up in this?"

"I certainly am not," Scott said sternly. "Sarah isn't involved in any of this. The poor girl is traumatized from all she's been through."

"And being a management consultant," Kerbich said, pronouncing the title with a slice of sarcasm, "you are somehow wise to the slick ways of the police and needed to protect your daughter from them."

"That is accurate."

"But you are worldly and tough enough to take us on all by your lonesome."

"Maybe. I consulted my attorney, separate from the woman representing my daughter, to avoid any potential conflicts, before coming down here, and he assured me I can stop this interview any time and ask for counsel. In case you get too slick for me."

Scott drew out the word "slick," matching Kerbich sarcasm for sarcasm. "There's also nothing I know that would be of any use to you in this investigation."

"Where are you from? I mean before Scarsdale and your elevation to Mr. Know-It-All?"

Scott couldn't help but laugh. He found it difficult to dislike the detective. "Brooklyn. A long time ago."

"Nah," Kerbich said in mock surprise. "Would have never guessed. Another Brooklyn boy made good."

"As long as we are doing origin stories, how does someone who gets named for a writer wind up as a cop? I had to do research, to find out more about Delmore Schwartz, to be honest. I was pretty intrigued by your first name."

"My father was an English professor at Queens College, my alma mater. He was a disappointed writer himself and despaired about the lack of interest most of his students showed toward literature. My brother is named Homer."

"You're kidding."

"Not at all."

"And this led you to police work?"

"I'm sure you don't have time for my life story, busy as you are."

"Fair point. But I have to say, in preparation for this, I read some of Delmore Schwartz's early short stories. It's not my thing, fiction, or poetry, but like I said, I was intrigued. Sometimes I think I would have liked to have been part of a much earlier generation. But you can't pick the era you're born into, right?"

"*One of life's many injustices,*" Kerbich said. "*There's a question I need to ask you.*"

"*Which is?*"

"*You had motive and you had access.*"

"*And?*" Scott said, though he knew exactly what was coming next.

"*Did you commit the murder, Scott?*"

– 1 –

It all began mundanely enough.
Scott's daughter, Sarah, was bringing a guest to her childhood home for dinner. It was the first time Scott and his wife, Meredith, would be meeting him. For weeks, he'd heard snatches of conversations about it. That was more than he could say about any number of earlier wife-daughter conspiracies, when he was kept completely in the dark. Meredith always knew way more about their daughter's life than he did. That seemed natural enough. Mothers and daughters, etc., etc. But their planning around this event was next level.

The three members of the Morgan family sat down in the spacious but rarely used living room. The facts presented to Scott Morgan were these: the approaching Saturday, Sarah would bring a man to join them for dinner in the family home, the home where she'd grown up, the somewhat drafty, 1950-built colonial in Scarsdale, a ritzy northern suburb of New York City. Worth about $2.7 million, maybe $3 million if the housing market stayed tight, Scott figured. A solid investment. Sarah and the man would travel together by train from the city. Scott would pick them up at the station. It was important, their daughter said, Meredith nodding, that the man not be referred to as Sarah's boyfriend.

"It's such a silly word," Meredith said. "What does it mean? It could mean anything."

It was Sarah's turn to nod. "We are grown-ups. We don't use it. We know what we are to each other."

"Okay, I've got it, 'boyfriend' is out," Scott said. "So, who is he?"

The first words out of Sarah's mouth, before she even stated his name, was that he was a writer, a novelist. He'd taught at the retreat she'd attended the prior summer. His name: Ed Blaus.

"Blaus," Scott repeated, "don't think I've heard of him. Though I don't get into fiction much."

Sarah said Ed Blaus was tremendously gifted. She mentioned the title for which he was best known. It sounded vaguely familiar to Scott, like something he might have heard about earlier in life, perhaps in the years right after college.

"When did that come out?" he asked.

Long silence. Then Sarah quietly mentioned a year three decades back.

"How old is Blaus?"

Meredith stared at him, angrily. Why? Was this not a basic question about the nonboyfriend their daughter was bringing home for dinner? Sarah uttered a number: fifty-five.

"Well," Scott said, "that clears that up. About not using 'boyfriend,' I mean. Any word connected to boy would be entirely inaccurate."

"Ha ha," his wife said, scowling.

"Dad," his daughter scolded.

Scott felt anger building inside him, gathering force at his center, just above his stomach. The guy was old enough to be her father. Well, that was obvious. Three years younger than Scott. He thought any man that age who'd take up with a twenty-eight-year-old had to be lecherous, egotistical, clearly devoid of redeeming qualities. He fought hard not to show the turmoil now rising up near his throat, urging him to speak. To protect his daughter.

"Age isn't important," Sarah said. "It's about what two people have in common."

"How can you have things in common if all his references are a generation behind yours?" Scott asked.

Meredith moved her hand up and down, signaling for him to tone it down.

Sarah said she needed to get back to Manhattan. Meredith volunteered to drive her to the train station. When Scott and his wife were alone in the house, he asked her to join him in the dark-paneled den, his office and sanctuary.

"Let me get one thing straight," he said. "This guy, Blaus, he is her boyfriend, right? I mean in the traditional way the term is used. I mean that's their relationship. Umm, it's romantic, and physical, right?"

His wife shifted her thin shoulders under the blue, oversized button-down shirt she wore.

"Yes, that's right. No need to be graphic."

He thought he'd done everything imaginable not to be graphic.

"Did it start at that writing program?"

"Yes and no. They met there, of course. He was one of the instructors. They started dating after she graduated. Last fall, when they were both back in New York."

"Too bad," Scott said. "I was thinking maybe charges could be brought against him. I believe that sort of thing is forbidden now, teachers dating students. Maybe not illegal, but wrong. And don't call it graduation. It's not a real school."

"She got a certificate in creative writing."

"We already sent her to a real school. An extremely expensive one. A recognized college. This was one month and a row of cabins. Also expensive, especially considering the returns."

"That's not fair. She's had a few of her poems published since."

"On internet sites no one looks at, for which she doesn't get paid."

"Pardon us if poetry isn't as lucrative as management consulting."

"Pardon us if all I've done is make something of myself and provide pretty damn well for this family so you can carry on as you like and Sarah can dally around in her writing program and in her expensive apartment in the city."

Meredith walked out of the den. He returned to half-heartedly watching a college football game with the sound off. A few minutes later he opened his laptop on the low-rise coffee table in front of him. He should move to his desk. Stooping over the laptop from his perch on the edge of the couch made his shoulders ache. But he did not move. It didn't take much looking to discover a number of internet pages filled with links to information about Edgar (Ed) Blaus, American author and writing instructor. Scott lost track of the time as he wandered from one site to another, starting with Blaus's Wikipedia page. He read news articles about Blaus through the years and even spent a few minutes watching parts of Blaus's lectures to aspiring writers, which had been preserved on YouTube. Scott's early impression was this: Blaus's résumé might be long as far as teaching credits, but his overarching literary achievement boiled down to a well-received debut novel published when Blaus was in his midtwenties. Clearly, his lovestruck daughter saw something very different in her man. Scott had to credit Blaus with one thing: he looked good for fifty-five. Blaus had all his hair and didn't try to hide the gray creeping up the sides. He was trim and in some photos looked a decade younger than he was. Scott didn't approve of the way Blaus dressed, Converse high-tops and tight jeans, as shown in one photo. Trying too hard to look hip. It was undignified. In more recent photos, Blaus sported a short haircut. In an image from a few years earlier, Blaus's hair was pulled tight over his forehead, the remainder squeezed into a ponytail that slid down to his neck. Maybe it was the ample hair that bothered him the most. Scott didn't have much left of his own.

Next to the laptop, Scott placed a yellow legal pad, and with a blue pen he created small circles and filled them with ink hard enough so that the impressions appeared three pages down. Next to each bullet point he jotted some discovered fact about Blaus. It was a method he used at work during meetings to collect his thoughts, to emphasize for himself the key points of some complex financial engineering plan or a multistep business strategy. Younger colleagues kidded him for his continued employment of pen and paper. That's what your laptop is for, they said. There are apps on your phone specifically for taking notes, they said. He persisted in doing it the way he always did. Something about physically writing things down fixed them in your mind the way tapping a few keystrokes did not.

He went on to a second page. Then he underlined the highlights of the highlights. Blaus's first novel was a hit. Not a blockbuster, but more than commercially respectable for a literary tome by an unknown writer. It was almost universally well reviewed, and those reviews spread Ed Blaus's name through New York's literary and journalism establishments. Overnight, he became a hot commodity. The reviews were followed in short order by news features and question-and-answer interviews that spread Blaus's name and reputation to an audience well beyond the group of serious readers who would actually buy the book. The novel was called *A View from Below*, and although it didn't feature a traditionally linear story, it essentially told of a friendship turned love affair between two young people growing up in fractured, unhappy families. The young woman struggles and ultimately can't overcome her obstacles. She dies by suicide. The young man, overwhelmed by his inability to help her, continues on, a wounded artist in development, whose first subject is the woman he lost and whom he now believes he didn't do enough to save. The early scenes take place in a surreal version of Brooklyn. By the end, the young man, hands in pockets, poorly dressed for the harsh winter weather, wanders the streets of the Lower East Side of Manhattan, alive but tortured, uncertain of everything he once believed. The male protagonist, Scott assumed, was a stand-in for Blaus. Brooklyn was something he didn't expect.

That's where Scott grew up. Well, it's a big place. Lots of people were from Brooklyn. After all, the population was close to three million. It was teeming with people, its ethnic demographics seemingly undergoing an upheaval with each passing generation. Scott came upon a particularly in-depth profile of Blaus in a now-defunct magazine. It was written about a year after Blaus's debut novel was published. Its theme was what will Blaus do next? How does he top his strong start? Will he move on to new themes in his second novel? Sophomore jinx, anyone? The magazine writer got Blaus to take the subway with him back to where Blaus grew up in Brooklyn. Blaus was disdainful of reminisce. He told the magazine he wasn't going to romanticize his past.

"You know, it was what it was," Blaus was quoted as saying. "It was a polyglot place. The fathers of my friends drove their own cabs or worked as union printers or managed the meat department in supermarkets. The mothers raised us, and some had part-time jobs at clothes shops or behind the counters at stationery stores. A few had full-time careers. The fathers came home tired and didn't want to hear about anything. It was not inspiring. It was the antithesis of a creative life. You needed to travel over only one bridge to get to Manhattan, but it seemed a lot further away than that. Everyone called Manhattan the city, like it was Oz. Of course, we lived in New York City, too, but, you know, Manhattan was a place apart." There was a picture of Blaus in an oversized green army jacket. He had long, dark hair and a scraggly beard and stood glumly outside a squat, undistinguished apartment building. The caption noted this was the Brooklyn home of the novelist when he was growing up, naming the street.

"Holy shit," Scott called out loud. "Holy, holy shit." Brooklyn wasn't such a big place after all. Not as far as he and Ed Blaus were concerned. Scott grew up just a few blocks away, in a similar lackluster apartment house. Blaus, Blaus, why wasn't the name familiar? They should have gone to the same schools, from grade school up through high school. Sure, Blaus was three years younger, but still. Did Blaus have older siblings? The article made mention of a brother, but just a mention. There were no other family references except that the writer noted Blaus's parents were deceased.

– 2 –

"You've got a really lovely home," Ed Blaus said, waving his hand to indicate the wide scope of the living room where they sat with drinks. "Really outstanding. A lot of thought went into the design, obviously. A larger than usual number of windows. Probably makes this a quite sunny spot for a time each day."

"Most of the afternoon," Meredith Morgan replied.

"Unusual for the time it was built, I am guessing. They were more interested in cookie cutters right after the war."

"Yes," Meredith said. "Agreed. This block and the surrounding area had some older houses already established, so they couldn't create a subdivision with all the houses going up at once. That avoided the sameness. I think the original owners were quite cultured, particular people."

She looked at her husband for affirmation. Scott grunted agreement.

"You have no idea how jealous a large, beautiful home like this makes us city dwellers, we in our cramped, noisy spaces."

The two women laughed. Scott grunted again.

At dinner, Ed Blaus continued the flow of compliments, aimed mainly at Meredith. The salmon and broccoli were amazing. How did she prepare the glaze? Scott could tell from the way she tilted her head to one side and stretched her neck that Meredith was enjoying Ed's words. This was her flirtatious pose. Why was Ed paying so much attention to Meredith? She was at least the appropriate age for him, and, smarmy or not, he was a handsome man. And a writer. Scott watched all this: Blaus addressing his wife, putting his arm around Scott's daughter. He was within and without: there, of course, but also at a distance, as if he was observing the action unfold on a screen.

"Okay, we've got to get back before the trains stop running," Sarah announced soon after Meredith served bakery-bought cookies for dessert.

"I'll drive you," Meredith said.

When she returned, Scott studied her face, which was slightly flushed, looking for clues.

"What?" she said.

"Nothing."

"Well, I thought he was very nice."

Scott decided not to reply.

***

It was a Sunday in July. The car's air-conditioning was on full blast. There was a lot of traffic as they rolled into New York City. *At least it's Sunday*, he thought. *Maybe there will be a parking spot somewhere in the West Village. Why didn't someone build a few more parking garages down there?* They found a spot on the street a half dozen blocks from the restaurant where they were meeting Sarah. They walked past small apartment buildings. The stench of garbage festering in the heat emanated from the banged-up metal cans. He did not like being dragged into Manhattan on a weekend. He had to come into the city every weekday for work when he wasn't traveling. Outside of that, he preferred to stay in Scarsdale. It's just brunch, his wife had said. We'll be back early. By the time they got to the restaurant, Scott was covered in perspiration.

The eggs, treated variously according to the diners' separate tastes, had been delivered to the table when Meredith moved her eyes at her daughter in a way that meant get on with it.

"I've got some news," Sarah said, not fully looking up from her plate.

"Promotion at work?" her father asked.

"No, though work is fine," she said. "Ed and I are going to move in together."

Scott put down his fork.

"You think that's a good idea?"

"Obviously."

"I mean, among other things, there's the huge difference in your ages. You are young, you have a lifetime ahead of you. He's used his up."

Sarah looked at her mother. "Do you two think you're all used up? Done? Ed's not used up either."

"How about children?" Scott asked. His voice grew louder. "What if he has a stroke?"

"Scott," Meredith interrupted.

"You'll wind up playing nursemaid." Now he could be clearly heard by strangers at nearby tables.

Sarah half rose in her seat but settled back into it. "If that's the reaction, let's end the discussion right now and move on to something else. You've been notified."

In the car, Scott said to his wife, "How long have you known about this?"

"It doesn't matter."

"Where is his place anyway? Sarah's new address. I guess she can rent her's out."

"She's not going anywhere. He's moving in with her."

"What!" Their car jumped, nearly hitting a passing vehicle in the left lane.

"Scott!" Meredith bellowed. "Control yourself. You're going to get us killed."

"Of all the gold-bricking, gold-digging phonies. He doesn't care about her. She's just a meal ticket."

"You have no idea."

"And you do?"

They drove the rest of the way in silence.

− 3 −

Scott devoted most of his time—when not working or sleeping—to finding out more about Ed Blaus. Sarah had had romantic relationships before, but none reached the stage of cohabitation. Here she was taking this big step with a has-been writer Scott was sure had nefarious motives. Sarah owned a one-bedroom apartment in a building in Chelsea, one she could never come near affording on her salary. She owned it thanks to Scott. His foresight. His investing knowledge. His money. During a temporary downturn in New York real estate when Sarah was a senior in college, Scott bought the place in Sarah's name. It seemed, even then, a fortune for an 850-square-foot apartment on Seventh Avenue. Scott held his nose and put in the winning bid, sure in his conviction that as crazy as apartment prices were then, they'd only go higher. He was right about that.

After school, Sarah got an entry-level job at a small nonfiction book publisher. She then switched to a literary agency and now was a full-fledged agent, which, as best Scott could determine, was a loosely defined title. Anyone could declare herself a literary agent. It all depended on which editors you could sell to and the commercial power and talent of the writers you represented. From what Scott could tell, Sarah led with her heart rather than her head when taking on newcomers or peddling the prose of her clients. Nobody on her list was going to author a bestseller. Meanwhile, she harbored ambitions for her own poetry. That's what led her to the Blaus-instructed educational adventure.

Once Scott squeezed all he thought there was to squeeze out of basic Google searches and follow-ups, he believed he had a decent life summary for Ed Blaus. After the critical success of his first novel, *A View from Below*, Blaus was for a time supercool. *The New York Times* wrote a short piece on how he spent his Sundays; he wrote a couple of reviews of others' work and took an adjunct spin teaching creative writing at Columbia University. Over the next couple years, Blaus published a short story in *The Atlantic* and one in *The New Yorker*. The commentary on them (Scott didn't bother to actually read the stories) was not broadly positive. Blaus was given credit for writing stories far different from his hit coming-of-age novel, for stretching his horizons rather than repeating himself. One of the stories was about two soldiers drafted to fight in the Vietnam War. The other imagined an idealistic high school teacher turned cynic when faced with the tough realities of his chosen field. The consensus view was Blaus didn't have the same feel for the new material that he did for the love story gone wrong at the center of his smash debut novel. After those stories, Blaus's literary citations trailed off. *Vanity Fair* did a whatever-happened-to-Ed Blaus story roughly three years after his novel was published. *Publishers Weekly* focused its contemporaneous reporting on the delays to Blaus's long-awaited second novel. In its final article on that subject, the magazine noted the book was nearly four years beyond the deadline set by his publishers. The second novel, according to Scott's reading, was eventually published.

Blaus's short marriage to an aspiring actress had ended in divorce. Soon after, he found himself the focus of the tabloids, which decided the recently cool literary firebrand deserved a new title. Front-page headlines screamed that he was a "Deadbeat Dad," refusing to acknowledge fatherhood of a boy born to a woman who'd been his girlfriend. From trendy literary cat to sensationalist fodder. Scott shook his head. It seemed like such a familiar story, but usually involving young Hollywood types or musicians who couldn't handle the rush of fame and money. But a novelist from Brooklyn? Well, maybe that was the New York equivalent of a big-screen star. The media clearly decided the Blaus paternity suit story had legs, and covered it with large photos of the purported father and the undisputed mother caught separately coming and going from the courthouse. Blaus would cover his face or rush into cabs trying to avoid the cameras. In court, scientifically sound evidence was presented. The judge made things official. Blaus was the father and child support payments were in order. Blaus, through a spokesman, finally conceded paternity and said he would strive to be a good parent. Amid all this, Blaus's much delayed second novel appeared, and bombed—all six hundred pages of it. The period of time taken to create it was certainly long enough to justify the length, but at least one critic decried the wastefulness of all that paper. An article noted the meager sales and quoted publishing gurus opining that Blaus would have trouble securing a significant advance against a third book. Scott read this part of the research with grim satisfaction. He saw the path that had led Ed Blaus from wunderkind to instructor at the literary getaway where he met Sarah.

Intrigued as Scott was to find Blaus had a son (did Sarah know?) who'd be in his early twenties now, he remained convinced there was a darkness to Ed Blaus that the public record—despite the glee with which some journalists had marked his downfall—had yet to reveal. In business, he learned early to step back when on assignment and to have an internal conversation. Was he looking at the situation as rationally and objectively as humanly possible? Was there some subjective factor or factors that were pushing him toward a suboptimal decision? That long-established ability to test himself, to separate emotion and psychological baggage from empirical markers, was, Scott believed, key to his climb from a modest upbringing to the middle-aged, affluent, respected person he now was. He needed to exercise the same disinterested rigor in the Ed Blaus project, but it was much harder. This time the project was rooted in emotion: Scott's urge to protect Sarah from getting hurt, emotionally as well as financially. Why was he so sure Ed Blaus was no good? There was the age difference between Blaus and Sarah, his clear financial need, his denial of responsibility for his own child. But Scott believed deep within himself there was something more. What it was he had no idea. He was skeptical of hunches, of knowing without really knowing. The only way to find out and quiet the gnawing in his gut was to come up with hard evidence. If it existed. Too bad he couldn't hire a management consultant the way his firm's clients did when they found themselves in a jam, knowing Scott and his colleagues wouldn't be influenced, as the clients themselves were, by ego and emotional encumbrance. The consultants could be pragmatic. In this instance, Scott would have to be both client and adviser.

Was he simply a concerned father? That's what he'd like to think. Or was something else lurking? Something less admirable. Might Scott be jealous of Ed Blaus? Might envy be the real reason he wanted Blaus gone from Sarah's life? Was he frightened that Blaus would nudge Sarah even further away from him? Blaus had written an acclaimed novel, one that still popped up on syllabi in college modern literature courses. Blaus had achieved a level of fame that Scott—despite his pride in his own accomplishments—knew he couldn't match. Ed Blaus was free from the travails of the routine workaday world; he was fit and handsome and able to attract the adulation of women more than twenty years his junior. Whatever. Factor in envy. Okay. Did that override the objective negatives about Blaus as a partner for Sarah? No, it did not. The bottom line was Scott was Sarah's father, and it was his job to keep her safe. Time to put the focus back on Blaus.

After achieving literary hero status with his first novel, Blaus hadn't achieved much. Scott knew his daughter wouldn't agree. Art was not a competition, she'd say. A successful novel didn't have to be topped and topped again. Sarah remained committed to quality literature for its own sake. That's what prompted her to keep working at improving her own poetry. There had to be something that would convince her otherwise. It was up to Scott to find it. He realized everything he'd read about Blaus dated from after the publication of *A View from Below*. That was natural enough. Before that, Blaus was nobody. There'd been that one long article that took Blaus back to the neighborhood of their youth, tipping Scott off to their closely shared backgrounds. If he had a decent sense of the post-success Blaus, he had almost none about what preceded it. That was an area that needed scrutiny. The time when they were both young, before Ed Blaus became Ed Blaus the writer. Scott still wondered why he didn't recognize the Blaus name from the old neighborhood. To satiate that curiosity, he would have to go back to that time and those people, something he'd assiduously avoided doing almost his entire adult life.

— 4 —

One evening, several weeks after they'd met Sarah in Manhattan for brunch, Scott said "What the hell" out loud to his empty study. He rubbed his hands together and opened his laptop. For the first time in a long while, he signed on to Facebook. Under the general theory that the less publicly known about you the better, Scott had provided minimal information about himself for his Facebook profile. He'd never added a photo, so he was a faceless blob. He'd ignored a number of invitations to join Brooklyn-based groups. Now he looked at them again, some closely for the first time. He saw a Facebook group composed of people who attended his high school. He divulged a few more facts about himself, including his graduation year, and he was welcomed into the group. He looked through the postings that became available with his membership.

Unexpectedly, Scott enjoyed rifling through the posts. Most of them were written by retirees, which made sense; they had more time on their hands and probably a stronger need to fight loneliness and remember their youth. One post was from Etta Friedhof, class of 1962, who provided a funereal catchup about a few of her contemporaries who she'd come to learn had died during the previous two years. She wrote a few words about each of them. "Eric Sconts, 76 years old, I think he was a dentist. When we were kids, his family lived in the building next to mine. We played tag when we were in grade school. Carey Dolenz, 78. She lost her son in the south tower of the World Trade Center on 9/11." And so on.

About a week after joining, Scott got a notification that he'd been tagged in a post. It turned out to be a welcome to new members from the volunteer, John Biggio, who administered the site (remember the group's rules, Biggio cautioned: no politics, no arguments). Within days of that notice, Scott received five generic-sounding direct messages from people saying they were glad he'd joined. Scott figured this was the website's welcome wagon. A couple of others claimed to know him from high school, but their names were not familiar, and when he consulted his yearbook, they weren't included among the rows of headshots of the seniors. *Maybe they think I'm Freddie*, he thought, his younger brother, who'd died soon after his class graduated. That realization made him want to leave the site.

Then he received a direct message from Mickey Genz.

"Goddamn it. Scott Morgan. Just about the last person I'd expect to show up on the high school Facebook page. You dying or something? Getting sentimental after all these years about the old neighborhood?"

Scott groaned as he read. This was the downside. Having to deal with jerks he thought he'd put permanently in his rearview mirror. Another beat and Scott changed his mind. Wasn't Mickey Genz exactly the sort of person he needed to hear from, the talkative bully who traveled along with Scott from kindergarten until they marched across the scuffed wood flooring of the auditorium stage and were handed their high school diplomas? God, he wanted absolutely nothing more to do with Mickey Genz. But. Did he want to learn more about Ed Blaus or didn't he?

"Hey Mickey. Good to hear from you. I hope you are doing well. Long time, long time. The good news is I'm not dying, at least not right now."

"No shit, long time. Where you been hiding yourself? The neighborhood's not good enough for you?"

"I'm not far," Scott rejoined. "Lots of good memories from the neighborhood."

The messaging went on like that over a few days. Scott ignored Mickey's juvenile insults and gave away little information about himself. Not that it mattered. All Mickey needed to do was Google him and that would quickly reveal Scott's successful life as a management consultant and his ownership of a house in Scarsdale. Still, Scott's instinct was to be stingy with details. The jokey small talk revealed an important fact: Mickey still lived in the old neighborhood, which meant the nosy, streetwise character was in a good position to know something about the Blaus family. Worth putting up with the rest of Genz's schtick. Mickey offered that he now lived in an apartment above a deli. He was surprised when Scott didn't recognize the name of the shop. "It's been here like forever." Asked what he did for a living, Mickey answered, "This and that. You know, I get by. I could never do the straight time in an office—or a classroom, if you remember."

Scott remembered.

"Do you know anything about a family named Blaus? Son is named Ed. A few years younger than us."

"The writer?"

"Yep, that's the one. "

"Yeah, I recollect the family. There was Ed. I think there was a brother. Maybe a sister too? I'd have to think about it. Why do you want to know?"

Scott had been expecting the question.

"Personal interest," he wrote.

"Geesh, that sounds like something important, or something peculiar. Well, well, personal interest. You want something from me, but you're not giving anything away here, Scott."

"I'm old-fashioned. I don't like all this typing. It feels artificial. How about I call you on the phone?"

"How about you buy me a steak at Laverno's? It's still around, believe it not."

Shit. How did he get himself into this? Bad enough communicating with this scoundrel. Now they'd have to meet face-to-face? And back in the old neighborhood, no less. Where he hadn't been since they put his mother in the grave—a year after his father—and he closed up the apartment. Deciding there was nothing there worth hanging on to. Well, he could still cut and run. Erase himself from the conversation, end his membership in the Facebook high school group. The young people called that ghosting. He'd return to his structured, contented life, far from the streets where he'd grown up. Yes, he could do that. But then he'd never know more than was publicly available about Ed Blaus. And he couldn't shake the feeling there was more to know.

On the three-block walk to the restaurant from where he'd parked on a residential side street, Scott worried about the safety of his year-old BMW X5. He had no sense of the current neighborhood crime rate or car theft statistics. He'd generally grown wary of the city, limiting his visits mainly to his twice-daily trek back and forth from Grand Central Terminal to his office. The restaurant was dimly lit, and the dark wood paneling added to the unnerving gloom. The red-and-white-checked tablecloths formed a sharp contrast, but the light was too weak to do justice to the lively pattern. The place seemed familiar, but Scott wasn't sure if he'd ever been inside. His family hadn't eaten out much, and it would have taken quite a special occasion to shell out for a meal at Laverno's. By the time Scott had his own resources to pay for a nice dinner, he was dining far away from the old neighborhood.

Scott was told his companion was already seated, and he was led to a side table where a man sat facing the front door. Mickey Genz. Would Scott have recognized Mickey if the two had passed on a Manhattan sidewalk? He doubted it. But in context, Genz was familiar. He wore a long black vintage leather jacket that didn't sit properly on his shoulders. Why was he still wearing it inside the restaurant? Mickey called the hostess Shirley and thanked her. She was a short, round woman with bottle-blonde hair piled high on her head. Her overly rouged cheeks, Scott thought, went well with the decor and the look of the few patrons who dotted the large dining area. Mickey was sipping a dark cocktail.

"Mickey," Scott said, "you're looking well."

"Eh, I'm still here, right? That's all I can say. It's more than some can say."

Mickey ordered the most expensive steak and two sides, mashed potatoes and corn. Scott didn't eat much beef these days, but he thought asking for something else would send the wrong message. He got the smallest steak and a side of broccoli.

Scott pasted a smile on his face. He was the one seeking a favor, and Mickey already made clear he wasn't the type to easily give things away. Scott tried winning Mickey over by making light references to their childhood, but Mickey's responses made clear he wasn't interested. Scott realized that while they had moved through the same grades and the same schools, from middle school on they had traveled on parallel tracks, rarely intersecting. Scott stuck to friend groups that generally hewed to the straight and narrow, broadly in step with their parents' wishes that they get their basic education, attend college, and move up the social and economic ladder. Mickey and his friends went after something different. Well, Scott thought, he's had his drink and there's a decent steak sitting in front of him. He got me out to Laverno's. That should be sufficient payment.

Scott asked what Mickey knew about Ed Blaus and his family.

"Listen, partner, we haven't even touched our main course. I bet you didn't treat your wife like this before you were married and you two were out on a date. So eager to get her back to your place that you rushed everything. Take it slow."

His face flinched into a crooked smile.

Why is he bringing up my wife? Scott thought. What does he know about Meredith? Or was it just a stupid, off-color crack? Probably only that. Take it easy.

Mickey's joke reminded him how much he hated that he was here—back here—and that Mickey Genz was again involved in his life. He was doing it for Sarah. So it was important. Certainly not the first time he put up with crap. But he'd earned his way out of most of that on his rise to higher corporate status.

Mickey was talking again.

"Before we get into what I know, I need to know why you want to know. You think you're this smart business guy talking to a Brooklyn *stupido*. Is that it? How much is this information worth? You're not the only businessman at this table."

"It's like I said, I have a personal interest."

"Is it a million-dollar personal interest or a $10,000 interest? That's what I need to find out."

Scott chuckled, trying to break the tension.

"There's no big dollar value here," he said. "No dollar value at all, really. It's simple: we have a long-standing client company. The CEO of the company has a wife who likes to do good works. She's involved in many of the big charity events in the city. Now she's putting together a fundraising dinner to help with literacy, to benefit charities that help people improve their reading. Immigrants who are learning English, kids struggling in school. The idea she has, since it's about literacy and it's in the city, is to feature a few native New York artists, writers. Fiction writers to be specific. Anyway, the CEO is overly concerned about anything messing this up, especially these days when anything about anyone's past can come up and become a huge deal. Go viral on social media. They want to make absolutely sure everyone on the program is clean. No hidden controversies. Ed Blaus is one of the artists they plan to invite. Since he grew up here, like me and you, I volunteered to check him out and I want to be thorough."

Scott had come up with the story on his drive from Scarsdale.

Mickey looked directly in Scott's eyes. Then he returned to what was left of his huge steak, carefully cutting a few small pieces at one go, like you would for young children so they had a few things to pop into their mouths before you had to start cutting again.

"Uh-huh," he said. Then he started slowly chewing.

Mickey's silence prompted Scott to continue talking, though he'd already run through the script he'd devised.

"Yeah, well, they already went over the basics, of course. Checked out everyone's social media, going way back, and anything else that's easy to find out that might be a problem. They don't expect 'angels.' Hey, after all, they're writers. Just nothing that would be an unpleasant surprise. All good, so far. But the CEO, he wants to be extra sure, so he asked us if we knew a way to take a deeper look. I saw Ed Blaus's name on the list, and here we are."

"Uh-huh," Mickey said again, then went through his advance cutting-and-chewing routine. Scott took a bite of his own steak.

"I thought you were an accountant," Mickey said.

"No, not me. Full-service management consulting. Advice of all kinds: growth, mergers and acquisitions, efficiencies, what tech to use, financial planning, bankruptcy, you name it. Anything a company needs to function in the modern world, we help get them there."

"Thanks for the infomercial," Mickey said after he took his final swallow. "You know better than anyone that information has value. It costs money. That's why you charge that CEO whatever big number you charge him. Because you provide advice as well as information, including the lowdown on Ed Blaus. If you want what I know, you better see me as a colleague. Temporary worker, subcontractor, whatever you want to call it. The important thing is that you understand it's a paid position."

With that, Mickey stood up, glanced at his empty plate, and adjusted his ill-fitting jacket.

"Thanks for the steak, I won't stay for dessert. I have other business to attend to. Think about my proposition. See you on Facebook."

– 5 –

Meredith Morgan slid her keys into the locks on Sarah's apartment door, painted an unappealing institutional green. There were two, at least one fewer than her neighbors had. Three locks seemed a lot. Were burglars targeting the building? Sarah hadn't said anything. Meredith made a mental note to talk with her daughter about adding another lock. Otherwise, Meredith was pleased as she looked around. The freshly painted hallway walls and clean carpeting told her the building was well maintained.

Meredith had been shopping with a Manhattan friend. She saw a blouse she thought was simply perfect for her daughter. It was green and silky, too youthful for Meredith, but definitely right for Sarah's age and fuller figure. She knew Sarah was at work. Meredith planned to set it down on the kitchen counter with a note, maybe add something about getting another lock. Her daughter would have a pleasant surprise at the end of the day. Buying nice things, Meredith thought with some chagrin, was one thing Sarah and Scott would agree was her strength. In her husband's estimation, the list wouldn't get much longer than that.

The blouse, in its small way, was an attempt to buttress her relationship with Sarah, to revive the regular, familiar interactions they had enjoyed when Sarah was younger. It was getting more difficult. Meredith knew an adult woman needed to make her own life, didn't require daily contact with her mother. But there was no denying the hole that had left. Meredith exited her job in property management when Sarah was born. No maternity leave, she had simply resigned. She'd been that certain of her decision. Scott was already working long hours and traveling, so she knew most of the parenting would be her responsibility. There were options, of course, but Meredith thought it best this way. Once she determined there would be no more children, she stayed home throughout Sarah's childhood. She didn't regret the choice, but now she was acutely aware she'd given up a lot by never resuming her career. All she had left was freedom, which translated into a surfeit of empty hours. Scott had his work. Sarah had her work too, and her city life. Now she also had a man, Ed Blaus. A special man, a writer, an artist. Not at all like the husbands of Meredith's friends.

Meredith was three steps into the apartment when she heard a rustling noise coming from the bedroom. *Oh my, how stupid.* She thought the apartment would be empty at midafternoon on a weekday. But Sarah didn't live alone anymore. And Ed Blaus had no office to go to, just like Meredith. Now here he came, moving quickly out of the bedroom and standing just steps from Meredith at the edge of the living room.

Meredith put a hand up just below her throat. "Oh my, that was frightening."

"Didn't expect you, either," Ed smiled. His longish, gray-streaked hair was tousled, and he hadn't shaved. He wore a stretched green T-shirt and blue sweatpants. He was barefoot.

"Yes, of course," Meredith said. "So foolish of me. I haven't adjusted to Sarah not living alone."

"Understood, it's not been that long."

"I also forgot that you, uh, work from home."

"Yes, when I'm not off teaching somewhere. It's the one instruction I try hardest to impart to my students: if you want to write, it is all about facing a laptop and staying put in your seat. Simple. The greatest privilege in the world is having the time needed to create. Not having to waste your hours earning your keep."

"I imagine most of them are doing just that. Working, not writing, I mean."

"Sad, but true." Ed Blaus spread his hands and bowed slightly. "But here I am, being a terrible host. May I offer you something to drink? A glass of water? Oh, it's nearly three. Late enough. How about a glass of wine? I think there's a half-done bottle of chardonnay in the refrigerator."

"I really should let you get back. I barged in unannounced."

But instead of heading toward the door, Meredith moved a few steps deeper into the apartment and placed the small shopping bag that contained the blouse on the kitchen counter, as planned.

"A little something I picked up for Sarah while out shopping with a friend," she explained.

"How thoughtful," Ed said, and he stepped past her to open the refrigerator. He took two wine glasses from a glass-fronted cabinet and poured generously into each. He took a seat on the living room's soft couch, another present from Scott and Meredith, and motioned her to join him. Meredith instead sat in the straight-backed chair opposite him.

"That's not a very comfortable chair. I'm not sure what Sarah sees in it," Ed said.

"Style ahead of comfort, I guess." She felt Ed's eyes examining her. She touched her hair. Meredith was confident in her looks. She was tall and thin and always careful in her choice of clothes. When she looked in the mirror each morning, she noted her aging but was still pleased with what she saw.

Meredith was only three-quarters through her wine when she thought the room was tilting slightly. She was no stranger to a daytime glass of wine. So why this sensation? She'd had a particularly light lunch, a small salad with no protein. Dieting again. The chair really was uncomfortable. Ed sat smiling on the couch, the wine glass in his right hand resting on his knee, which was crossed over his left leg. His left arm stretched out along the top of the couch. He was a handsome man, Meredith thought, even unshaven and uncombed and in sweatpants. He'd avoided the most obvious signs of middle age. His stomach showed only the slightest hint of flabbiness. His biceps, left uncovered by his short sleeves, were firm. Meredith found the bulging, weight-lifting-enhanced biceps of younger men unappealing. They looked like cartoon versions of masculinity. They couldn't possibly be interesting if they spent all their time working on their bodies. Ed's look was the right one. Staying trim made him youthful. Meredith's friends always told her she was too thin, but she believed they said that with more than a touch of jealousy. She subscribed to the idea there was no such thing as too thin. Her shoulders searched futilely for proper support from the chair's back, which ended abruptly. *Who designed this chair?* She thought for a moment about joining Ed on the couch. He did look comfortable. There was the issue of his arm being draped along the top. Would he remove it if she sat next to him? Put it on his lap? Or would he stay exactly where he was, his arm hanging precariously close to her shoulder? She told herself not to move.

"I know this makes me sound dumb—though I did take literature classes in college—but it still strikes me as a sort of magic, what you fiction writers do. Conjuring things full-blown, in such detail, out of nothing but your heads."

"Persistence, not magic," Ed said, smiling. "Another thing I tell my students."

"Am I keeping you from pershisting? I mean, persisting. I should go."

Meredith started to stand and swayed to the right, her left hand lifting her wineglass above her head. Ed rushed over and took her left elbow, slowly helping her lower her arm and the glass. He put his other arm on her hip to steady her.

"Oh my, that's embarrassing," she said. "I'm a pretty cheap drunk."

With that she managed to remove herself from Ed's grip.

"Are you sure you're okay? Want to sit back down?"

"No, no, fine," Meredith said. She exaggeratedly wiped her hands down the front of her expensive light-blue pants, as if that was a sign of stability. "I'll be terrific once I am outside in the fresh air."

"If you say so," Ed said. His smile was wide.

The train ride back to Scarsdale gave Meredith enough time to sober up, but still she hesitated before getting in the car she had left at the station for the short drive home. It wasn't even a full glass of wine. She started the ignition. Meredith was honked at twice during the trip. She was driving that slowly. Once she was in her driveway, her thoughts turned back to Ed Blaus. He was something. Not only good-looking, but so interesting, and he seemed to take her seriously. She could tell by the way he trained his eyes on her when she spoke, listening intently, like what she had to say was important. What a contrast to Scott. It was amazing that only three years separated them in age. They seemed like they were of different generations. There was nothing cool about Scott, while Ed, well, he was a writer, a free spirit. Unconventional. Lately, it seemed, every time Scott did want to talk with Meredith it was to complain about something—mostly about the existence of Ed Blaus in Sarah's life.

When Meredith thought of Sarah and Ed, she had to wonder.

Would Sarah prove enough for Ed, over the long haul? Of course she had her youth, which was always overvalued by middle-aged men in their desperation to fend off their own aging. She was an attractive girl and carried herself well, though she clearly didn't believe, like her mother, the adage that one couldn't be too thin. Not that Sarah was overweight, exactly. But this wasn't about looks. Sarah simply hadn't lived enough. How worldly could you be at Sarah's age? No, some things could only be acquired with age. Physical attraction always diminishes. There's got to be something more to hold a man like Ed. Meredith wondered if she should send Ed an email. She would apologize again for bursting in on him like that. She would mention she usually held her wine a lot better. Was sending an email the proper thing to do? What if Sarah saw it? Would she think it odd? Her forgetting that Ed would be in the apartment could be explained and excused easily enough, but staying for a glass of wine, getting tipsy, then sending a follow-up note? It would surprise Sarah that Meredith hadn't mentioned the encounter. Meredith had no intention of doing so. She doubted etiquette manuals had a section on appropriate communications from the mother of a man's live-in girlfriend who is a contemporary of that man after arriving uninvited at their apartment and getting drunk. She decided to send the email, confident Ed would keep it to himself.

– 6 –

Scott wanted nothing further to do with Mickey Genz. The man was clearly a grifter. Which made Scott the victim, or the potential victim. All brought on by his own actions. That's what made it infuriating. He'd handed Genz the advantage with his need for information on Blaus. Scott should just walk away. It was the only logical thing to do, since Genz had leverage over him. In many tense business situations over the years Scott always stayed on plan. He looked only at the numbers and advised his clients accordingly. If this was work, and he was his own client, he'd say walk away. The risk-reward ratio is not in your favor. The chances of Genz digging up damaging information on Ed Blaus and his family were hard to figure, but they were likely slight. The downside was money spent and being at an informational disadvantage to a creep. Genz had demanded $5,000. All of that said walk away, just as Scott had walked away from the neighborhood when he graduated from high school and hardly ever turned back. It was partly about getting away from the Mickey Genzes of the world, with their schemes and big dreams that had no chance of realization. The place got his younger brother, Freddie. His brother wasn't like Genz. If he was, he would have had a much better chance of surviving. "Just walk away," Scott said aloud. Even thinking about Freddie and the neighborhood was proof of Genz's negative impact. But there was Sarah. She needed to be saved. Blaus had already moved in with her. Already serious. What if it went further? Meredith was bugging him about going down to the city to have dinner at their apartment. Sarah's apartment, he corrected her. The one we bought for her. What was that going to be like? Like dining at the tennis club with another couple, Meredith said. Swell, at least one of the pair was the right age for that. The problem was the other person was his daughter, and she had no business being part of that couple. It was obvious Meredith wasn't going to do anything about it. Sarah is an adult and it's her life, Meredith said. It was up to Scott. Him alone. He'd been in that position before. With his brother, Freddie. Look what happened there.

He sent a direct message via Facebook to Mickey Genz. He was willing to meet. And pay.

It was cold for late September. Scott looked right and left, right and left, as he approached the schoolyard, afraid of being recognized even while conscious of the absurdity of the fear. He hadn't walked around the old neighborhood in about forty years. Anybody who was still around wouldn't recognize him. Still, his head kept swiveling. He told Meredith he was driving to the office. On Sunday morning? She was incredulous.

"Big deal brewing," he replied. "I can't say anything more or they'll lock me up. You too. And they'll keep us in separate cells. I wouldn't want that."

He smiled at his wife, keeping things light, trying to be charming, something he hadn't attempted in quite a long time. Meredith didn't show any sign of noticing.

Mickey Genz had beaten him to the otherwise empty schoolyard. He was seated in a far corner, on a bench that looked like it hadn't been replaced since they were kids at the school. Mickey was in the same long black leather coat. It had seemed odd when he wore it in the restaurant, but now it might not be warm enough. Wind whipped through the schoolyard, rattling the chain-link fences that enclosed it. Mickey was hatless, and his black hair, full of gel, was combed straight back.

"What do you think?" Mickey said and spread his arms.

"About what?"

"My office out here. Not as fancy as yours, I bet." Mickey laughed.

Scott grunted. "You need to put in some heat."

"Hey, I don't know where my manners went, but I never asked you about your family. Are your parents still with us?"

"No, neither one. It's been a bunch of years. How about you?"

Scott felt obliged to ask. He stuffed his hands into his jacket for warmth.

"Yeah, well, you know, my father was as good as dead to me since second grade. That's when he ran out on us. He's dead for real now. Mom went last year."

"Sorry."

"So, you're all alone now, I mean your family when we were kids. I think we were not in touch when I heard about your brother. Tough break."

Scott pulled a thick envelope out of the inside pocket of his jacket. He didn't want to talk about Freddie, certainly not with Mickey Genz. He took another look around before he handed it to Mickey. If anyone was watching, he or she might think it was a drug deal.

"You can count it," he said.

Mickey stuffed the envelope inside his coat. "No need."

"So."

"So, I did a lot of legwork on this one. Those Blaus people were not exactly well-known. Barely anybody even remembers Ed—I guess it was a long time ago that he was sort of famous, and then famous again when he had the court fight with his baby mama. The Blauses lived in that apartment . . ."

"Knew that."

"Yeah, the father ran a little luncheonette. It did okay, but then he dropped dead there one day of a heart attack. Probably wasn't even our age. That leaves the mother and the two children. Ed is the younger. When his mother died, Ed was already out of high school. Maybe early twenties. I don't have exact dates and math isn't my strong suit."

He smiled, and Scott saw he was missing a couple of teeth on the upper left side.

"The older brother—his name is Michael—has some sort of big problem, like he couldn't advance beyond a certain point as far as his learning and thinking. Didn't get very far. I'm not sure what the appropriate words are. I think the brother is our age, maybe a year older, but we wouldn't have known him because he had to go to a special school for those kids with, well, you know, those issues."

"You don't know where the brother is now?" Scott asked.

"No clue."

"Anything else?"

"I found this old woman, ancient, the kind who is only leaving that building in a box. Lived there forever. She says after the mother died, she started seeing Ed around the building again. Hadn't been around for a few years. The brother was there too. He'd always lived with his parents. It was a short period, she said. She couldn't remember how long exactly, and then one day she realized they were both gone and a new family was in the apartment."

Scott got up and said he was leaving.

"So, you ain't gonna ever say what this is really about?" Mickey asked, producing the missing-teeth smile.

Scott pointed to Mickey's coat, where he had stashed his envelope full of twenties and fifties.

"You got the answer that's important to you."

Was that worth $5,000? Scott wondered as he headed for his car. Impossible to know. Hiring a private detective could have been just as much or more. Scott knew that because his consulting group sometimes hired private eyes, not that they called themselves that. They preferred "security professionals." It could be a delicate matter for a client that needed a discreet investigation. Those bills ran up. So, yeah, who knows, $5,000 for a few facts. Maybe. He hoped he never had occasion to see Mickey Genz again.

– 7 –

Scott would have preferred a restaurant, but Sarah insisted they have dinner at the apartment. She'd been taking an Asian cooking class and wanted to show off the results.

"Where does she get the time for a cooking class?" Meredith asked on the drive down to the city. "She already works every day."

"Maybe she's happy not to be in the apartment with him," Scott said. "To have a night out."

Meredith frowned.

"You know, you can be a real ass sometimes," she said. "I expect you to be cheerful at dinner."

Scott grunted. Once they were there, it was obvious Ed Blaus's charm offensive was on track. He fell over himself telling Meredith how great she looked.

Sarah yelled hello from the kitchen.

"Don't come near here. I'm just at the crucial stage. Talk to Ed."

The kitchen was only half hidden from the living room, whose windows looked down on Seventh Avenue. The rest of the apartment moved right. The doorless kitchen and then the short corridor that took you to the one, albeit spacious, bedroom. The bathroom was another few steps down the hall on the opposite side, along with a linen closet.

Ed hustled to get them drinks, a tall white wine for Meredith, a club soda for Scott. He was driving, he said. Dinner was a combination of fresh, lightly cooked vegetables with diced chicken and cashews. It was surprisingly good.

"Ed, tell us something about your family," Scott said as Sarah and Meredith cleared dishes.

"Let me help," Ed said, rising from his seat.

"It's okay," Sarah said. "I know this is as sexist as it gets, but it's fine. Mom and I will clear."

The men sat on opposite sides of the embroidered white tablecloth set on the folding table that stood in the corner of the living room, near the big television set. The folding table was for company. Ed and Sarah usually ate at the small round table in the kitchen.

Scott was about to repeat his question when Ed said, "I have an adult son, Justin. That's all the family I have."

"No siblings?"

"Yes, but we're not close."

Ed Blaus's face went hard. His eyes locked on the window behind Scott's head. He looked to Scott like a poker player with a losing hand who'd trained himself not to let his expression give himself away, but who didn't have quite enough self-control. Scott sensed that if he pressed further, he'd run the risk of antagonizing Blaus, which he was loath to do with Meredith and Sarah present.

"You know, I understand we grew up in the same neighborhood in Brooklyn," Scott said.

"Yes, Sarah mentioned it. Quite a coincidence."

"I'll say. Do you go back often?"

"No, no. I'm afraid I'm a Manhattan elitist now." Ed smiled tightly.

The two women reentered the room.

"I was just telling Sarah I finished reading *A View from Below*," Meredith said. "It's embarrassing, of course, that I didn't read it when it was first published. There was so much to-do about it. But now I'm glad I didn't, because I can say that after however many years, it's still really great. It's timeless. What a terrific story. Really so moving."

Sarah stood smiling. Ed Blaus looked down. "That's awfully kind of you to say. It was a long time ago."

"That doesn't matter," Meredith intoned. "Most of us, we don't get a chance to make something, something that lasts, of value. Maybe I'm not expressing myself clearly."

"You're quite clear," Scott said.

Saturday morning. Meredith was in the shower in the big bathroom attached to their master bedroom. She'd had it redone twice in the time they lived in the Scarsdale house. Now there were two sinks, a separate bath, and shower stall. The shower was built with an adjustable ceiling head that featured everything from an almost mist to a fire hose of water drilling into your head and shoulders. Scott scampered out of bed and headed to the kitchen counter, where Meredith kept her handbag. He rifled through it and quickly came away with her ring of keys. He was hurrying, but Scott knew he had a lot of time. Meredith's shower would be followed by at least twenty minutes devoted to drying her hair. Her plan was for lunch with a couple of friends, a typical Saturday activity. Scott located what he thought were likely the keys to Sarah's apartment, separated them from the chain, and returned the rest to the bag. There were three, one for the lobby door and two for the apartment. He didn't know which were which, but that would be easy enough to figure out on the spot. He planned to hustle down to Home Depot once Meredith was gone and have duplicates made. When she showered on Sunday morning, Scott would return the original keys to her ring.

On Tuesday at 10:00 a.m., Scott tried the first of the keys on the vestibule entrance. His second choice worked. He knocked vigorously on the apartment door. No answer. Sarah was at work. Blaus was who knows where. Scott was supposed to be at a medical appointment. No big deal, he told his assistant, just a checkup. But he might be a while, he warned. The doctor was one of those who perennially fell behind schedule. He clicked open both locks and closed the door quietly behind him. He would have told the truth if a neighbor questioned the strange man entering the apartment: he was Sarah's father. But no one was in the hallway. Scott stifled an urge to look around. He took off his coat and placed it at the back of the straight-backed chair in the living room. He angled the chair so he would immediately be seen when someone entered the apartment.

It was nearly eleven when Ed Blaus walked in. He had a diner's takeout coffee cup in his hand.

"What the . . . " Blaus began.

Scott stood up.

"Oh, it's you," Blaus's voice steadied as he recognized Scott.

"Apologies for the surprise," Scott said in a tone that was not in the least apologetic. "But we need to talk. Right away."

Blaus walked to the kitchen, put down the coffee, and wiped his fingers with a dish towel. He returned to the living room with the paper cup.

"Important enough that you had to ambush me, rather than call and set up a meeting?" Blaus said.

"Here's the thing," Scott said. "How much is it going to take?"

Ed Blaus smiled from the couch. He crossed his legs.

"You are direct, aren't you? I'm not for sale."

"Everyone has a price," Scott said. "And from what I know about you, I'm certain you can quickly come up with a number."

"You are sitting in the apartment in which I live . . . . "

"Which I paid for."

"In which I live, and you make me a corrupt offer. What am I to think of you? What have I done to deserve that?" There was mockery in his tone.

Scott leaned forward in his seat. He tried to be menacing. "I don't give a rat's ass what you think of me. You are a user, and I want you out of my daughter's life."

Blaus laughed. He walked to the kitchen, spilled his remaining coffee in the sink, and tossed the empty cup into the white garbage liner. He returned to the couch, but stood in front of it.

"I'm not going anywhere, Scott. I'm your worst nightmare. I'm in for the long haul. Maybe Sarah and I will even get married one day. You can walk her down the aisle."

Scott started to go for him, then thought better of it. He stood up straight and put on his Burberry raincoat.

"Think about it, Blaus. The offer won't be on the table forever."

He started for the door.

"What do you think Sarah will make of this encounter when I tell her about it?"

"Your word against mine."

"She's in love with me, Scott. You're the stern dad who doesn't like her lover. Who do you think she's going to believe?"

"Think about it," Scott said. "The offer won't be there forever."

Scott decided to walk back to his office from Chelsea, though it would be a good forty minutes and the breezes were stiff. *Moved too soon. Gained nothing from the element of surprise.* Blaus was going to be a tough adversary, clearly a man who wouldn't be easily blown off. Scott should have waited. By showing his cards early, he had appeared desperate. His emotions had gotten the best of him. Emotion was the enemy of all success, whether in business or warfare, he believed. Blaus probably did the numbers in his head and figured whatever

Scott could offer in lump sum would pale in comparison with a lifetime ride on the purse strings of a younger woman, supplemented in her income by that same dad. Add in the benefit of taunting Scott with his presence for decades. *What if they did get married? What then? And when Scott died? Would he, in effect, have an heir in Ed Blaus? No, that was not going to happen. Could not happen.* Scott had worked way too hard for too long to let that happen.

– 8 –

Meredith's hand shook as she knocked on the front door of the apartment. This time she'd emailed Ed Blaus she would stop by sometime in midafternoon, if it wasn't too much of an inconvenience, to drop off a houseplant of hers Sarah had admired. She'd make it a gift. Not at all, he replied. She'd spent much of the morning selecting what to wear and settled on a recently purchased top and sharply pressed tan pants. She wore flats and had applied little makeup. The look was supposed to say *Typical day in the city. Nothing special or different. Not trying to hide anything. Not trying to look younger. Not trying to compete with my daughter. This is who I am.* Once inside she apologized again for interrupting Ed's writing.

"Don't worry," he said. "I could use a little break. It's, uh, not flowing very well."

"I'm sure it's terrific," Meredith said.

Ed smiled briefly and tucked his head toward his left shoulder. "Wine?"

"Why not?" Meredith replied. Rather than choosing the straight-back, this time she slipped out of her shoes and sunk into the far corner of the couch. "Not sure I'll be able to get up again," she smiled out of the deep cushion. "Especially after the wine."

Ed sat in the middle of the couch, not right next to Meredith, but perched where the two cushions met. His descent lifted Meredith up slightly, as if the couch cushion was a seesaw. They talked about Ed's current writing project, but he was reluctant to go much into detail.

"Anything and everything could still change," he said. "When I started this thing, it had a totally different trajectory. Sooner or later, I have to stick with what I have and finish it. It's just, well, I'm just not ready to commit. Not yet."

"I'm sure it will be wonderful," Meredith said. "I'm sure you are your own harshest critic."

Ed offered a second glass of wine and Meredith accepted.

On the train into the city, Meredith had tried to step away from herself and analyze what she was about to do. She was a woman anticipating going to bed with a man her own age. A man who was not married. Of course, there was the issue of Sarah. Meredith downplayed it. *Who knows how serious Sarah and Ed really are? How long it will last?* Meredith also expected whatever happened to be a secret between Ed and herself. *No one else will ever know.* Looked at in a certain way, she would be carrying out the bigger transgression. She had a husband, though not one who seemed to notice she existed, not as a physical, sensual being. A woman who still desired and wanted to be desired. How different from when it all began with Scott. They met as seniors in college, he at Binghamton University, she at Ithaca College. She was at Scott's school for a weekend, visiting a friend. They went to a party at Scott's fraternity. Meredith was used to male attention; she had long legs and a slender figure, blue eyes, high cheekbones and a warm smile. She'd always taken care to dress stylishly in an unostentatious way. Scott wasn't like the boys she'd known. He was certain of himself and direct. Handsome, too, at six feet and ramrod straight. Back then he had a full head of wavy brown hair. He told her tales of his Brooklyn youth, insisting that he was never going back. There were heights he was certain to climb, even if back then he wasn't exactly sure of their nature. Meredith thought his rougher upbringing accounted for his maturity and driving ambition. She hailed from a more affluent family in southern Connecticut. Scott made clear from that first evening he wanted Meredith. His attention was non-stop and that pleased her. Soon, they were spending every weekend together. Meredith began to imagine a happy life with this confident young man, seeing in him someone who could be depended upon as a future husband and, eventually, a father. Over the many years, things had dramatically changed. Now, when Scott spoke to her at all, it was about Ed. That he was no good, that he was using Sarah for a nice place to stay and someone to pay his bills. Scott insisted there was something even worse going on than Ed sponging off their daughter. There was something Ed was hiding, something important. Scott was certain. Meredith told Scott he was paranoid, imagining things because he was so irrationally upset Sarah had taken up with Ed.

As they drank their wine, Ed moved next to Meredith on the couch, causing them to sink further into the cushion. They laughed. He placed his hand on hers and they sat like that, not talking, for a while. Then Ed rose, his hand entwined with Meredith's. They walked to the bedroom. It occurred to Meredith to ask what time Sarah was expected home from work. No, mentioning Sarah would be a mistake. She didn't want to think about her daughter. The wine helped on that front. If there was any danger, Ed would say something. She was not dealing with a man who lacked guile. Meredith pushed Scott and Sarah out of her mind. This wasn't about either of them. This was about her. For a change, it was about what Meredith wanted. Ed closed the bedroom door, which Meredith thought strange in the otherwise empty apartment. Then he turned and embraced her, running his hands feverishly up and down her back. He kissed her hard, pushing Meredith's head sharply backward. She felt her balance slipping away, but Ed's arms were firmly around her, so she didn't fall.

– 9 –

Action, not inaction. That's what a former boss of Scott's used to say. When the group was paralyzed with indecision, when a junior staffer pleaded they didn't have enough information to proceed with a plan or make a confident recommendation to a company, the boss would shake his head. Action, not inaction. We have to move. Pick your best bet and get on with it. He didn't want to hear that it would be only a guess, that one choice could be just as faulty as another. He didn't want to hear about mistakes made along the way. They had to keep moving. Action, not inaction. Choose. Scott told himself to move.

Mary Jenseth, Ed Blaus's ex-wife, agreed to see him. She invited him to lunch at her apartment in the East Village.

"I Googled you and am mostly convinced you aren't an ax murderer," she wrote in an email to Scott. "Still, two of my friends know you are coming over and one of them will stop by soon after you arrive."

Scott frowned as he read it. Hell, he would have been happy to go to a neighborhood coffee shop instead of being considered a threat to Mary Jenseth's safety in her own home. Mary was Ed Blaus's only wife, since he and his child's mother had never married. She agreed to the lunch after email exchanges and one phone call in which Scott honestly discussed his worry about Sarah being involved with the older and, in Scott's mind, disreputable Ed Blaus. He told her of his need for additional information about Blaus that would either set his fears to rest or confirm them. His expressed concern for his daughter won Mary over. She had a son in college, she said. She understood how a parent worries about a child. Her son had become too serious in high school with a girl she never liked. Her protestations just drove him to spend more time with the girl. Luckily, the relationship dissolved on its own once he went off to college.

"I know what it's like to worry about a child in an inappropriate relationship," she said.

It was a small but tidily kept apartment, a postdivorce place, Mary said. Not post-Blaus, but after her second marriage had broken down. The second round was a lot more successful than the first, though it still didn't last. Not the way we're told when we're young. Marriages are supposed to be forever, she said. "Made it to fifteen years the second time; that should count for something." Mary laughed. Her son's room was nothing more than an alcove. "His father has a bigger place," she said, "but most of the time he prefers to be here." She laid out cut-up sandwiches filled with vegetables picked up at an organic place down the block. Scott thought they didn't look particularly appetizing, but he nibbled on one to be polite. They drank tap water.

"What exactly do you want to know?" Mary asked.

"Everything."

"Ha. We don't have that much time. My friends will really think things went wrong if we sit here for hours. That's what it would take."

"Okay. How about his family? Did he say much about that when you were together?"

"No, it would irritate him when I even asked. He liked to say he escaped from his family. From Brooklyn too. That what I saw before me was a person built purely by his own invention and will power. A self-made man, though he would say self-created artist. He was pretty full of himself back then. His book came out just before we met, and it was a big hit. Not sales so much, though they were decent, but the way it was received in New York by the people who mattered. The reviews, the articles about him, proclaiming the latest young literary bigshot, it all went to his head, which was understandable. I also had dreams back then. About acting. Mine never took off."

"Sorry to hear that," Scott said.

The marriage lasted just two years. Even as the accolades continued to sail in, Ed's writing was going poorly. They made him feel worse because he couldn't get going on novel number two. He would be a one-book wonder, he feared. He drank more heavily. There were other women. Mary said she forgave the first transgression after Ed took a knee and promised it wouldn't happen again. She pretended not to know about the second. Looking back, she said, she realized she had hung on to Ed even after he began sleeping around because he was her ticket to the exciting lower-Manhattan life of writers and journalists, visual artists, and working actors and theater directors. They provided her with a busy social life. People she considered friends. Some of them, yes, might even be able to help her career. Her motives weren't pure. The help for her career never arrived. And by the fourth known affair, she couldn't take any more. Mary left.

None of this surprised Scott, and none of it, he knew, would do any good with Sarah. No doubt Ed had already admitted it all. It was decades in the past. His public fight with the mother of his child over financial support was slightly fresher—though still old news— and more scandalous than these infidelities. Even the parenting fracas likely hadn't deterred Sarah. He's a changed man, Ed probably told her, and Sarah believed him. Everyone has the ability to be better after they make mistakes. He's grown. He's different.

Scott was eager to steer the conversation back to Blaus's family.

"About his family, when he did talk about them, what did he say? Did he ever mention his brother, Michael?"

Scott took another bite of the sandwich. Way too many sprouts.

"Believe it or not, I never laid eyes on Michael. Ed's parents were dead by the time we met. If there were uncles or aunts or cousins, Ed didn't want anything to do with them. Our wedding was attended mainly by friends. It was a counterculture thing. An unwedding, he called it. My parents and sister made it. Michael didn't attend. He lived in a group home on Staten Island. I don't remember being told anything specific by Ed about his condition except that he shouldn't live alone. That he couldn't fully care for himself."

"Please, I know it's been a long time since you were with Ed, but it's important. Did Ed ever say anything that made you think something was amiss about his past?"

The doorbell rang. It was a blond-streaked woman, who, like Mary, appeared to be in her early fifties. Mary's friend. They were both in good shape and stylish on a budget. Mary's friend carried a rolled-up yoga mat.

"All okay," Mary said when she opened the door. "Thanks for stopping by."

"Your friend is welcome to join us," Scott called from the kitchen table, eager to prove to anyone interested he was not a threat. But the friend had things to attend to. She would call Mary's cell later on, just to stay on the safe side.

Scott repeated his question. It occurred to him, not for the first time, that something unusual must have happened to the Blauses back in Brooklyn, as it did to the Morgans, something that cracked apart an otherwise typical neighborhood family. With Scott's family, it was his brother's drug addiction and early death from an overdose. Did the Blauses also have a family secret? That so little was known about them, combined with Ed's reluctance to talk about his upbringing, could mean only one thing: something went wrong. It was simply a matter of how wrong. "Mary, is there anything more about Ed's brother? Did Ed ever say anything?"

"You know, it's funny, I haven't thought about this in a very long time. But one night we came home from a party. The usual thing. A lot of smart and pretty young people, a lot of pot consumed. When we were back in our apartment, I washed up, getting ready to go to sleep. When I opened the door to the bedroom, Ed wasn't there. It was a small apartment. He was out in what we facetiously called the family room, which was just a space off the kitchen. Ed was at his writing desk, with his head on his forearm. He was crying. That was really unusual. I thought he had too much to drink or smoke and that he was feeling sorry for himself. Because the novel he was working on wasn't going well. I admit I was impatient with the self-pity. Here I couldn't get a single break doing what I wanted to do and he'd already written this fabulously received book. It was too much. I said something like 'Stop feeling sorry for yourself and come to bed.'"

Scott leaned forward in his chair and stared intently at Mary. His six-foot frame was nearly bent in half.

"He kept crying, sobbing really. He mumbled 'Michael, Michael' a couple of times. He said he smoked too much pot and it seemed like a different kind of pot, like there was some special ingredient in it. I felt a little more sympathy, because he was clearly in a bad way, and I asked him if he wanted to talk about it.

"So he tells me—the one and only time—about how, after his father died, his mother found out she was sick with cancer. The diagnosis was bleak. There likely wasn't a lot of time left for her. Her worry was what was going to happen to Michael after she died. Like I said, I don't know specifically what Michael's issues are, but the closest Ed said was that it was like he was perpetually a young child intellectually. He'd gone to a special school, but at the point when his mother was diagnosed, Michael was maybe twenty-five, so school was long over. He lived at home. He went down and sat on a bench at the playground when the weather was nice. He went grocery shopping with his mother. Sometimes they went to the library."

Mary's cell phone buzzed, breaking the intensity of her tale and causing them both to jump in their chairs. She looked down at the table and canceled the call.

"Anyway, Ed's mother consulted a few people. Someone suggested a lawyer, and the lawyer recommended a trust be set up for Michael. The lawyer and his firm would oversee it. They would arrange for Michael to stay in the apartment after his mother died, and they would pay the rent and all the bills he needed from this fund, which they would invest in something safe, like Treasury bonds or an annuity. There wasn't a ton of money, though the father had a small business that sold after he died. There was enough that with interest it would stretch out for a while. Her son's needs were modest. The apartment was rent stabilized. The mother's biggest fear was that Michael would be sent away somewhere. She thought he was too sensitive for that. That he'd be so scared in an unfamiliar setting. That it could be the end of him. This was all a very long time ago, of course. Things were different. She believed he'd be better off in the apartment and the neighborhood, where he knew what was what. She told Ed she knew he had his own life to lead but she hoped he would keep close tabs on Michael under that arrangement. Make sure things were running the way they were supposed to run. That Ed would visit Michael very often."

"What was Ed doing at that time?" Scott asked.

"Ed was working as a busboy or a dishwasher or something, sharing some dilapidated Lower East Side place with three other guys and trying to write. He dropped out of college to write. That night, when he stopped crying, Ed told me he said to his mother that he had a better idea. She shouldn't get involved with the lawyer. Who knew if he could really be trusted? They might rescind everything after she was gone. Find some legal loophole to keep the inheritance money and freeze Michael out. The lawyer wasn't family. Ed's idea was that his mother should leave all her money to Ed and Ed would take care of Michael. They would live together in the Brooklyn apartment.

He'd invest the money just like the lawyer suggested. No magic there. Anybody could buy Treasury bonds. The money would mean Ed could write and look after his brother. He would give up his crappy job. They would stay in the apartment so Michael would feel at home. Their mother agreed. She was dead within a year.

"At first, Ed said, it all went according to plan. He quit his job. He moved back into the apartment where he grew up. But Michael was much more work than he expected. He really missed their mother. He couldn't really understand that she was gone forever. At times, Michael refused to do anything, wouldn't eat, wouldn't get out of bed. Ed wasn't getting any writing done and Michael seemed to be getting worse, regressing. Ed liked it better when he was dirt-poor and working all night in restaurant kitchens."

Scott was impressed Ed had taken on responsibility for his brother.

"How long did that go on?" he asked.

"Some number of months. Then Ed said he realized it wasn't sustainable. He looked around and found a hospital-type place. It was run with city and state grants. Because Michael was an adult and Ed was just a brother, not a parent, there wouldn't be any fees for Michael living there. The money that was inherited was all in Ed's name. From the city's point of view, Michael was indigent. The institution said it had modern ideas about how to help people like Michael. There'd be medications only if necessary and activities and educational projects to help him feel and be productive. They took a taxi there one morning with Michael's things in two suitcases. Ed told him they were going on a vacation trip. When they got there and Michael sensed what was going on, he got hysterical. The check-in person told Ed it was probably best if he left, his presence was just making Michael more agitated. They said give it a couple weeks and then come back and visit. Later, Michael moved on from that place and went to live in a group home."

Mary stopped talking. She inhaled deeply. "It's funny how this is all coming back. It's weird."

"Please, please continue," Scott said, his eyes imploring.

"With Michael deposited, Ed used the inheritance money to get himself a decent apartment in Manhattan. He didn't have to get a job, and he could concentrate on writing. Within a year, year and a half, he finished *A View from Below*. Oh, and that night, the night he broke down, Ed said he never went back to visit Michael. He rationalized that seeing him again would set Michael back from having adapted to his new surroundings. He never visited. Not once. That's what he said he felt most guilty about."

"He told you this all in one evening?"

"Yes, by the end of the story it was morning. He made me swear I would never tell anyone, and he never talked about it again, at least not to me. One time I suggested he ought to visit Michael, that it might do him as much good as it would Michael. He snapped at me, told me I shouldn't talk about things I didn't understand. Funny, but I kept my word. I never mentioned it to anyone . . . until now."

"Thank you. Thank you. This is important for me to know. But I am curious. Why share now, after all the years of keeping his secret?"

Mary drew her finger along the rough wooden table, like she was gathering an imaginary line of dust.

"I'm not sure," she said, "you seem like a sincere guy, trying to look out for your daughter. I sort of wish someone had tried to look out for me way back when, you know? I don't think people change. I bet Ed hasn't."

46

– 10 –

Michael Blaus pulled on his brown leather jacket. There was some cracking at the elbows and just above the elastic band at the bottom. It looked to him like spiders were living on the coat. He didn't mind. Spiders didn't scare him. He liked the idea of insects tagging along with him. It meant he wasn't alone. He was with friends. He waved to Perry, the overnight supervisor at the front desk.

"You are going to be too warm in that coat. It's going to be in the seventies later."

Too warm? He didn't feel too warm. Michael was told time and again that he should listen to the supervisors who sat in a glass-fronted office between the front door and the suites in the group home. They had the residents' best interests at heart. But he loved the coat and he didn't want to take it off. His mother had bought it for him. Before she got sick. And then died. When he had the leather jacket on, it felt like part of her was with him, along with the friendly spiders. He and his mother used to go everywhere together, to the supermarket or on walks around the neighborhood.

"Come on, Michael," his mother would say, "let's get some air."

You were supposed to listen to the supervisors, but Michael wanted to keep the jacket on. He smiled at Perry as he advanced to the front door. Perry smiled back and shook his head, as if to say, *Okay. I warned you, you're going to sweat in that thing.* Michael moved forward. To break his routine was confusing, and becoming confused meant becoming anxious. And that was hard to shake once it descended on him. "Anxiety" was the word the psychologist kept using when she and Michael met for their weekly forty-five-minute sessions.

"Don't participate in activities that increase your anxiety," she said. "Do what makes you feel peaceful."

Once he left his suite, which consisted of a good-sized room with a connecting bathroom, it was so much better to keep going, to follow the well-established order: out the front door, left turn, five blocks up and another left, two more blocks and into the back entrance of Good House Burgers, the fast-food joint where he'd worked in the kitchen for more years than he could count. It wasn't yet 7:00 a.m., and the sun was still weak.

Of all the group home's supervisors, Michael liked JoAnne the best. She was always nice to him and she was beautiful, especially, Michael thought, when her light brown hair fell down around her shoulders. Sometimes she wore it tied up in a twisty thing that she played with a lot, setting and resetting it so that finally the small amount of hair squeezed by the contraption sat atop her head like a little crown. After dinner, served to the residents every night in the big dining hall at six, Michael would wander out toward the front door to see if JoAnne was busy.

"Going out?" she would ask, and when he hesitated, she would often say, "You know, you are free to go out any time you want, Michael. You just have to let us know if you are going to be back after ten."

Whenever she said that without looking up from her laptop because she was busy, Michael did go out. He didn't want JoAnne to think he was just pretending and was really hanging by the front door hoping he could talk with her. If JoAnne wasn't busy, she'd invite Michael to take the seat alongside her desk, and the two of them would chat. That was always nice. Whenever he did leave the building even though he really didn't want to, Michael was never sure what to do next. It wasn't like the neighborhood where he grew up. Those streets he got to know and was comfortable navigating himself, always confident he could find his way home. But the neighborhood surrounding the group home never became familiar like that. He'd been there a long time, ever since the people at the place where Ed had dropped him off told him he didn't need to stay there anymore. That there was a new facility where, they said, he would be happier. "Independence," that was the word they used over and over. "Progress," that was another one. The group home was progress, progress for Michael and for everyone. Michael would have his own suite. He could get a job. Sometimes when he went out after dinner to show JoAnne he wasn't in the hallway near the front door just to talk with her, he walked over to Good House Burgers. His place of employment was open twenty-four hours. It meant he always had a place to go if he needed one. Michael wouldn't order anything. He'd have just had dinner, but he'd sit for a while at one of the small tables and watch the customers come and go. He'd sometimes approach the counter and try to peer into the back to see who was working in the kitchen. Occasionally he'd see a worker he knew from the dayside who had switched shifts or been asked to work overtime. Michael would wave, and if the coworker saw him, Michael would get a wave in return. People at Good House liked him.

When he first got the job, the head supervisor at the group home had a conversation in Michael's presence with a manager at Good House. Sam said it would be good if Michael could put in the same hours every workday, no variance. They settled on 7:00 a.m. to 3:00 p.m., and even though Sam no longer worked at the group home and the manager who had made the deal no longer worked at Good House, those work hours never changed. Michael proved more flexible than Sam had imagined, and while he was not asked to work nights, Michael was always happy to work an extra day if they were short-staffed. The managers appreciated that.

On the best evenings, JoAnne invited Michael to sit facing her in a straight-backed chair that was just to the left of her desk. They talked about Michael's workday and about upcoming events at the home. The home staged special meals from different national cuisines and celebrated every holiday the staff could think of by showing a film or hosting a talk by someone who knew about the holiday's history and significance. More than once JoAnne had asked Michael if he would like to learn how to use a laptop. She'd be happy to show him, but he demurred. He had a television in his room, with cable channels. He'd developed a fondness for soccer and often watched matches, not caring if the announcers spoke Spanish, which he couldn't understand. He also liked to watch wrestling. One night, JoAnne asked him to talk about his family. He said the most about his mother. He remembered his father too, but he died before his mother did and he was away from the apartment more because of work. He spent the most time with his mother. JoAnne asked if he had any brothers or sisters, and Michael mentioned his brother, Ed.

"Do you talk to him on the phone?"

Michael shook his head.

"I don't see him come around to visit. Does he come when I'm not here?"

Michael shook his head again.

"Would you want to find out where he lives, so maybe if you wanted to you could contact him?"

When JoAnne asked that, she looked so directly into his eyes that it almost hurt. Her eyes seemed to soften even as he watched them. He didn't reply. She motioned him to bring his chair around to sit right next to her. He felt strange sitting on JoAnne's side of the desk. Like he was a supervisor now too.

"Come on," she said, "Let's take a look. It can't hurt."

It seemed impossible to Michael that somehow Ed could be hiding in that little folding machine, with its colorful screen and typing pad. Ed was gone. Just like his mother was gone. They had been with him, and now they were not. Michael couldn't tell you the year Ed had dropped him off or how long it had been since that day, but the vision was still clear in his head. Michael had screamed, screamed louder than ever before. His heart was pounding like a big drum he had heard once when he walked by a group of street musicians: boom, boom, and then an even louder boom. It was hard to breathe. Finally, the people who worked there helped him calm down and he was taken to what would be his room. He was happier where he lived now.

JoAnne typed a few keystrokes. She paused, and then in a flurry she typed more. All of a sudden, Michael saw a picture of Ed pop up on the screen. Then there were three more. In a couple, Ed looked like Michael remembered him, maybe even younger than when Ed had dropped Michael off. In the others the man looked somewhat like Ed, but Michael wasn't sure, since those photos were of an older man. Could it be his brother? How could he be the young man Michael remembered and the old man in the last photos? He felt like he was going to cry. He pushed backward in his chair so brusquely that he almost toppled over.

JoAnne reached for the back of the chair to steady him. "Are you okay?"

Michael landed the chair back on its four legs. He sniffed and put his sleeved arm to his nose. He nodded yes. JoAnne returned to the words on the screen and clicked on an article about Ed that featured yet another photograph. Michael read along with her, but there were many words he didn't know, and it became a frustrating, dizzying chore. His mother had made him read for thirty minutes each day, often books with pictures that helped him understand. Once he'd finish, she would read something to him, which was always a highlight of the day. After she died, he slowly gave up the habit of reading and now only read when someone in authority told him he had to, like reading the papers he signed before he could start working at Good House Burgers or the rules posted for keeping his suite tidy.

He took his eyes off the laptop screen.

"Listen, Michael, here's what I'm going to do." JoAnne's voice had a sweetness to it. "I am going to write down what I think is your brother Ed's current address on this piece of paper. I don't have a phone number for him, but I'll keep looking for that. Maybe some time you'll want to get in touch, even visit."

– 11 –

Meredith thought it is really too bad cigarettes can kill you. The after-sex cigarette was a true pleasure, even if it was a cliché. No chance of lighting up now. Not in her daughter's smoke-free apartment. Meredith tried to recreate the memory, the indulgent pleasure of inhaling the hot, scratchy mixture of tobacco and nicotine and then pushing smoke out through nostrils or open mouth, each languid motion the perfect reflection of her body's attitude after the pleasures just experienced. When was the last time she actually smoked a cigarette in such a setting? She couldn't recall. She thought she'd had too much wine that afternoon. Best to stick to a single glass. Especially these days, when she wasn't eating much. Now that a weekly rendezvous with Ed at the apartment was an established event, she needed to look her best.

"You know, this is actually the better relationship for you," Meredith said to Ed, who'd just emerged from the hall bathroom. She pulled a closed thumb and forefinger away from her mouth as if she had just taken a long drag. She audibly exhaled, nothing but air. "Not just because our ages match better."

"A hidden affair with a married woman is healthier than living with and being a full partner with Sarah? That's a novel thought." He smiled.

"I mean you shouldn't be in a full-time relationship with anyone. Not just my daughter specifically. A weekly fling like this is what's best. Being full-time with someone keeps you from doing your best work."

He frowned.

"I suppose you think I'm brazen by mentioning my daughter."

"Whatever. I am at ease with the unconventional."

"Me too. I mean, I'm not, but I want to be. Now. I've lived too long stifled in every way."

He smiled at her. His smile, she thought, was never endearing. Something about the curl of the lips.

"I mean it, though, about the writing. Neither of us is getting any younger."

Ed's face reddened. "Listen, this is fun. And if it helps you rebel against what you see as your humdrum, too average suburban life, well okay, that's fine too. But please don't start lecturing me about writing."

"I just meant that I make no claims on you, leaving you free to pursue your art. I don't want or expect anything more than meeting you once a week as long as it seems like something we are both interested in doing."

"How very noble of you."

Meredith didn't like the sound of his sarcasm.

"And how very unorthodox to sleep with me and then urge me to dump your daughter," Ed said. "For the sake of my art. Good God. Or is it a Machiavellian scheme because you don't think I'm the right man for Sarah? Just like your husband. He's certainly made it clear enough. Are you sacrificing yourself on the altar of my bed in order to save your daughter?"

He smiled again. Each new smile seemed uglier to her.

"Don't be an idiot," she said.

– 12 –

Michael Blaus pulled on his brown leather jacket, more appropriate now with the onset of colder weather. He immediately felt better with the jacket on, safer, almost like how he used to feel when his mother gave him a big hug. JoAnne was waiting for him in the supervisor's area, near the front doors. Michael was thinking about Good House Burgers as he carefully descended the stairwell from his third-floor apartment. The positive vibes from the leather jacket faded, replaced by a slow rumbling in his stomach as he thought about not going to work. Maybe he should just go to his job and forget about this being a special day. He would tell JoAnne that he had changed his mind, that he was needed and expected at work and that's where he was going. He wouldn't be able to go on the trip they'd spent weeks planning. If he didn't go to work, what would his boss, Manny, think? Would he and the others be angry? Would they think, *Michael, you didn't show up, and that meant more work for all of us?* Would they say they didn't need him to come back to work anymore if they couldn't count on him to come when he was supposed to? That they could get along without him? That would be terrible, too terrible. He tried to push the thought of being banished from Good House Burgers out of his mind. It was difficult. If they didn't want him, what would he do then?

JoAnne had assured him it would all be fine. People missed work once in a while for a variety of reasons. She herself had missed work a few times because she was sick. She'd called Manny a few days earlier and explained the situation. A family issue had arisen, and Michael needed to be away for one day. Just one. She told Michael his boss couldn't have been nicer. He was fine with Michael missing a day. In fact, he wished Michael would take more days off. They didn't have paid vacations at Good House, Manny said, but they didn't hold it against anyone who needed time to themselves. When Michael first heard all this, he felt better. But now, when missing work was a tangible reality, it was different. Still, he trusted JoAnne. She was smart, and if she said Manny had given the okay, it really should be okay. And he liked JoAnne. If he went with her, it would be a chance for them to be together for the day. Just the two of them. He would be brave. He would go with JoAnne.

The first big step was the ferry ride to lower Manhattan. Michael stood outside at the rail and enjoyed the sharp, damp wind as it hit him in his face. JoAnne pointed to the Statue of Liberty in the distance. He'd seen pictures of it in books. Now he got to see it for real. Then there was the subway uptown. The strange rumbling cars, the dark and dirty platforms, the long flights of stairs to climb before they were up, finally high enough to walk onto the sunny sidewalk and out of the gloom. When they reached the building, JoAnne pushed a small button on the wall. She knew Ed Blaus's phone number, but had decided not to call ahead. Given that Ed hadn't seen his brother in more than thirty years, JoAnne thought advance warning wouldn't work in favor of a reunion.

A voice came crackling out of the same metallic wall covering that JoAnne had pressed. "Hello?" Michael wasn't sure it was Ed. Maybe. JoAnne gestured for Michael to answer, but Michael couldn't find a word to say. Despite the silence, a buzzer sounded, and JoAnne was able to open the door to the lobby. She ushered Michael to an elevator, pushed floor five, and quickly stepped out before the door closed. "Remember, 5G. Knock on the door or ring the bell. I will be waiting for you right here. I will not go anywhere until you come back down."

Michael required a couple of trips around the hallway before he was certain he was standing in front of 5G. He wasn't sure if the bumpy thing at the side of the door was a bell to ring. He knocked. Nothing happened, so he knocked again. Ed Blaus opened the door a crack. He saw an older man with close-cropped hair, gray in patches, and cheap-looking, plastic black eyeglass frames. The man was wearing a brown leather jacket. The jacket looked familiar. "Oh my God," Ed said. He opened the door wider to take in a full view of Michael. "Oh my God." He felt for a moment like he was going to fall backward. He steadied himself and took Michael's forearm and led him into the apartment. He helped Michael off with his coat and half pushed him down into the soft, enveloping couch. He took the hard-backed seat across from him.

"Mikey, my God. What a surprise to see you. I wasn't expecting . . . How did you get here? How did you know I live . . .?" Ed kept interrupting himself. "I almost didn't recognize you, but that jacket, I remember that jacket, when Mom bought it. Do you want a glass of water?" Michael nodded.

After Michael had a couple more minutes to observe Ed, who sat facing him, pensively perched at the edge of the chair, it seemed more likely this man could be Ed, the brother he grew up with, the young, long-haired man who took care of him for a time when they lived together in the family apartment after their mother had died. Together, until the day Ed had taken Michael to the new place. Ed never came back. Michael thought he was gone for good. But here he was. If Ed was still here, still alive, though in this different apartment, which they had had to reach by boat and underground train, Michael thought, maybe, just maybe his mother also could be found somewhere after a certain amount of travel. Maybe a bigger boat or even an airplane would be needed. Maybe his mother also was simply somewhere else, not dead, though it was hard to imagine his mother would ever leave him and never come to visit if she wasn't dead. If she had a choice.

"It's good to see you, Mikey," Ed said. "It's been such a long time. But I've kept up with you. I know you have your own room now in a nice place full of good people."

"Is Mom somewhere else now too?" Michael asked.

"Mom?"

"Does she have a different place somewhere else?"

"Mikey, Mom is dead. Remember. Dead for a long time. We went to the funeral together."

Michael nodded. He sipped at his water. Ed was right. They went to the funeral. They watched their mother's casket lifted and then gently settled into the hole in the ground. Then men poured dirt over it. That was the difference. There had been no funeral for Ed.

"I have a job," Michael said. "At Good House Burgers."

"That's great, Mikey. I bet you are a really good worker."

"I didn't go today. I didn't go to work. I came here. I hope they aren't mad."

"They won't be mad, Mikey, I know they won't be."

"Is that your daughter?" Michael pointed to a photo on a low-slung mica table of Ed and Sarah, arms around each other. "Uh, no, that's a friend of mine. She lives here too."

"I wish I had someone to live with."

They talked for a few more minutes. Ed continued to sit at the edge of his chair, as if ready to spring up at any moment if circumstances warranted. He tried explaining what he did all day, writing. "But don't you go to work?" Michael asked.

"This is my work," Ed said. "I just get to do it at home, not in an office."

That did not seem like a good plan to Michael. He imagined being cooped up in his room all day, by himself. He'd much rather be with his friends at Good House Burgers. There was a knock on the door. JoAnne introduced herself. She said she wanted to make sure Michael was all right. She'd been waiting downstairs, but then she became concerned and decided to check to make sure Michael had found the right apartment. Michael smiled when he saw her. Ed invited JoAnne in, but she remained just inside the front door frame. She didn't want to intrude. Ed wanted to ask if she was behind the surprise visit. What was its purpose? Who was this woman to spring Mikey on him like this after all these years? Unannounced. Leaving him unprepared. What gave her the right? Why didn't he have a say in the matter? He felt his face heat up. He kept his mouth closed. Better just to wait it out. Now that she was here, the visit couldn't last much longer. Michael sipped his water. Ed faced his brother.

"You look well, Mikey. You must like it where you live."

Michael nodded and studied his water glass.

"Are you ready to go back?" JoAnne asked after a couple minutes' silence. Michael said he was.

"Is there anything else you want to know, Mikey? From me?" Ed spread out his arms.

Michael considered. "Why can't we live in our old apartment anymore?"

Ed narrowed his arms, hands matched against each other and directed toward Michael, who thought it looked like Ed was pointing a pretend gun at him. "It's better this way, Mikey. There are people at the place you live now who can help you, who know what you need. Like I didn't. Like I couldn't."

– 13 –

"No, no, I definitely don't want more spaghetti." Justin Skilbahl pulled back from the kitchen table and patted his narrow stomach. "I've got to keep my physique in shape for leading man roles."

His mother smiled and put the pot back on the stovetop. She wiped her hands on a paper towel and joined him. His expression suddenly stiffened, and Emily Skilbahl wondered if he was going through an acting exercise.

"I'm thinking seriously of changing my name to Blaus," he announced.

"Whatever for?" she asked.

"I know he's not famous anymore, but in the New York arts world some people probably still remember it, the name, I mean. It's unusual enough."

"I don't follow. Whenever you talk about him, it's always negative. His no-shows at birthday parties, school plays, all that, that negligence."

"Of course he's a bastard. I'm not contesting that. Or changing my mind. But that's the thing. Maybe this is a way to finally get him to do one single, solitary thing for me, do me some good. It might work, because he doesn't actually have to put himself out. Anyone can change his name to Blaus. You don't need Ed Blaus's okay. I'm thinking if people remember his name, then Justin Blaus, not Justin Skilbahl, might get more audition calls, maybe even parts."

"I'm trying not to be offended that our last name isn't good enough for you anymore. I'm trying to be practical. So practically speaking, I'm not sure anyone remembers him, maybe some literature students," Emily said.

"The way things have been going, I don't have much to lose. I can just as well be a waiter called Skilbahl or Blaus, or 'Hey you, why's my dinner taking so long?'"

Emily looked down at the backs of her blue-veined, nearly translucent hands and shook her head slowly from side to side. Justin had a bad habit of feeling sorry for himself. She'd brought it up to her son often enough. It would be better if he let Ed Blaus go. She had, at least during her waking hours. Ed still too regularly visited her dreams. Often he asked her to join him on a journey—in one dream he actually showed up with a magic carpet, patted it, and asked her to hop aboard—and then, at the last moment, some terrible event, a storm, a fire, some other catastrophe, always left her behind while Ed escaped. In one dream, she fell from a train. In another, she ran, gasping for breath, after a beat-up Volkswagen sedan as it drove away. She couldn't see him, but she knew Ed was driving the car. In certain dreams, she wasn't the only one abandoned. Sometimes there'd be a baby too, crying. Then he'd be in her arms as she limped away, covered in dust, near railroad tracks. Whatever the scenario, Ed Blaus was always gone.

Sitting in her cramped apartment in Astoria, Queens, with her grown son, Emily thought of all the legal battles she had fought with Ed, the unwanted publicity, the exorbitant attorneys' fees, and the stressful trips to court. One newspaper had run a large photo of Emily that she still remembered, thin and fragile, wearing a long, hippie-style skirt spread wide by a gust of wind. The photographer had caught her heading into the court building to face Blaus and his lawyer. Justin, just a baby, was with one of her friends. She had won the case, just as she did subsequent judgments, but they were in the main pyrrhic victories. Ed never lived up to the court orders. He sent money for a while, as obligated, but then he would stop. He worked irregularly. Much worse was what Ed's neglect did to Justin. As much as Emily tried to be an ever-present, loving mother, she couldn't do anything to assuage the pain of rejection created by Ed's notable absence. In the early years there were excuses—he was teaching in one place or another. He sent an occasional present, usually a book too advanced for whatever age Justin was. Later, when Justin was a teen and Ed lived mainly in New York City, Justin started reaching out directly. Ed would raise Justin's hopes and then dash them with last-minute cancellations of lunches or dinners.

"After everything he's put us through, put you through, it seems so odd to honor him this way," Emily said.

"It's not about honoring anyone," Justin said, getting up abruptly. "It's about trying to survive."

"If you do decide to go through with this, you should get in touch with him, tell him about it. He'll probably be quite pleased that you are taking his name. His ego and all that. Maybe it will soften his heart."

Justin snorted. "As if there's a heart there to soften."

Still, he agreed to contact his father before taking any steps to change his last name.

−14−

Scott kept thinking about the story Mary Jenseth had shared, how Ed Blaus had taken the inheritance meant to assure Michael's future and instead used it for himself. He dumped Michael off, the very outcome their mother, knowing she was dying, had plotted to avoid. Ed did the very thing he promised his mother he would not let happen. Once the older brother was dispensed with, Ed never visited. It was a terrible tale. In Scott's mind, this was worse than Blaus's infidelities, worse than denying he was the father of his child. Scott was confident Sarah wouldn't be able to ignore this, wouldn't be able to say Ed Blaus had grown and therefore previous indiscretions no longer mattered. That he was a changed man. Some things were too big to run away from. A crime against your own family was one. Certainly, Scott knew, the world required compromises, corners cut, that there were times to look the other way. But your family. Hell, your family was the reason you dirtied your hands in the first place. Scott had no doubt the way Michael was treated spoke to the centrality of Ed Blaus's character. This was it. This was the something Scott had expected lay hidden from the moment he met Blaus. Now he had it. And yet. And yet. Scott felt no jubilation from confirming what he suspected. He thought the information might well lead his daughter to get out of her relationship with this no-good older man. *That was the goal from the start, right? Right. Okay then, keep your eye on the ball.*

What kept coming back to Scott, though—in fragments of old conversations, images of his parents' bewildered expressions, slices of his own incoherent dreams—was Freddie. His brother, Freddie, in pain, reaching out for help, his help. Freddie. Not strong enough to make it alone. Then, earlier scenes: Freddie on the Little League field, clumsy but happy, his curly brown hair poking out from all sides of his dirty cap. Having no sense of what in a few short years would befall him. Freddie's death was a subject Scott was usually successful pushing to the back of his consciousness. Freddie was gone. Scott was helpless to do anything about it. Life was for the living. Mantras repeated over and over. Scott's work and ambition and the time-consuming trudge of it all made it possible to move on from Freddie. It was easier after Scott's parents died. He hated to admit it. But it was true. Finally, he no longer had to look into their haggard, beseeching faces, etched in a pain that never diminished, even years after Freddie's death. They never accused him of bearing responsibility, but Scott saw it in their faces. They suffered the worst imaginable pain any parent could be asked to endure: the death of your child. Scott severed already tenuous ties with other relatives as soon as his parents passed away. Their broader family life consisted of Meredith's larger, generally happy clan, and that was fine with Scott. He also broke off all connections with the neighborhood of his youth and moved to Westchester. That made it easier to live without thinking too much or too often about Freddie. But Ed Blaus's arrival blew it all apart. It had prompted Scott to join his high school's Facebook group, get in touch with Mickey Genz, and travel back a couple times in pursuit of information about Ed. Now that he had what he was looking for, the reputation-damaging story that should sway Sarah, there was no sense of triumph. Freddie was back too, preying on his mind.

 Freddie was three years Scott's junior, and the brothers couldn't have been more different. Scott fit in pretty much everywhere; Freddie never did, or at least felt he never did. Scott wasn't the smartest or the best athlete or the bravest in his age group, but he was close enough to each of those superlatives to be accepted by the pack. He was generally well-liked. He found the right balance of youthful rebelliousness and compliance. His parents were proud of him. Freddie was tall and lean and wasn't any good at sports, which was tough on a boy growing up at that time. In the preteen years, athletic ability determined your fit in the social hierarchy, the amount of respect you received or taunting you suffered. Freddie had little cache, and while Scott had protected him a number of times from bullies, he was also frustrated by what he perceived as Freddie's nerdy ways.

 Freddie did find a group. They wore their hair long when that was no longer the style and rode skateboards up and down the streets, jumping from any curbs or higher concrete they could find. Freddie developed an interest in drawing and took some art electives. But then he began hanging out with other kids who were more interested in illicit drugs than any of Scott's friends. And more quickly than anyone in the family thought possible, Freddie was into hard drugs, bad drugs, even heroin. It made him feel, he said during one of the times Scott confronted him, like he was gliding, like the world made sense and he was the master of it. It made him feel like he never felt in what they called real life. Scott was disgusted and told him he was going to wind up a sick, shivering junkie. One of those strung-out, desperate people they stepped around or crossed the street to avoid on their way to school. Then Scott was off, quickly ensconced in a new life at Binghamton University, while Freddie remained in Brooklyn and followed the path his brother had warned him against.

Eventually Scott's parents became aware of the seriousness of Freddie's drug problem. They didn't know what to do. They'd never imagined this issue would invade their home. Freddie stole from them and from neighborhood stores. He didn't eat. Forget about graduating from high school. There were cycles, but whenever Freddie entered a new downturn, it seemed worse than the one before. They looked to Scott, their successful son, to supply them with answers. Scott knew he should take charge, but he also didn't want to derail his life on campus. He counseled tough love. Offer Freddie help, try to get him into a detox program, which was no easy task for people with limited means. But only when Freddie came to them and said he was ready. Ready to be helped. Because without that, without Freddie truly buying in, rehab would not hold. If Freddie didn't come to them and say he wanted help, they needed to be firm. He couldn't sleep in their apartment. They should change the locks so that Freddie couldn't steal from them anymore. They shouldn't have anything to do with him. When Freddie was ready to ask for help, they would be there. But Freddie had to be the person to fight his own addiction. All this advice came from books Scott read as Freddie deteriorated. It made sense to twenty-two-year-old Scott. His parents had no better ideas, so they went along. They put their trust in Scott. They locked Freddie out of the apartment. They ignored him when they passed him and his friends in the neighborhood, whispering and clearly up to no good. Scott's mother said it almost killed her to do that, to turn away from her own son, whom she had carried and brought into the world. They said Freddie was barely recognizable. Scott told them to stay strong, to stay the course. Freddie never came to them for help. Instead, he died in a basement hideaway from a heroin overdose. He was a month short of his nineteenth birthday.

The walls Scott had so sturdily erected over the years to distance himself from that story cracked apart after he talked with Mary Jenseth. But what happened with Freddie was different from what Ed had done to his brother. Scott knew now that his young self had been stubborn and foolish to think that if Freddie just put his mind to it, he could decide to straighten himself out. But Scott's intentions were good. Yes, yes, he told himself, his intentions were good. That was not the case with Ed, who had placed his brother in a frightening situation and never looked back. Scott had wanted Freddie to get well. He'd thought his recommendation would turn Freddie around. But addiction was all-powerful. From his fifty-eight-year-old perspective, Scott could see that Freddie had needed more help than his parents were willing to offer because of Scott's advice. Freddie couldn't take the first step toward them. He was in too deep. Too in thrall to the drugs. They should have gone to him and gotten him off the streets and into a program. Scott should have taken the lead. He should have gone home and made it happen. He knew his parents could not. It was on him, and he simply didn't want to become too involved. Instead, they all stood by and watched until one day Freddie went too far. This was not the same as Ed's behavior toward Michael. Scott told himself this over and over again. But that point didn't banish the thoughts of his dead brother.

When Scott called the group home to see if Michael Blaus lived there, the woman on the phone was suspicious of his interest in Michael. Scott pretended to be an agent with the Internal Revenue Service who needed to confirm Michael's mailing address before his tax refund could be released. Faced with the prospect of Michael being denied his deserved money if she refused to engage, the woman relented. Yes, you can send it here, she said; he'll get it. That phone call was the last piece of the project. All was in order. Scott would present incontrovertible evidence of Ed Blaus's baseness to his daughter. *In case you don't believe me, he would say, just ask Ed to tell you about his brother. Oh, and if he tries to lie about it, or actually doesn't know where*

Michael is now, I can help: he lives on Staten Island in a group home. Here's the contact information. Still, he kept putting off telling Sarah. He returned to the group home's website. With a few clicks he found various protocols, including rules for visitors. He imagined himself driving to Staten Island to visit Michael Blaus. He could say he was a friend of Ed's, or that he knew Ed; the latter was certainly true. He just wanted to see how Michael was doing, spend some time so Michael would have someone with whom to hang out. Maybe take in a ballgame together if Michael was so inclined. Scott clicked out of the home's site and firmly shut the cover of his laptop. What was he doing? He was not going to visit a stranger in a Staten Island group home. What was going on with him? This was getting ridiculous.

At dinner, Scott summarized for Meredith what he found out about Ed Blaus.

"Wait, what did you do, hire spies to dig up dirt from his past?"

"It's all pretty much there for anyone to find," Scott lied. He didn't worry about Meredith finding out about the $5,000 payment he had made to Mickey Genz. He controlled the couple's finances. Meredith was content to have a credit card with no spending limit attached. She could buy whatever she wanted any time she wanted. Why worry about anything else moneywise?

"And you plan to tell Sarah this, this tawdry story about Ed?"

"That is the plan. Right now, I am talking to you about it."

"I think the problem is you are applying traditional, bourgeois values to a realm where they don't belong, because artists, real artists, can't be bound by such conventions."

"Is that so?"

"Don't be sarcastic. It is so. And yes, I have a better understanding of these things than you do. I have an aesthetic perception. I took a number of literature classes."

"And that aesthetic perception says that if you write a book, you are not subject to the bounds of human decency? That you can screw your brother out of an inheritance designed to take care of him?"

"That's your interpretation. Another might be Ed realized he couldn't adequately care for his brother, so he brought him to a place where trained professionals could help him."

"Which one is it? He did the right thing for Michael's care or artists can do whatever they want?"

"Don't be so rude," Meredith said. She stood and picked up both their dinner plates. She walked from the dining room, where their table was large enough to accommodate many more than two, and took the plates to the adjoining kitchen. When she returned, Meredith was ready for more.

"You really should try not to be such a philistine. There's an old saying, maybe you've heard it: talent does what it can; genius does what it must. It's true. Ed had to answer the burning need to create. He simply had to. And he needed to find a way to support himself while he wrote. That's how it works. That's in addition to the reality that his brother was better off where Ed placed him."

"Oh please, Meredith, that's absurd. Ed Blaus is not an artistic genius. If anything, he's an artistic con man, using women, ignoring people who depend on him. That's the truth. You've stopped being able to accept simple facts about Blaus. Sarah, I think, can still see them."

− 15 −

Justin Skilbahl texted Ed Blaus. "Hey, it's been a while. I need to talk to you about something. Let me know a good time. Face-to-face would be best for this."

He got a reply the next day. "Hello Justin. Kind of busy these days and I may have to go out of town soon. Would prefer phone talk if okay."

On the phone, Justin stammered out his idea of changing his last name to Blaus. There was a long silence, and then Ed Blaus asked, neutrally, "Why?"

Justin was prepared with a spiel he thought would appeal to his father. When he had thought it up and rehearsed it, he convinced himself there was truth to it too. "Well, as you know, we haven't always gotten along or been tight—and I am not intending to rehash any of that stuff now, don't need to, don't want to—but I thought, I guess, that if we shared a name, especially one that was passed down to you over generations, it might help to bring us closer."

"I'm not real big on tradition, Justin. In fact, I think it's a load of crap, passing down a name and all that. It's a name, and in this case, a blunt, unmelodic name. At least it's short."

"Uh, I, uh, thought you'd be pleased."

"I'm afraid you're wrong. This isn't the way to appeal to me, if that's your intention. I'll be honest: whatever you use as a last name is not going to change our relationship. It will not bring us closer. What we have is what we have. So let me give you some fatherly advice, for once. Here it is: stop thinking about me. Stop thinking about Blaus. Everyone, even those with attentive, affectionate fathers, has to invent themselves sooner or later. It's on the individual. Not on the parentage.

You might as well get on with it."

"I am getting on with it," Justin shouted. "What the hell do you think . . ." Justin stopped when his voice cracked on the last couple of words. He composed himself and was about to begin speaking again when he realized Ed Blaus was no longer on the line.

– 16 –

Scott looked at his watch. Not bad. The Metro-North train was going to be only a couple minutes late as it approached the Scarsdale station. The long workday was a blur of half-concentrated-upon meetings. Scott was preoccupied with various scenarios under which he would tell his daughter about what Ed Blaus had done, years earlier, to his defenseless brother. Hell, you could argue Blaus's artistic reputation was made possible by a theft. He thought of his wife's comments about a moral free pass given to artists. That was ridiculous. Could Sarah possibly believe the same? Was she so smitten with this man that nothing would penetrate?

Scott gathered his things, patted his jacket pocket to reassuringly feel the bulk of his wallet, and stood to leave the train. He knew he should have talked to Sarah already. He was stalling. There was something he couldn't fully strike down. It stuck around like a dull pain in a back tooth, never acute enough to sideline you or demand immediate action, but also never fully out of your consciousness. Try as he might, he couldn't disconnect the story of Ed and Michael Blaus from the story of himself and Freddie. Scott never stole anything their parents intended to go to Freddie, nor had he double-crossed his brother. But Michael Blaus was still alive. Quite possibly, as Meredith had maintained, in a better situation. Ed Blaus, like Scott, wanted to get on with his life. In Ed's case, to write. He wanted to avoid being tied down in the old neighborhood. That would stop him from realizing any of his dreams. As Scott pulled his car into the wide driveway, this thought sat in his head: *Blaus's brother is alive. Mine is dead.*

Scott found his wife in the living room, but not in a chair or on the sofa. She was sitting on a low stool, meant for your feet when you sat in one of the overstuffed chairs that framed the room. No one ever used it. They didn't spend much time in the living room. Meredith's head was down and in her hands. Her dark fair fell limply over her thin fingers. A Delmonico glass half full of what smelled like Scotch sat beside her on the rug. Scott suppressed a groan. What melodramatic act was this? He thought of how Meredith had said she had an aesthetic understanding of life Scott didn't share. Another way of saying she was intellectually superior to Scott. Meredith could be so over the top, especially lately. Another term for aesthetic whatever was "self-centered." Scott removed his bag from his shoulder. He walked over to Meredith, but didn't touch her. She didn't look up.

"What's wrong?" he asked without evident concern.

She didn't answer.

"Meredith, what's wrong?" he said more firmly.

"Call your daughter," she said weakly. "She'll explain."

"Sarah? What happened to Sarah?"

"She's okay," Meredith said, finally looking up. Her dark eyes were red, streaked with veins. Her mascara was smeared. "She's not hurt . . . physically. I just can't bear to talk about it. Can't talk about it. Call her."

Scott strode into his den, closed the door, and rang his daughter. She sniffled on the other end.

"Daddy?"

"What's wrong, sweetheart?"

"Mom didn't tell you?"

"She just said to call you. She said she couldn't talk. She's being quite dramatic."

"Of all things, like she's the injured party. Unbelievable."

"Please, Sarah, just tell me."

"Mom and Ed are having an affair."

The sniffling resumed, more audibly.

"What!"

"Unbelievable, right?"

It was more than unbelievable. Scott couldn't speak.

"A few times recently, I'd come home from work and there would be a faint odor in the apartment. Stronger in the bedroom. I couldn't put my finger on it. Today, I left the office early. My boss is on vacation, and there wasn't much going on. I walked into the bedroom to change, and there was that smell again, but stronger. I was laying out my work clothes on the bed before hanging them up. That's when I noticed the bed was made up a little differently than usual, like someone remade it. Then it hit me. The smell was Mom's perfume. It's so distinctive, and she's worn it for years. She can only get it at a few places here in the city. It's from Italy.

"I didn't think much of it, but I asked Ed if Mom was here today, and he said no, of course not, why should she be? I just shrugged. Then, in the kitchen sink, I saw them. Two wine glasses, just about empty. And Mom's lipstick smudge on one of them. I knew instantly it was her. It's a shade no one else I know wears. She has to be distinctive in everything. It's pretty annoying, really, you know, her insistence on being unique. I guess he figured he had time to clean up the glasses and hadn't gotten around to it. Like I said, I got home earlier than usual.

"I can't believe I am saying this so casually. My mother is having sex with the man I live with. Who does something like that? What is she?"

What is *he*, Scott wanted to interject. Forget your mother for a moment. How about the nonsense about how Ed had changed, how he'd grown, that he doesn't cheat anymore. Scott had the urge to tell Sarah right then about Ed's brother. *You think this is bad*, he wanted to say, *wait until you hear what I found out*. But he did not say anything about Blaus. Instead, Scott asked his daughter to continue to recount events.

"Eventually, he admitted it all. Said he didn't think it was a big deal. Can you believe it? He is having an affair with my mother and he said it didn't mean anything. Why was I so upset? Yes, he said that. Why was I so upset? Sometimes it's like he's from another planet, Ed. No emotional connection on either side, he said. Just some physical contact between bodies. Said Mom was lonely and a little sad. At one point, he said the whole thing was really your fault, if you thought about root causes. Root causes, like he's a sociology professor. Because you don't pay sufficient attention to Mom. He made it sound like he did nothing wrong."

"Unbelievable," Scott said, conscious of the weakness of the word and unable to locate an appropriate replacement. "Where is Blaus now?"

"I don't know. I told him he had to leave. Probably went to stay with one of his writer buddies. He's got a decent number of them. He was sure to take his laptop before he left. Probably afraid I would use a hammer on it after he was gone. I just might have too."

"Are you okay there? By yourself, I mean, with all this?"

"It's funny, I thought for a moment after Ed left that I'd take the train up to you guys and stay at the house. Just to have some company, you know, have other people breathing nearby and all, maybe call in sick at work tomorrow. But then I thought that's over now. It's not a refuge anymore. Mom's there. The problem is right there, sitting there, in the house."

Scott looked at the closed den door, which separated him from Meredith, who he presumed was still on the stool, head in hands, in the living room.

"What are you going to do?" Sarah asked.

"Me?" Scott said, surprised by the question. He hadn't thought of himself as a participant. He was concentrating on Sarah and Ed. That it was now over between them. He quickly realized what Sarah's question meant. Meredith had betrayed him as well as Sarah. What was he going to do about his wife having sex with his daughter's lover? Good God.

"I don't know. I guess I have to do something."

"I would think."

Scott told Sarah he would check back with her. To call him for any reason, or no reason. He was willing to drive down if she wanted. She told him no, she thought she would be okay on her own.

"Just remember, I am always available," he said. "At a moment's notice."

They ended the call. He looked again at the thick door of the den. He had no interest in leaving his comfortable desk chair. So, he sat. Eventually he flipped on the laptop and half-heartedly scrolled through a few news articles. He didn't absorb any of the information in front of him. He had no idea what to do next.

– 17 –

They met late on a Saturday morning for brunch, which was Sarah's favorite meal to eat out. It was the same place in the city the three of them had gathered—Scott, Meredith, and Sarah—the day Sarah dropped the news that she and Ed were planning to live together. That bombshell had inspired Scott to double down on his research of the man, as if Sarah's life depended on it. To convince her with hard evidence that Ed Blaus was a bad person. Someone with whom she shouldn't be involved. Well, here they were, and sure enough, he'd uncovered the goods on Blaus; he'd succeeded in his mission. The data was in, and it proved his case. That's a thing Scott learned as a young man making his way in business. Believe the data, not your gut. Or find the data to confirm your gut. No one's gut is enough. Those who said they built fortunes on it, well, at some point, their guesswork returned to the mean. The smart ones, after a big strike made by trusting their instincts, those smart ones bought villas in the south of Spain and enjoyed themselves. They left the game ahead.

Scott did the work, and he had the goods. He knew Blaus's most damning secrets: that he had cast aside his brother, rejected his own child, and carried on affairs behind the back of whomever he was in a relationship with at any given moment. And now he knew he would never need to use any of it, because Blaus had outdone himself. Blaus proved the makeup of his character once and for all by having an affair with Meredith.

"How are you holding up?"

"Ha! What a question!"

Sarah removed a tissue and dabbed at her eyes in what seemed to Scott a practiced motion. Even after she removed the tissue, tears continued to slowly stream. Sarah didn't seem to notice. She kept on talking as if nothing was happening higher up on her face. It was painful for Scott to look at.

"To be honest, I can't fully process it. Not yet, maybe never. How am I ever going to face my own mother again? My own mother . . . " she trailed off.

"I know, it's still so raw. But in time you'll remember she is your mother and you only get one. Like it or not. In time. She's flawed, like all of us."

"Flawed! Flawed! Come on, Dad. Are you kidding? Flawed is having a short temper or maybe drinking too much at parties. Flawed is you can't cook a steak without burning the thing. Sleeping with your daughter's lover: that is one hell of a lot more than flawed."

"I know, but . . . "

"And what about you? Your wife of thirty years has an affair. With a guy we all know you don't think much of, not from the start. Are you so Zen about that? That's not you. That's not the father I know. What are you on? If this is what it does for you, I'd like some."

Scott smiled. She had a point. Mother and daughter didn't know him as a forgive-and-forget type of guy. And yet. Maybe he also was still processing. Maybe it would hit him later. Could he separate his own reaction, apart from feeling for Sarah? If so, would it be closer to pity for Meredith? Understanding even? Maybe what he should have felt for his brother, Freddie, when Freddie couldn't get out of the addiction that killed him. Instead, he'd been angry at Freddie, disgusted with him, his failure to be a real man, to straighten out. As for Meredith, to do what she did, it seemed to him, meant she had lost all self-respect. Not that he was going to take responsibility for Meredith's stupidity. Hell, no. They'd both let the marriage drift. Things were good in the early years. The best times were after Sarah was born. She became the center over which they connected. It was all new and exciting. After a troubled pregnancy, Meredith thrived as a mother. Work started demanding more from Scott as he advanced: more hours, more travel, more time away from Meredith and Sarah. The separation was ever-widening. Once Sarah went off to college, Scott felt the thread of connection between Meredith and himself just about give way. He doubled-down on career and didn't dwell on what Meredith thought about their marriage and how she viewed the road ahead for herself. He convinced himself that what he and Meredith had left was the most one could realistically expect after so many decades together. They weren't divorced; they weren't at each other's throats. They shared a house and a daily life full of small rituals. He imagined they both understood this. They had Sarah. They had a family, because of Sarah. He thought they both put that above all else. Family. The one certainty when everything else lost meaning. Obviously, he was wrong. If Meredith felt the way he did about Sarah and family, she would not have bedded down with Ed Blaus. If she wanted to have an affair, she could have picked someone else. A man from their tennis club. Or one of the trainers at the gym. Clichés, of course, but they were clichés because of the regularity with which they happened. Meredith didn't have to go and blow everything up. But anger? At Meredith? No. That was reserved for Ed Blaus, who wasn't satisfied with his own long résumé of destructive behavior, but had to keep adding more.

"I went to see Blaus's ex-wife a while back."

"Why did you do that?"

"You know I was against your relationship from the get-go. It wasn't just the age difference. I knew he was a bad man. I wanted to find out more. To convince you . . ." Scott stopped there.

Sarah reached across the table and put her hand on her father's.

"Oh, Dad, it's so nice to have you looking out for me. I really mean it. Clearly, no one else is interested. And, unfortunately, you were right and I didn't see it. I appreciate not hearing 'I told you so.'"

Sarah's gesture and words warmed Scott in a way he hadn't felt in a long time.

"Well," he said, "you'll know what it's like when you have children."

"Meanwhile, he keeps texting me," Sarah said.

She removed her hand to show Scott her phone. The first communications were abject, apologetic. Blaus again admitted to the affair, begged for forgiveness, repeated there had been no emotional attachment between him and Meredith. After a couple days of that, Ed Blaus's tone changed. "Sarah, please respond to me. Your silence, I have to say, is an immature reaction to the situation. I say that with love." Then: "Sarah, this is insane. I have apologized. Again and again. You are a sophisticated woman. You know sex can be meaningless. A physical act. That's what it was with Meredith. Why throw away what's been real between us? True and deep." Then, still lacking a response,

Blaus became matter of fact. "I would like to arrange an acceptable time when I can come to pick up my things. If it is too difficult for you to be there while I do this, I can let myself in one last time."

"Do you want me to write him and tell him to leave you the hell alone? That I'll kill him if he contacts you again?"

Sarah smiled weakly. "It's okay. You don't need to get involved. I'll eventually tell him he can come and get his stuff. I just can't communicate with him . . . not yet."

"If I were you, I'd change the locks and throw his crap out with the next trash."

"I will change the locks, once he's come and gone the last time."

"But, meanwhile, he's out there somewhere with your keys. He could let himself in any time, even while you are asleep."

"Dad, he's a creep, a bad guy, as you would say, but he's not that."

Scott wasn't so sure.

"It's funny, though. Right after I found out about Ed and Mom, I went to the kitchen drawer where I keep an extra set of keys and put them in my purse. You know, just to have them and make sure Ed didn't. Then I realized that didn't make any sense, since he's got his own keys."

"So, you *are* worried."

"I guess, no, not really, just in a daze and not acting rationally. Mom's got keys too."

"I don't think you have to worry about her sneaking into your apartment. Not anymore, anyway."

"Where is she? There's been complete silence from her. Which I appreciate."

"She's with her sister, Aunt Carole, in Connecticut. As for not contacting you, I'm sure she wants to but can't imagine what to say."

"Have the two of you talked since . . . "

"Just briefly, to exchange information," Scott said.

Sarah excused herself to use the restroom. She looked exhausted. "This has taken a lot out of you," Scott said when she returned. "I mean, just coming out to eat."

Sarah nodded.

"Just one more question. I know you said Blaus was staying with one of his writer friends. Do you know specifically where he is?"

"Not a hundred percent sure," Sarah said. "But most likely with his friend Henry Levitt on the Upper West Side, near Columbia. Henry teaches there. He's a poet."

Scott nodded and stood up from his chair.

"Why did you ask? You're not going to . . . "

"No, no," Scott assured her. "I was just curious. I wish he was farther away from you than Upper Manhattan."

– 18 –

Henry Levitt wasn't difficult to locate. Poetry circles aren't large, and nothing about their makeup would have prompted Levitt to take protective actions online. On a Monday morning, a few minutes after nine o'clock, Scott stationed himself across the street from the apartment house on Riverside Drive. A steady breeze blew in from the nearby Hudson River. Winter was giving in to spring. The street wasn't busy, and it felt a world apart from hectic Midtown. Scott figured office workers who lived in the area had already headed off. Now he witnessed a menagerie of individuals emerging and meandering in different directions: mothers pushing strollers, a few unkempt student types who looked old enough to be graduate level, and one man who might as well have worn a sign that said "I am a professor" based on his tweed jacket that looked too light for the weather. His thinning, windblown hair and dirty white sneakers completed the package.

It was nearly eleven. Scott was about to abandon his post to find a public restroom when Ed Blaus emerged from the prewar building and looked both ways before heading south. He made a left on 105th Street, and Scott caught up to him before he got to West End Avenue. "Blaus," Scott said loudly as he strode alongside the startled man, "we need to talk."

"Shit," Ed Blaus exclaimed as he backed toward the exterior of one of the buildings lining 105th. "What's wrong with you, coming up on someone like that?"

Scott smiled.

"Where would you like to have our chat? Back up in the place you're staying?"

"What makes you think I have any interest in talking to you?" Blaus recovered himself. "This is the second time you ambushed me. You like playing at being a cop or a spy or something?"

"I think the least you owe me is a conversation."

"Ah, grow up. I don't owe you anything."

"Okay, if that's how you look at it. You mentioned cops. Maybe I am on my way to file a police report about a quite expensive family heirloom, an exquisitely painted antique vase worth tens of thousands of dollars, that disappeared from my daughter's apartment. I can let the police know we have our suspicions about who might have taken it."

"I don't have any goddamn vase."

"Sure, the vase might turn up later. It could all be a big misunderstanding. But my guess is you don't need the police poking around your possessions right now."

"You can buy me a coffee at the place on Broadway," Blaus said. "I don't want to be alone with you."

The two men completed the walk to the coffee shop in silence. It was after breakfast and before lunch, so they were able to snag a booth.

"What is it with you, anyway?" Blaus said after Scott had returned from the bathroom. "Sarah told me from the get-go you wouldn't approve of me, and you confirmed it the moment I met you. Then you try to pay me off to leave."

"You should have taken me up on that offer. You were so confident you could squeeze Sarah and me for more, for a lifetime, you didn't even pick a number. I can tell you from long experience, that is piss-poor negotiating. Always pick a number. Shoot for the moon if you want, but by all means pick a number. You had leverage."

"I am an artist, not a businessman," Blaus said. His disgust was clear when he spat out the word "businessman."

"As for why I was against you from the start: I knew you were scum, and you proved me right in a way I never imagined."

The insult didn't seem to faze Blaus. *The man was used to it,* Scott thought. *Or felt himself above it all.* The writer waved his hand dismissively.

"'You're scum,'" he repeated in a mocking tone. "Where did you come up with that? In some superhero comic book? Come on, we're from the same neighborhood, right? About the same age. Don't try tough-guy bullshit."

"Bullshit? You had an affair with my wife while you were living with my daughter. How do you expect me to feel?"

"Yeah, yeah. If you were some evangelical preacher from Indiana, I'd buy it. The moral-outrage routine. But not from you. You're an operator; you just do it in an expensive suit."

Scott felt oddly complimented. "I made something of myself, by myself. I didn't spend a lifetime using people."

"I've got a theory about you," Blaus said, a wry smile spreading over his face. "I've been thinking about it because it could be useful in a novel. Something for the future. You want to hear it?"

"Shoot."

"The reason you get so worked up about me is because you secretly want to be me."

"What!" Scott's voice was loud enough that the few other patrons turned around. Scott noticed the unwanted attention and quieted down. "I figured you for an egomaniac, but that's ridiculous."

"Here's how I see it. Yeah, you've done fine materially, but God knows exactly what you do for all that money. Your daughter says you were remote and severe and worked all the time when she was a teenager. Your wife obviously isn't in love with you and hasn't been for some time. Deep down, you don't really care about that, but you know you're supposed to, so you go around huffing and puffing about it. You're starting to get old, and now you're realizing it's all pretty empty and there are plenty of people with a hell of a lot more money than you've accumulated, so you really didn't even win on that score. You've got your story: self-made man, working your way up from old Brooklyn to the wealthy suburbs. It's not original—I'd be laughed at if I tried to do a novel on that today."

Scott scowled at Blaus. The writer continued.

"See, what you missed is this: what's really appealing to women is the creative thing. That's what I have and you never will."

"Is it appealing to be such a bastard? To try to deny your own son. To trick your brother out of his inheritance?"

Blaus removed his hands from the coffee cup and put them at his sides. He lost some color from his face. For the first time since he had recovered from Scott's sudden appearance on the sidewalk, Blaus looked frightened.

"What do you know about my brother?"

"I know enough. I know he wound up abandoned in an institution after you talked your dying mother into leaving you her money with the promise you would take care of him."

"You don't know anything . . . "

"You see, Blaus, the reason you're a failed writer is in the end you aren't really that smart. Or maybe it's you're too lazy to work hard. You summed me up pretty well, but all on the surface. You don't dig deep, so you underestimate me. I'm just another striver who made it to the fancy suburbs, blah, blah. Old story. You think you are the savviest guy out there, the guy who got out of the old neighborhood, who made it as an artist. Ha. You were a flash in the pan. You wrote one book as a young man that some people liked. That hit at the right time for a guy like you to tell his Brooklyn story. After that, there's been nothing for thirty years, but you still think you're the sharpest guy in any room."

The I-don't-care sarcastic smile was back on Blaus's face. "I'm surprised you have the gall to talk about brothers. Maybe you forget, but your brother and I were in the same grade. We weren't really friends, but you know how it was back then. You knew something about everyone your own age. You'd see them around. You might hang out for a while in the same pack. Nice kid, I remember, quiet. Then came the drugs. What a waste to die so young."

Scott felt his hands roll into fists under the table.

"Stay away from my daughter," Scott said. "Stop texting her. Don't call her. She'll let you know when you can come by to pick up your crap. It's more than I would do."

Scott dropped a twenty-dollar bill on the tabletop, though only two coffees had been ordered. "If you don't stop contacting Sarah, you'll see me again." He walked toward the door of the long, narrow restaurant.

"Very good, tough guy," he heard Ed Blaus laughingly call from the booth. Blaus held up the twenty-dollar bill. "Hey, can I keep the change?"

— 19 —

Justin Skilbahl showed up at his mother's apartment unannounced. He looked like he hadn't shaved in days. Or slept much.

"What's going on?" Emily asked. He slumped down in the white, sculpted plastic chair at the kitchen table, his usual spot.

"Do you want something to eat?" she asked.

"Water."

She handed him a glass and watched as he gulped. He looked a mess, which Emily took to be indicative of his broader life, and with every day he grew older, she felt it less and less healthy for him.

He squinted. "Why the hell did you get involved with that lousy bastard in the first place?"

Emily looked at the floor. "The call didn't go well."

"That's good understatement. Well done. Perfect timing. Just a few words and then the sad, resigned look. Maybe you should be the actor instead of me. I'm obviously shit."

"You have a lot of talent, Justin. It's just you've chosen such a difficult field . . ."

"My father succeeded in a difficult field. I should probably stop using that term, 'father.' He obviously doesn't see our relationship that way."

"Do you want to tell me what he said?"

"In a sentence, 'Get the fuck out of here.' He doesn't want me to change my name. He doesn't want to be any closer. He doesn't want anything to do with me." Justin hung his head. "What did I ever do to him? Why doesn't he care about me?"

Emily saw that this time Justin wasn't overemoting, which he called acting, as he was wont to do. She smoothed his dirty hair. "You're right, he is a bastard, and no, looking back, I don't know why I got involved with him. Except I am so glad that I did. I am thankful for that every day. Because if I hadn't, I wouldn't have you. And if he's too stupid or pigheaded to realize how wonderful you are, that's on him."

Justin had the night off from the restaurant and went to a friend's grubby apartment on the Lower East Side. Several guys he knew were there. They drank cheap vodka, mixed with a little 7Up. When the 7Up ran out, they dashed in some water. Those drinks tasted terrible, but they sloshed them down anyway. The room spun, so he lay down, half on the floor, half on an unsheeted mattress in a corner. Guest accommodations, no doubt. He told the group of his recent talk with Ed Blaus, followed by a condensed history of Blaus's dismissal of him as a son.

"You shouldn't put up with that shit," one of the guys said, dragging the word "shit" out until it was barely recognizable. The others found that hysterical. "Yes," another one said, "you should take some revenge."

"Seriously, that dude needs to be fucked with. Needs a lesson taught."

Justin nodded. He took another sip of vodka and water and winced at the taste.

"Cut off his ear," Justin's friend screamed. "Like they did to Van Gogh."

"Van Gogh cut his own ear, dipshit," another guy said, and they all laughed uproariously, Justin included.

– 20 –

Another day off. He had every Saturday off, and then a second off day on a weekday, usually Wednesday. One of the things the shift managers liked best about Michael Blaus, in addition to his reliability and general good humor, was that you could slot him into the day schedule anywhere there was a hole because another kitchen worker had a family emergency or just got fed up, pulled off his apron, and walked off the job. Michael didn't care when he worked, and he didn't care if you told him he had to switch days off. Michael was always good for Sunday work. It was the hardest day of the week to schedule. Michael wished there were fewer days off. He'd told his boss that and got a puzzled look in return. Michael understood that most of the full-time workers had two consecutive days off each week. That would be terrible. The off days stretched too long for Michael. He was deprived of the structure imposed by work. The alarm clock would ring. He would shower, put on his uniform and walk to Good House Burgers. This Wednesday morning it took him a long time to pick out what to wear, and then he couldn't find two socks that matched. He went to the front lobby. His face sagged when he saw JoAnne was not at the desk. Then he remembered she wouldn't be here this early. She started midafternoon. He asked the bearded young man at the desk whether JoAnne would be working later that day. He checked the online roster. "Uh, no," he said. "Looks like she's off today."

Michael couldn't decide where to go. In the past, even on a day off, he went to Good House and sat at one of the tables. He could sit contentedly for a long time, watching the comings and goings of customers and placidly observing the animated hustle of the order takers and drive-through specialists. Even though he wasn't in the kitchen, where he worked mainly doing clean up, he felt better for being in a familiar place. But one time, the shift manager came out and told him he shouldn't do that. Come to the restaurant on his day off. This wasn't Manny, Michael's regular boss. This manager spoke slowly but firmly. It was for Michael's own good, the man said. He should enjoy his time off, do something, go somewhere, and not hang around the very place where he spent forty hours a week. "Work and nothing else is wrong. Do something else on your day off," the man said, putting a hand on Michael's shoulder. "You understand me?" Michael wanted to tell him he liked sitting at Good House. He didn't mind the extra time there. No one ever bothered him about being there too much when he wandered over in the evening if JoAnne was too busy to talk with him. It was too difficult to think of new things to do. But Michael sensed from the man's tone it wouldn't matter how he responded. The man was a manager, someone above him. He had to listen. So he left. Now, on days off, Michael tried to stay away. If he did go to Good House Burgers, he would try to ascertain if the manager who told him to leave was working before he opened the door.

Michael walked around the block and then did it again. He thought about his visit with JoAnne to see Ed. On the ferry back from Lower Manhattan, Michael had asked JoAnne if it was okay to again stand by the rail. The wind felt like sharp caresses as it relentlessly whipped against his face. Its force made him squint.

"What did you think of your visit to your brother?" JoAnne asked.

It was hard to hear her above the dull roar of the engines and the wind. Michael was happy enough just thrusting his face into the wind and watching the ferry kick up spray as it moved. What did he think? He didn't know how to answer. He liked seeing Ed, though he almost didn't recognize his brother, who now looked old. Once Ed started talking it was easier to believe it was really him. But since he'd been gone so long, Michael had considered him dead. Like his mother. Would his mother stay away like Ed if she was still alive? He didn't think so, but there were so many things other people did that he didn't understand. If she was hidden somewhere like Ed, why didn't she visit him? Why didn't they live together anymore? Had he done something wrong without knowing it? Is that what kept Ed and his mother away? He couldn't think of any answer to JoAnne's question on the ferry ride back to Staten Island. So he just smiled. JoAnne smiled too.

Weeks passed from that trip, and Michael heard nothing from Ed. JoAnne asked Michael about it a couple times. He asked her a couple of times. Then the subject was dropped. But on this clear Wednesday morning with nowhere to go, Michael was focused on Ed. The ferry was within walking distance. He knew the way. In his pocket sat twenty-five dollars in small bills, paper-clipped to his photo ID from the home. The residents carried some money and their ID, clipped together. In case one of them got lost and couldn't explain things, the ID, with the name and phone number of the group home, would help a nice person sort it out. Most of the residents, including Michael, didn't have cell phones.

When he got to the ferry terminal, Michael thought about a ticket. He couldn't remember if JoAnne had taken care of that when they traveled together. He heard a crew member call "All Aboard" and was caught up in the crowd, which swelled into the belly of the ferry. It seemed no tickets were required. Once they slowly started on their way to Lower Manhattan, Michael again went outside and stood at the railing, waiting for the Statue of Liberty to come into view.

When they docked in New York and a crew member called everyone off, Michael shuffled along with the others. The excitement of the ride quickly wore off. He stood in the middle of the sidewalk's cement squares and was jostled by people rushing by. One man told him to get the hell out of the way. He moved over to stand in the shadow of a tall building. Down the block he saw a subway station entrance. It read "South" something, South Front? No, that wasn't it. As he got closer, he was able to make out "South Ferry." It had a big number 1 in a circle. He remembered that "1" was in front of the train he and JoAnne had taken on their trip to visit Ed. Numbers were easier for Michael than letters. Michael could not remember the stop where they had gotten off once they were on the 1 train. Did it have a name or a number? He carefully walked down the stairs to the subway station. The sharp sunlight disappeared when he was about halfway down the stairs.

– 21 –

Scott saw Sarah's name pop up on his phone and quickly answered. All he heard on the other end was harsh panting.

"Sarah, are you there? What's wrong?"

"Ed," she managed, and then repeated his name. "Blood, in the bedroom. Dead."

"What are you saying?"

"Ed is dead. He's in the bedroom. Blood all over. Oh my God, he's dead."

"Did he fall?"

"I don't know. I don't think so. There's so much blood. I couldn't really look."

"Have you called anyone else?'

"What, called? No, I called you."

"Okay, Sarah, listen to me. You should walk out of the apartment. Don't touch anything. Don't go back to the bedroom. Walk out and stand on the street until I call you back. Answer when I call you, okay? I'm going to call 911."

"Okay," she said.

"Did you understand what I said?"

"I think so."

Scott called the police.

Stuck in crosstown traffic behind a single-lane snake of cars and trucks on a one-way street, Scott cursed loud enough for the taxi driver to turn around.

"Something the matter?" he inquired with more than a little hostility.

"No, I'm just in a hurry, that's all," Scott replied.

"Yeah, well, in that case, it's best to stay out of New York."

Sarah wasn't in front of her apartment building when Scott arrived. A half dozen police cars and a boxy ambulance were. It took him five minutes to persuade the cop at the door that even though he wasn't a lawyer, as a father he was an adviser and needed to see his daughter if the police were questioning her. When he got to the open apartment door, another uniformed cop stretched his arm out, palm raised.

"Where do you think you're going, pal?"

Scott began to answer. He saw Sarah seated at the kitchen table. She looked up. "Dad," she said, and waved weakly. A man roughly Scott's age wearing a blue-fleece vest like those favored by Wall Street and tech types turned to also look at Scott. The uniform looked into the apartment. "It's okay," the vested man said. "Let him in." Scott walked carefully toward the table. He could see down the short hallway a clump of people—some in police garb, some not—huddled near the doorframe of the bedroom. He couldn't see inside.

"So, this is your father," the vested one said.

"Yes, I'm Scott Morgan," Scott said. He was about to extend his right hand, but pulled it back before it got very far.

"Sit," the man said.

Scott sat.

"I'm Detective Delmore Kerbich, NYPD, Manhattan."

"That's an unusual name, Delmore." Scott automatically had broken into business negotiation mode. Start friendly. Find out something personal about your opponent. Establish a rapport. Opponent? Was the police detective an opponent? Best to assume he was.

"My father was a devotee of the writer Delmore Schwartz. Have you read him?"

"I'm vaguely familiar with the name, but I'm afraid my reading is made up mostly of corporate reports, industry analyses, that sort of thing."

Sarah looked at them with an expression that both men read as saying *Is this conversation about first names, long-gone writers and financial statements really happening with a dead man lying in the other room?*

Detective Kerbich cleared his throat. "Your daughter was just recounting her movements prior to making the unfortunate discovery in the bedroom."

"I don't mean to be rude, Detective, but I rushed over here to tell

Sarah that she shouldn't answer any of your questions. Not until she has a lawyer sitting next to her."

"And why is that? Does she have something to hide?"

"No, of course not. It's nothing personal. It's just that any civilian needs legal counsel in such a situation when dealing with the police."

"Dad, I don't mind . . ."

Scott held up his hand. "Please, Sarah, I've been through enough issues to know this is for the best. I have a couple of people I can call."

Detective Kerbich smiled.

"No offense taken. But out of curiosity, what line of work are you in that you would have familiarity with these sorts of 'issues'? Are you a lawyer?"

"Management consultant," Scott replied evenly. "Senior partner." He handed the detective a business card.

"I know business can be cutthroat these days, but murder? You have experience with murders?"

"Is that definitive in this instance?"

"Oh, yes, there's no question about it."

Sarah started crying. She lifted a balled-up tissue to her eyes, but it was beyond being of any use.

–22–

A few days later in the precinct, Detective Kerbich repeated his question.

"Did you commit the murder, Scott?"

"No, of course not," Scott said firmly.

Kerbich slid down a bit in his chair. He was on the short side, but not so small that it would be the first thing you noticed about him. He was slim, but not hard. Scott assumed he didn't spend a lot of time in gyms. Probably liked to walk. He wore glasses with thick black frames in a European style that made them the most noticeable thing about his face. His hair was cut short. His blue button-down shirt was pressed but faded, like it had been well cared for but kept in service for more years than it should have been. Scott thought he could be someone's uncle from a Central European country who had just landed at Kennedy airport for a visit. The kind you'd have to remind to watch his wallet and keep his wits about him, because it wasn't always friendly in the Big Apple.

"Yet Sarah said you knew when Blaus would be in your daughter's apartment, alone, packing up his things. That spells "access." Or "opportunity," if you prefer. I like the word access. Of course, we know you've got motive."

"Motive? I think not."

"Do I have to spell it out? You took an instant dislike to Ed Blaus. You thought he was leeching off your daughter, that he was an old, washed-up writer who would take her money. Then he goes and has an affair with your wife. Your *wife*. This, of course, is devastating to your daughter. Boyfriend and mother conspire to deceive her. What a betrayal. Meanwhile, you are cuckolded by the guy, and you also have your daughter in distress."

Scott worked hard to be measured. "Difficult things happen to people all the time. Pain caused by other people. Someone must have run the data on this. I'd wager an infinitesimal number of those who are wronged by someone resort to murder as a response."

Kerbich let go a whistle, low and long. "Infinitesimal. That's the kind of word I read but wouldn't dare use in conversation. I'd be afraid I'd bungle it."

"Yeah, if I'd thought about it before saying it, I would have wondered the same. I won't chance it again."

"Infinitesimal or not," Kerbich again pronounced the word correctly and made clear by his steady tone the fun was over, "enough people do resort to murder to keep us at the precinct fully employed. There's pressure to get this one solved fast. It's always good to start with the most obvious people. You already have two elements—motive and access—that put you in the spotlight. Do you happen to collect knives?"

"You're getting ahead of yourself, Detective. Opportunity, access, whatever you call it, is a nonstarter. I was in my office all day."

"What time did your daughter call you?"

"I can check my phone for greater precision, but I believe it was at seven."

"And being a busy consultant, you are often still in your office at 7:00 p.m.?"

"I'm not sure about often, but it's not unusual."

"A big man like you has a personal assistant, right?"

"I do."

"She works late when you work late?'

"Well, my assistant is a he, not a she. Generally, that's the case, about working late. If I don't need Kyle's services, sometimes I'll tell him it's okay to knock off even if I'm staying."

Kerbich opened a reporter's-style notepad and started flipping through it. He flipped and flipped. Scott found it theatrical.

"That's right, your assistant is Kyle. Kyle Humphries. One of my colleagues spoke with Kyle, not me, that's why I assumed he was a she. A sexist assumption, no doubt." He grinned and paused for a response, but Scott offered none. "So, this is what Kyle told one of the other detectives." He pulled the notebook closer to his face and read. "On the day in question, Kyle had a dental appointment. He left the office around 3:30 p.m., done for the day." Kerbich looked up at Scott. "Seems poor Kyle has gum issues. I am sure you are aware."

"I did not remember that," Scott said. "About him leaving early. I know about the gums."

"No reason you should remember," Kerbich agreed. "We know how busy you are. But it does mean, hypothetically speaking of course, that you could have slipped out of the office any time after 3:30, since there was no Kyle standing sentry outside your office."

"He does not . . . "

Kerbich cut him off. "There's another thing my colleague noted. He's a good man. Sort of junior, but eager, by the book. You know the type?"

Scott didn't answer. "Maybe playing by the book doesn't get you very far in your line of work?" Kerbich continued. "Anyway, Detective Forster disclosed to me another interesting detail about your office building: you have to use your company ID to get through the turnstiles to get in, but you don't have to use it to exit."

"That's true," Scott said.

"No Kyle standing sentry after 3:30. No need to record your exit from the building. Capisce?"

Scott stifled the urge to repeat the word capisce.

"I am going to make an appointment with Kyle," Detective Kerbich said, his dark eyes aimed directly at Scott's forehead. "Not to see you, but to get a sense of the setup in your fancy offices. See it for myself. Who sits where? How many steps from your office to the elevator bank? Who else do you have to pass on your way out the door? That sort of thing."

Scott shrugged his shoulders.

"And your wife is where?"

"Uh, staying with her sister, I believe. In Connecticut."

"You haven't been in contact since the discovery of her activities with the deceased?"

"Occasional. I'd rather not delve into a very painful part of my private life, Detective."

"But delve we must, since this investigation is all about your private life. Your family is at the heart of the matter." Scott had no comeback for that. He was getting fidgety in the chair. It was so damn uncomfortable. Probably set up to be that way. Then he thought:

Fidgety looks suspicious, even worse on video. He willed himself to stay still.

"Do you possess keys to your daughter's apartment?"

Scott hesitated just a second, but long enough for it to be noticed. "Yes," he said.

Delmore Kerbich again checked his notes. He flipped through a lot of pages. Then he started tracing something with his finger. "Funny," he said finally, "we asked your daughter who besides herself and Ed Blaus had keys. She didn't mention you."

"She must have forgotten. As I've noted more than once, this has been traumatic for her. Obviously."

The interview went on for another fifteen minutes. Nothing else substantive came of it, at least from Scott's perspective. But it was clear Kerbich was focusing on him as a suspect—a disturbing notion, to say the least.

Once it was over, Scott walked swiftly out to the hectic street. The controlled chaos of the city seemed incongruous just steps from the suffocating confines he'd just escaped. He questioned whether it was smart to have come without a lawyer. Then he shook it off. Nothing of any real consequence was revealed. Nothing the police didn't already know or could easily find out. A lawyer would simply have advised him to answer every question in as few words as possible and never veer off track. Wise advice he'd heard many times delivered to his own clients who were in hot water. Yet before this, he'd always been on the outside looking in at legal predicaments. Sure, he was all-in for the client, no matter who it was or what the CEO or company was accused of doing. But when the stuff hit the fan, it wasn't Scott's business that was going down the drain or, worse, his ass that was going to prison. He was on the outside no longer. And as much as Scott considered himself a realist, a man without illusions, it still came as a shock that he had just been across a table from a police detective who at any moment could have slapped handcuffs on him and deposited him in a jail cell, under arrest for murder. Hadn't he spent his entire adult life constructing walls of money and respectability to protect himself and his family from just that sort of possibility?

−23−

Scott texted Meredith. "We should talk on the phone with Sarah," he wrote.

"What about?" was the quick text reply.

"Phone only," Scott typed. He wanted as few words written down as possible. He'd seen some of the brightest people he knew write self-incriminating things in texts and emails. They knew better, or certainly should have, but they did it anyway. It always came back to haunt them. Maybe the exalted think nothing can touch them. Scott was not exalted. He knew he was vulnerable.

"Sarah has agreed to join?" Meredith asked.

"I will get her and then call you. 8:00 pm."

Scott called Sarah. "How are you holding up?"

"Ehhh."

"The police talks were long?" he asked.

"Insanely long. They went over the details of my day, you know, that day, so many times. Josie finally jumped in. She said it was getting to the point of harassment. I guess they were trying to find some contradiction in my story. Then they went on forever with questions about my relationship with Ed, when we met, when we moved in together. I told them about him and Mom and how I found out. I had to, I thought. Josie agreed. Josie was a big help. Thanks for bringing a lawyer into this, but there weren't any questions she said I shouldn't answer."

"Josie Horvitz is a good one. She's represented a number of our clients quite ably. Did they ask you anything about me?"

"What you thought of Ed. What you thought of our relationship and how you reacted to Mom's affair with Ed. I told them. I tried to keep it short."

"That's fine."

"Also, it came up that you'd gone to see Ed's ex-wife."

"Came up?"

"I guess I told them."

Scott was silent, wondering what that information might mean to Delmore Kerbich. Would he eventually know the full extent of Scott's investigation into Ed Blaus? If he did, it would only exaggerate the target Scott already felt etched on his back.

"Not to worry," he said weakly.

"And they told me to stand by for more," Sarah said. "They said as they investigate, they are sure they will have more questions for me."

"Did Detective Kerbich ask most of the questions?"

"Delmore?"

"Delmore?" Scott repeated.

Sarah laughed. It was good to hear that.

"You're the one who made such a fuss about his name. The first thing you said when you arrived at the apartment that night. There were a bunch of cops who asked me questions. That was their excuse for asking the same ones over and over. One of them would say, 'I want to hear this directly from you.' But I guess Delmore spent the most time with us. I kind of liked him. He didn't seem like a cop, really. More like, I don't know, a college professor."

"His father was one. Anyway, if they call you for more questions, make sure Josie is with you before you answer anything."

"Got it."

"I am afraid I have another challenge for you. At eight tonight, we are going to get on the phone with Mom."

"*Why?*" Sarah shrieked. "I don't think I can. I don't think I am physically able to speak with her."

"I wouldn't ask if it wasn't important. You don't have to say much. I just want to gauge where she's at and find out if the police have spoken with her. We may be broken, but we're still a family, and if the heat is on one of us, we need to stick together."

"You don't think Mom . . ."

"I've given up assuming anything."

At exactly eight, Scott announced that the three of them were successfully connected. Meredith started crying.

"Sarah, are you there?" she blubbered. "Honey, I am so, so sorry for what I've done."

"Meredith, please stop," Scott interrupted. "The purpose of the call is to discuss the police investigation. Sarah made clear to me she's not ready to speak with you about, uh, other matters."

Meredith stopped talking, but continued to audibly cry.

"Okay, let's get to the point. Sarah and I have been separately interviewed by the police. We likely will be again. Meredith, how about you?"

"Yes, a detective traveled up here to talk with me."

"Kerbich?"

"Yes, he asked that I call him by his first name, Delmore. He's an odd, little man."

"And what did he ask you?"

"Where I was the day Ed was killed. And about our, ugh, relationship." She started again to blubber. "And whether I thought either of you killed Ed."

"To which you replied . . ."

"Well, that it was absurd to think Sarah did it. I told them you, Scott, were obsessed with Ed, that you believed he was evil. I also said you can be cold, very cold, but that I doubt you are a killer."

"A ringing endorsement," Scott muttered.

"Do you expect me not to tell the truth?"

"Of course you should tell the truth," Scott said, articulating the words slowly and loudly, as if Detective Kerbich was listening in. "You just throw in the sloppy, amateur psychology with the price of admission."

"I said I didn't think it was likely you were a murderer."

"Understood. I just wanted to say we are all in this up to our necks, nothing to do about that. We should think before we talk so that we don't inadvertently raise suspicion."

"Spoken, as always, from total self-interest. I, for one, have nothing to hide," Meredith said.

"Mom, please stop." Sarah spoke.

"In fact, I am concerned about all of us," Scott said. "Including you, Meredith. No doubt there are other people who have legitimate beefs with Ed Blaus. It could have been someone we know nothing about. The police will come up with the right answer in time. I'm trying to figure out how to help them widen their focus to others.

"Also, we have to get ready for the mud. I've seen Sarah in news stories and online called his roommate, lover, girlfriend, gal pal, or latest touch, depending on who is doing the talking. Meredith, of course . . ."

They heard more crying. Meredith was being crucified on social media. The Ed-Meredith affair had leaked, and it astronomically ratcheted up public interest in the Blaus murder. *Next time, don't hop into bed with your daughter's writer boyfriend*, Scott thought.

"Given the facts we have to face here, I think the best thing we can do is lay low, not engage with anyone except each other and lawyers. No media, no interviews, nothing. Any accounts online should be taken down."

There was silence. "Am I understood?"

"Yes," each woman said quietly.

"One more thing," Scott said. "Let's keep the fact that this conversation happened to ourselves."

– 24 –

Mickey Genz hurried down the street, heading to his studio apartment above the deli. A newspaper was under his arm. One of his cronies, a guy they called Sad Sal or just Sad because his left eye drooped and was often watery, stepped out of the long-standing bar across the street from the deli.

"Hey, Mickey," Sad called. "Come have one with me."

It was nearly nine, so Mickey figured Sad Sal was well lubricated. Sad tended to start early. His usual was a shot or two of scotch followed by a steady stream of Budweisers. On many other nights, Mickey would have been in the joint too.

"Can't, got some business," Mickey called over the stream of cars slow rolling down the street between them.

"Business," Sad laughed and arched his back. "What sort of business could you have this time of night?"

Mickey Genz waved and smiled. He walked up the narrow set of steps that led him above the delicatessen to his large, messy room. There must have been a lot of demand for ham and egg on a roll from the deli grill, because Mickey could still smell it all these hours later. Never mind. There were more important matters at hand.

The cover of the newspaper screamed the latest in the Ed Blaus murder investigation, highlighting the juiciest twist that had been discovered since the local novelist turned up dead: "Mom Bedded Daughter's Lover." The smaller text, under the headline, invited you to read the story on page three, adding: "Louche Writer Got It on With Both Generations Before He Was Brutally Stabbed." The photo used to accompany this news was of Blaus trotting away from a horde of photographers who wanted to snap him as he left the paternity hearing for the now twenty-two-year-old Justin Skilbahl. The inset was a headshot of Meredith Morgan from a charity dinner some years back.

So, finally, Mickey knew why his old neighborhood guy Scott Morgan didn't want to tell him the real reason for his interest in the details of Ed Blaus and his family. This is why he wanted the dirt. Did Scott know about the affair when they had talked over dinner at Laverno's and then later when money changed hands in the schoolyard? Hard to tell. If he knew his wife was having an affair all that time, Scott certainly played it cool. One thing Mickey knew for sure: he'd been taken. Having suckered any number of people himself, Mickey knew it when he saw it, and it didn't feel good to be on the wrong side. Not at all. Scott was richer than Mickey thought. The article said he lived in a Scarsdale mansion. All Mickey got for his trouble was $5,000. Jesus. Pocket change for that fucker. But this play wasn't over. Far from it. Mickey knew it would be of great interest to the police that Scott Morgan was snooping around about Ed Blaus before the writer got himself killed. Scott wasn't closemouthed about the why of it all because he was protecting a client. Morgan was looking for the goods because both women in his family were under Blaus's spell. The way Mickey figured it, Scott's daughter and Blaus were a legitimate item. They lived together. Then Scott's wife tried to shoehorn her way in on the action and seemed to succeed for a time. What did Scott know when he approached Genz? The daughter thing was clearly underway and out in the open. Did Scott think digging something up on Blaus would break things up? Maybe. Mickey couldn't hand over a smoking gun, but his information was useful. And it was hard to come by. You had to wonder how Scott reacted when he found out about his wife and Blaus. Mickey would have liked to have been there when that discovery was made.

He sat at the edge of his unmade bed and smiled at the disheveled, egg-sandwich-smelling room. He had it figured. Once Scott Morgan found out his wife was with Blaus, on top of Blaus living with his daughter, he made his move. He would decide it was the only way to stop Blaus from wrecking his family. Yeah, that arrogant bastard is just the type to think he could get away with killing Blaus, whether he did it himself or paid someone to do it. And then not worry about a loose end like Mickey Genz, who knew something the police didn't know. Sitting right here where it all began, tucked away in the old neighborhood. Well, Mickey Genz was tired of playing the sap. It was long in coming, but his ticket finally hit. Scott Morgan was going to pay him and pay him well to keep quiet. No bullshit this time.

– 25 –

The old house made more noises than Scott remembered, creaking like an old man as he walked about it. Warmer weather was regular now, and Scott thought he should have the air-conditioning checked. He'd need it soon enough. Didn't they have an annual contract with a local outfit? He certainly paid a bill every year for maintenance, but maybe Meredith had arranged an appointment each cooling season. Another thing for his list. Check his records. He certainly had the time now that he'd asked for and received an indefinite leave of absence from the consulting firm. Not that the firm had much choice. They couldn't get rid of a partner just because his family name was now a staple of every social media platform and repeated in the furthest reaches of the digital tabloid world. No doubt some would like to do just that. One senior leader hinted at the case for resignation, but Scott ignored him. Scott knew that man wasn't speaking for the firm, because subtlety was not the firm's style. If they really wanted to move on him, he knew he would feel blunt force. Damn the consequences. But the downside was too big. Scott knew that's what he would advise if he was part of an executive leadership meeting on what to do if a different partner was in Scott's predicament. It wasn't about the money. Reputation was nine-tenths of the law. Getting rid of Scott—provoking him to balk publicly and file a lawsuit—would accomplish exactly what they were trying to avoid. The company would become more closely associated with murder and adultery. They already were too close.

People got murdered in New York City all the time. That Blaus was (once at least) a well-known writer juiced the story for eager eyeballs. The public revelation of Meredith's affair with Blaus (leaked, Scott assumed, by someone in the NYPD) blew the thing into the online gossip stratosphere. Scott hired security guards for a couple of weeks right after the murder to keep the swarm of camera people, scandal scribes, and wacko adventurers confined to the public spaces on the residential street and off his property. It was still often a chaotic scene, and he rarely emerged from the house. So when Scott got the consulting firm's elderly executive chairman on the phone to hash things out, he figured the old man would jump at the chance to have Scott take an extended leave, since it would provide a temporary separation from scandal. Once word of the leave seeped out, at least the photographers camped near the lobby of the midtown office tower would go away.

"For the record, I didn't do it," Scott said.

"Of course not!" the chairman affirmed. "No one here thinks that."

The chairman offered advice. "This is one of those times when the best defense is a good offense. The sooner they catch who killed this writer the better for you, for us, for everyone involved. Likely will be a break-in gone wrong."

Did anyone think that? There was no forced entry and nothing taken. No one in the building remembered seeing anyone or anything suspicious. It's funny, he thought, as he wandered into the kitchen for water: he never thought he'd wind up spending most of his time in the big house, let alone by himself. He often thought in nuts-and-bolts fashion about his advancing age, actuarial probabilities and the like, and he wasn't counting on early retirement. He hadn't cultivated meaningful hobbies or avocations. With Sarah established as an independent adult and his relationship with Meredith ever more distant even before the affair, work was what he had. It sustained him, enriched him, provided direction to his days. He knew the statistics: women usually outlasted men, so when he thought about the coming decades, it was Meredith he pictured remaking a life for herself after he was gone. Now that wouldn't happen. At least not in this house.

The absence of work held one benefit: Scott could turn his full attention to the capital P problem in front of him. The chairman was correct that the sooner the investigation was wrapped up, with a suspect other than him, Sarah, or Meredith sitting in jail, the sooner things could get back to whatever "normal" looked like after the murder. He had no illusion that the specter of Ed Blaus would ever truly leave his family.

Settled in his comfortable executive swivel in the den, Scott called up his digital Blaus file and reviewed everything he knew. It struck him that what was not long ago an individual pursuit to find out anything and everything he could about Ed Blaus now seemed to be the most popular national parlor game, aided and abetted by the journalists and true-crime bloggers who wanted to make hay, or at least a new post, about every scrap of Blaus's existence. Scott and his family got similar treatment. Scott watched as the world learned of Blaus's short, failed marriage to Mary Jenseth, though when contacted, Mary wouldn't speak with reporters. The press repeated the facts from the long-ago magazine profile of Blaus, where the reporter had accompanied Ed back to the Brooklyn neighborhood of his youth. Blaus was now uniformly referred to as a renowned novelist, and his novels, written long ago, were selling faster than book stores could stock them. Scott thought Blaus would have gotten a kick out of that. A few enterprising reporters went to the old neighborhood to interview locals about Blaus. As Scott expected, almost no one recalled him or the family. The few who said they did provided inaccurate accounts. Luckily, Scott thought, no one found Mickey Genz to interview. He wouldn't have done one without getting paid, in any case.

Nothing surfaced about Blaus's brother, much less the story of how Ed stole his brother's inheritance and broke his promise to their mother. The event in Blaus's fractured family history that was getting the most play online was his attempt to deny paternity and avoid supporting his son. Since Blaus was still a respected writer when that went down, the court appearances had gotten decent coverage in the mainly analog age a couple decades back. Despite the negative tone at the time of the paternity suit, the media was now generally going easier on Blaus. Someone even called him a loving father. *That's one way to improve your image*, Scott thought. *Become a murder victim.* Didn't seem like a worthwhile trade-off. Scott noticed as he read and reread the current coverage of the historic paternity battle that neither the mother, Emily Skilbahl, nor her son, Justin, was quoted in any of the articles or videos. They couldn't be reached for comment. Smart, he thought. Nothing to be gained by talking. Not then and certainly not in this circus. Scott, of course, was keeping his own counsel. The ingenuity with which some reporters tried to get to him amazed him. His cell phone number had slipped out, somehow, so he got a new phone and started a new account. A couple of reporters had even gotten his partners to email Scott and vouch for their credibility. Scott still wasn't talking.

Scott speculated about Detective Kerbich's view of the investigation. The killer might have been Scott in his most desperate act as a protective father, or an enraged husband, or some combination of the two. It might have been Meredith, angry that Blaus admitted to the affair, simultaneously ruining her relationship with her daughter and her husband. It might have been Sarah, incensed by the discovery that Blaus regularly had been having sex with her mother under their shared roof. Scott looked and looked again at the gathered materials. Emily and Justin Skilbahl: Two people who had reason to wish Ed Blaus ill. He knew nothing about them. He needed to talk with them. He would approach them as a fellow victim of Ed Blaus, depressed and distraught at how Blaus had blasted his family apart. Could they compare notes? Have a conversation somewhere out of the sight and knowledge of the press? Talk about the real Ed Blaus, the evil one? They would form a council of those Blaus hurt and used. It would be a hard sell, but an important one. Scott wasn't used to failure when the stakes were high.

– 26 –

The Facebook direct message from Mickey Genz said "We need to talk." Mickey Genz was the last person with whom Scott wanted to speak, so he ignored it. The next day another message came from Genz. Three words: "Not fucking around." Scott sighed. He was spending too much time in the house, though he feared going out, even for groceries. The television vans and still cameras on tripods and the churlish, microphone-wielding reporters were gone. They'd received no satisfaction. Still, Scott wasn't certain the coast was actually clear. He thought reporters and cameras could be stashed in any of the scattered cars parked on the block. All he needed to do was step out of his house or pull the car out of the driveway and they'd snap into action. But the house was oppressive. After a lifetime of commuting and traveling on business, smartly decorated, temperature-controlled offices and five-star hotel rooms had become his true homes. That is where Scott had made himself into what he'd become, the man who could afford the nice house in Scarsdale through dint of his hard work and his ability to win the trust of myriad business leaders with his clear-thinking advice. But clear thinking was hard to accomplish in the house Meredith had expensively designed to her own tastes, with frilly couch pillows and abstract paintings in bold color schemes that now mocked him as he wandered the empty place day and night. Only his den office bore his own touches: the big, dark wood desk and executive-style chair, the laptop, large monitor, and printer. For hours he sat there, shutting out the rest of the world, thinking mainly about Ed Blaus—his murder and what it had done to their lives. Now Mickey Genz was back and would have to be addressed. Mickey Genz was not fucking around.

"Hey Mickey," he wrote back. "Hope all is well. Been pretty busy on my end."

"We need to meet."

"Kind of tough now, I think you can imagine. Phone?"

"Meet. I don't care how tough it is."

They arranged a rendezvous for the next day on the Brooklyn boardwalk where it ran parallel to Brighton Beach Avenue. The day was breezy, but still, a number of people lined the boardwalk's wooden planks on benches and folding chairs, facing the beach and Atlantic Ocean. Scott stood by the railing, gazing at the near-empty beach and white-topped waves. It was hard to believe he was still in New York City.

He saw Mickey approaching. They found an unoccupied bench and sat. If not for the cutting wind, Scott thought, it would be a pleasant way to while away the afternoon, contemplating beach and water. But his bench companion removed any chance of pleasure.

"Now I finally understand why you wanted the dirt on Blaus. You coulda told me."

Scott shrugged his shoulders.

"The stakes got a lot higher. Two hundred thousand."

Scott looked straight ahead at the ocean. He spoke calmly.

"Two hundred thousand for what, exactly?"

"Two hundred thousand says I don't tell the cops you were sniffing around about Blaus before he got killed. And how you paid me for information."

"And knowing that will mean what to the police?"

"That you were after Blaus, obsessed with him. From way back. That you had motivation to kill him."

"They know that already."

"About me? Hell, they don't."

"About what they think is my motive."

"Yeah, but they don't know about me. The way I figure it is this: you tell your daughter what you can to make Ed look bad and she don't care. Then you find out about your wife screwing him. You need Blaus gone. So, you kill him. You think you're smart enough to get away with it. But you forgot about me."

"Nobody forgot about you, Mickey. You were already paid for your services."

Genz buried his right hand inside his coat, then poked Scott just above the waist. Was he carrying a gun? Scott didn't know whether it was a bluff. No one had stuck a gun into him before. He didn't know what the real thing felt like.

"No more bullshit, wise guy. Two hundred K. Small bills. I'll be in touch about when and where."

Genz stood up. Some of the confidence drained from Scott's voice, but he managed to keep it from cracking. "What makes you think I have that kind of money anyway?"

"I don't have to think. *You* have to think. I just have to collect or talk to the cops. What I have seals the deal for them. It's the missing piece of the puzzle."

Genz walked toward the steps that led to the sidewalk. Scott stayed seated. He'd come all this way. He was pretty sure no one had followed him. He watched the ocean rise and fall, the water dribbling to a stop as it met the beach, over and over again.

Did Genz have anything important? More evidence of Scott's preoccupation with Blaus, his willingness to pay for information. Could that really be the piece that convinced Detective Kerbich Scott was their man? If so, he feared, the police investigation would then focus exclusively on him. Wasn't that how it worked? He pictured a strutting assistant district attorney headed toward the jury box, making the case that Scott was determined to stop Blaus at any cost. *He even launched his own investigation of the man, looking for any scrap of negativity he could use toward his own ends. Paid good money to obtain it. When that didn't work and his hatred of Ed Blaus compounded when he discovered his wife was having an affair with Ed, well, ladies and gentlemen of the jury, that's when Scott Morgan put a knife into Ed Blaus. The only way to get his revenge was to end the life of Mr. Blaus.*

Scott smelled the salt in the air, breathed it in greedily, like a man unsure of when he'd again be in a position to enjoy the wind and the sand, the low rumbling of the waves, and the screeches of the seagulls as they drifted overhead.

A week later, the two men were back on the boardwalk. This time, Scott stood behind a bench with his back to the ocean as he watched Mickey Genz walk toward him. Genz took up a similar stance next to him. Scott had spent much of the intervening week thinking about tactics. Ultimately, he took a page from his work playbook. Flush out the emotions that make you feel weak and outmaneuvered. Find the best strategy and press it to the full. Don't relent. Whatever you had to work with could become the winning hand. You had to will it. Scott wondered whether Mickey was carrying a gun. Given the news he was about to deliver, he hoped not. He watched the old men and women walking the splintered planks of the boardwalk. Others sat on benches, heads cranked upward, trying to capture on their faces the comforting rays of the sun. Would Mickey risk violence with so many witnesses? How desperate was he? *Banish these thoughts. Don't lose the advantage, Scott told himself. Action.*

"I don't have any money with me and I'm not going to pay you. Not now, not ever," Scott said.

Mickey, surprised, reared forward as if struck. Then he composed himself. "It's your funeral." He took a step away.

"You're making a mistake if you go to the cops," Scott said. "Your information isn't valuable. It isn't smart to voluntarily walk into an open murder investigation."

"What do I have to hide?"

Scott allowed himself a smile, satisfied the encounter would not turn violent. Now that he made clear he wouldn't be blackmailed, the worst was over. "I would imagine a fair amount. I don't know exactly what you've been up to all these years, but I'm sure a lot of it doesn't line up as legal. This is the big time, Mickey. The murder of a well-known writer in a nice Manhattan neighborhood. The press and public can't get enough of it. Imagine the pressure on the cops who are on this case. They want to pin this on someone and close it down."

"Yeah, you. They are going to pin it on you. And once they hear what I have to tell, it'll help them do it."

"What about you?"

"Me?"

"Yeah. Let's look at it from the lead detective's point of view. You need to close this. A guy walks into your precinct with a story about getting paid to provide information about Ed Blaus to me, already a suspect. How come you're walking in now? Oh, I'm just a concerned citizen. So, the first thing the police do is look into the background of this concerned citizen. Who is he? What's his job? Where does he hang around and with who? And why did Morgan think he's the kind of guy who can dig up dirt on somebody?

"That scenario alone should be enough to keep you away from the cops. I imagine it would take only a little digging for them to have you cold on any number of charges. But I don't think that's all you have to worry about. Because this lead detective, I've spoken with him a few times already, he's a smart man. His father was a professor. He's named after a writer. Like I said, the pressure on him is enormous. He thinks, *This guy Mickey Genz, he's not exactly Mr. Chamber of Commerce. There are some dubious things we've discovered about him. Maybe I ought to ask Morgan about it.* When they come to me, I'm always going to tell the truth, right? I say, 'Yes, that's accurate, I paid Mickey Genz for information because I'm a worried father.' It's understandable I wanted to know as much as possible about Blaus, given that he was moving into my daughter's apartment.

"And then I ask how Mr. Genz came to their attention. They tell me he's a concerned citizen who came forward, and I say, 'That's interesting, because recently Mr. Genz asked me to pay him $200,000 to keep him from going to the police with this exact information.' You know, I'm not a lawyer, just a management consultant, but I think blackmail is a crime even if it's not successful. Even if no money changes hands."

Scott's confidence grew as he spoke. He saw in Mickey Genz's eyes he'd managed to frighten the small-time hood. "Once I say all that, the smart detective, his name is Delmore Kerbich, in case you need it, well, he thinks, *Maybe, just maybe, if this guy is willing to try blackmail, he's willing to commit murder.* He thinks: *Mickey Genz knew early on that Scott Morgan didn't want Ed Blaus in his daughter's life. This guy Genz, from what we can tell, he's always on the hunt for a big score. So he knocks off Blaus in order to blackmail Morgan.* This version of events will make the police very happy, because they need someone for this murder."

Genz stayed put. "Ha, ha, ha," he said. It seemed to take an effort. "Very funny. Me murder Blaus so I could blackmail you. What are you smoking? You think you are so fucking clever. We'll see if you can keep it up when they put the cuffs on you and parade you into the cop house. Mr. Smart-ass himself, in the can. Lock the door and throw away the key. I'll help them put you there." He walked away from Scott.

– 27 –

Three days past the boardwalk encounter with Mickey Genz, Scott felt good about what he'd pulled off, but the victory was minor. No progress had been made on the main event: helping lead the police to the arrest of a person whose last name was something other than Morgan. He walked the house. Over and over, he reviewed what he knew and didn't know. Was there an even stronger case against Sarah than himself? After all, she discovered the body. Why couldn't she have been the one, by dint of a few knife thrusts, to put that body in the condition in which she said she came upon it? She knew when Blaus would be in the apartment, and she had keys. It was her place. She knew every inch of it. Boy, did she have motive. Her live-in cheated on her with her mother in their shared bed. Was she strong enough to put a knife in Blaus against his resistance? She was much younger, though only five foot three. She could have caught him off guard with the first thrust, making anything that followed a lot easier.

Scott moved from room to room, settling first on a chair in the kitchen without any reason to be there and then wandering back to his office. Then he got up again and got a glass of water. All that in twenty minutes. God, the clock moved slowly away from work, away from purpose, with only the constant dread of accusation hanging over him. Scott's thoughts stayed on Sarah. He remembered regretting as Sarah graduated high school that he and Meredith hadn't had more children. After Sarah, Meredith said she'd had enough. She'd had a particularly difficult pregnancy, feeling lousy almost all the time, with various scares about her own health as well as worries for their unborn daughter. But Sarah was big and healthy as a baby. Meredith started to physically feel better once Sarah was born, but things were still tough on her. She was overwhelmed by the responsibility of caring for a newborn, this fragile thing dependent on her. Scott quickly went back to work. He didn't try to reduce his hours or his travel. To do so would have made him look weak, he believed, would have knocked him offtrack. Scott paid for help. He'd thought that was enough.

"We already have our family," Meredith said when, years earlier, he'd raised the subject. Sarah was two or three. There would be no more children.

Scott knew anyone looking in on him and Sarah when she was a child wouldn't consider them close. Was it because she was a daughter rather than a son? Maybe. Still, he imagined they'd had an understanding, unspoken but real.

He thought of a time he drove a twelve-year-old Sarah a couple of hours north to a horse show. Where was Meredith? Something was up. A sick relative? Who knew? She was somewhere else. Whatever the reason, it was rare that he and Sarah were on their own. He remembered they spoke little on the drive. Sarah asked if she could turn on the car radio, then tuned it to a pop station that grated on Scott's nerves. Sarah's horse infatuation began when she was ten. With a couple of friends, she had begun taking riding lessons.

Scott had found himself surprised and impressed by Sarah's performance at the horse show. She looked so small and inconsequential on the big animal, but her jaw was set, and she clearly had the horse under command, going through the various trots and turns and two jumps without a single obvious misstep. Through it all, under her black National Velvet-style helmet—the kind Scott was amazed still existed outside of television programs and movies depicting earlier eras—Sarah was wide-eyed and determined. A few of her moves spurred applause from the gathered families and other riders. She took home a ribbon for second place.

That summer, instead of going back to sleepaway camp for a third straight year, Sarah opted for a program where youngsters would be taught, in the words of the brochure, "the ins and outs of caring for horses."

"This is crazy," Scott barked at Meredith when she laid out the program to him after Sarah had gone to bed. "They charge us thousands of dollars so our child can become unpaid manual labor, cleaning up horse manure. Does she have any idea?"

"I think she understands it is hard work."

One Saturday afternoon, Scott was dispatched to pick her up. Meredith told him the session was over at four. "You mean her shift," he said derisively. When he arrived, he found Sarah finishing up in the stables, surrounded by horses. Her face was dirt streaked, and a line of perspiration ran down the back of her thin, short-sleeved shirt. Scott backed out of the place after taking a couple steps toward her. Flies swarmed all around and it smelled to high heaven. It had to be over a hundred degrees. Back in the car, Scott insisted Sarah sit on a towel so she didn't mess up his seat. As he turned around on the dirt path and pushed up the air conditioning, he waited for a torrent of complaints. When he looked over at his daughter, she looked serene. *A hard day's work*, he thought, *makes her feel good*. If she thought somewhere deep inside that she'd rather be cavorting with her friends in the Maine camp's cabins or diving into the cool lake instead of performing backaching duties in the unforgiving sun, she didn't let on. *Okay*, Scott thought, as he turned onto the paved road. *That's okay*.

He promised himself that if Sarah was arrested, he would confess to the crime. He'd describe how he snuck out of his office unseen. His assistant had been at the dentist. There'd be no record of his exit. He had the apartment keys he'd surreptitiously copied from Meredith's handbag. He could say he went only to confront Blaus, as any man would given what Blaus had done. But things got out of hand. There were threats. Something came over him, and the deed was done.

Sarah was staying with a friend uptown. Her apartment was vacant now that the police had closed their on-site investigation. Once permitted, she had a specialty cleaning company come in. Then she replaced the carpeting in the bedroom. Scott paid for all that. A friendly neighbor oversaw the work so that Sarah didn't have to go back. She wasn't sure when, if ever, she would be able to return to the apartment. Don't worry about that, Scott told her. It would be a luxury to live in a future where questions such as whether to return to live in the apartment where Blaus was murdered were the most pressing ones. So far, reporters hadn't figured out where Sarah was temporarily living. She stayed away from her office, able to work remotely. The literary agency was quite understanding, but it couldn't go on forever.

− 2 8 −

JoAnne Pesto put it off and put it off, but as she drove to work at the group home in her dilapidated compact she knew today had to be the day. If it didn't come from her, someone else was going to mention to Michael that his brother Ed was dead, murdered, stabbed. She could try to do it delicately. She knew Michael liked her best among the staff, felt closest to her, so the news should come from her. She was the first to make the connection. Of course she was. She'd done the research and led the two of them on the visit to Ed Blaus. Afterward, she wasn't sure it was a good idea. It's just that Michael seemed so alone in the world. He was such a nice man, who saw the good in others. Apparently, the very opposite of his brother. Not that she knew Ed Blaus, but any brother who avoided making a trip within the same city to visit a brother in, what, thirty years? What could you say about such a person? Even after they showed up unannounced on his doorstep, shaming him in a way that JoAnne was certain would prompt him to change, nothing happened. Ed Blaus never called after that. He never visited. Now he was dead. The staff was buzzing about it, and some of the residents knew. How could you avoid it? The murder of Ed Blaus was all over the television news, all over online, seemingly everywhere at once. After the news broke, JoAnne had had several short conversations with Michael when he arrived back from work. She looked for clues, hoping he'd found out about Ed and she'd thereby escape the burden of having to tell him. But he gave no indication he knew anything.

Michael walked through the double doors at 3:25 p.m. in his Good House Burgers uniform. He brightened and smiled broadly when he saw JoAnne behind the desk.

"After dinner, Michael, come see me, okay?"

"Yes, sure," Michael said, and he went to his room to change.

When the dinner plates were cleared, Michael walked over and took the seat at the side of JoAnne's desk. She thought it best to get right to the point.

"Michael, a sad thing happened. Your brother Ed is dead."

She saw no reason to describe the circumstances of his demise.

"Oh," Michael said. He thought about how he had tried to visit Ed on his own. Was it wrong to have done that? He never told JoAnne. His mother died and now Ed. His father died so long ago. Was it him? All the people who were supposed to care for him were gone. Would JoAnne be next to die? Oh no, he hoped not. "Is it my fault?" he asked. "Did I do something bad?"

JoAnne's eyes welled up, and she leaned over and put her hand on Michael's hand. "No, of course not," she said. "You didn't do anything wrong. You are wonderful. It's just, well, sad things happen sometimes. People die."

"Was he dead when I went to see him?"

JoAnne was puzzled. "No, Michael, no. When we went to see him, you spent time with Ed. You talked. I saw Ed too. He was alive."

"No, I meant the next time. Last time."

"What last time?"

Michael explained in a zigzag way that he'd had a day off and didn't know what to do, so he decided to try to again visit his brother. He was told by the bearded man at the desk that JoAnne wasn't working that day. He was pleased to inform her he again rode the Staten Island Ferry to Manhattan and viewed the Statue of Liberty. JoAnne's eyes widened, and then she took a deep breath.

"You went to visit Ed yourself? That was very brave. When was that?"

Michael couldn't remember. He knew it wasn't Saturday. Wait, yes, it was a Wednesday, his other day off. JoAnne thought back to all she had read about Ed's murder. What was the date? What day of the week was that? She didn't want to start tapping on her phone or laptop to find out while Michael was sitting there.

"Was Ed surprised to see you when you went to visit him by yourself?" she asked gently.

Michael shook his head. "I didn't see him." Haltingly, he told JoAnne the story of his descent into the subway station and his convoluted conversation with an MTA worker. After many minutes, the woman helped Michael buy a Metrocard with some of the cash he had clipped to his ID. He knew to take the 1 train, but he couldn't remember the stop to get off. The train kept going; people rushed in and out at every stop. There was a lot of noise and distracting conversations. At some point, Michael decided he must have passed the stop for Ed's apartment building. When the train pulled into a station and he saw the number 59 on the walls and poles, Michael left the train. He wasn't sure why he got off there, but he'd decided that he wouldn't be able to find the station for Ed's place. It was too much for him. There was a policeman on the platform. Michael explained that he was lost and showed the policeman his ID. The policeman walked with him to the downtown side of the tracks and waited with him until another 1 train arrived. Michael took it. He waved to the policeman after the doors closed and the train started slowly and noisily to move away. He repeated the name South Ferry to himself over and over during the ride so he wouldn't forget or get confused about where to get off. He stepped off at the correct stop. From there he found his way back to the Staten Island Ferry, and he eventually made it safely back to the group home.

JoAnne stood up and bent over the seated Michael and hugged him. She pressed her cheek against his, and a tear rolling from her eye wet his face. It made Michael start to cry too, quietly at first but then louder.

—29—

Scott needed to talk with Emily Skilbahl and her son, Justin. Two people deeply connected to Ed Blaus whose stories he didn't know. The substantive public information about them was decades old and confined mainly to the paternity suit Emily had brought against Blaus—and won. Emily Skilbahl seemed to have no social media presence. Justin, as a young, aspiring actor, had accounts on most of the platforms Scott knew about, but nothing particularly useful. There were attractive headshots of Justin and lots of rah-rah talk about obscure theatrical revues in which he appeared to have had small roles. Some of Justin's Instagram comments, mainly attached to photos of food, were hard to decipher and seemed aimed at an inside crowd of friends. Scott took from them collectively the impression that Justin was a waiter who was not advancing much in his acting career and was unhappy about it. So he made jokes about the dishes he served and the customers he waited on who were too cheap to leave a decent tip. The restaurant was never named. Justin might have worked at more than one over time. Justin didn't respond to direct messages Scott sent via social media. Nowhere could he find their home or email addresses or cell phone numbers. He did not know where Emily worked. It was time, he thought, to do what would never have crossed his mind before the murder of Ed Blaus. Even now, with his world so radically altered and his desperation mounting, it seemed extreme. But what choice did he have? He or his daughter faced the real prospect of murder charges. It was time to contact DARK DAY.

Scott had never seen DARK DAY's name written down anywhere, but when it was whispered among the senior partners of the consulting firm, Scott always imagined it in capital letters. When he was younger and working his way up, Scott had heard rumors about DARK DAY, a person or persons the consultancy called on when the need grew urgent to protect a client or itself against imminent danger. DARK DAY was brought in when all else had failed and the firm urgently needed results, even if it meant breaking the law. A successful outcome might mean a client company avoiding the loss of tens or hundreds of millions of dollars or avoiding legal consequences for one of its actions. When, as a younger man, he heard occasional loose talk about DARK DAY, Scott didn't give it much credence, because it came from peers who wouldn't have been in the trusted circles where decisions on hardball tactics were made.

Scott admitted this to no one, lest he be called naive—a particularly damning label at the firm—but he was skeptical DARK DAY even existed, let alone that it was a contractor of the company for which he worked. Just look at the multiple floors the consultancy occupied in its modern skyscraper. The professionally etched logos, the high-end office furniture, the top-of-the-line computers and expensive analytic services. The large, elegantly designed and decorated offices of the senior partners. It all spelled stature, legitimacy, permanence, power. An active cadre of compliance officers seemed to be everywhere. The idea of hiring a shadowy firm to do the dirty work seemed the figment of some anti-capitalist imagination.

In the past decade, however, once Scott had attained seniority and his loyalty to the firm was beyond question, he came to know the rumors were correct. Three times he attended meetings where the highest-ranking executives of the firm made the decision to call for assistance from DARK DAY. Once, Scott was put in charge of the effort, and he made the contact himself: calling a number to arrange a face-to-face meeting in a suburban New Jersey diner. He hadn't wavered when asked to take it on, though he knew it was the legally riskiest thing he'd ever done. As always, pragmatism colored his decision-making. Did he want to be here and enjoy the money and perks? Yes, yes he did. There was no question about that. He'd worked too doggedly for too long to get to that place. He'd get it done. He always had.

The assignment was this: Scott asked DARK DAY to make and record a heroin sale to the former girlfriend of a married CEO whose company was hell-bent on taking over a farm equipment manufacturer.

The farm equipment company was the consultancy's client, and the head of the company—descended from the founder—was adamant about not wanting the takeover to happen. The money was reasonable, but as the client told them, what was he without the company that his ancestor had started? No longer the industrial leader and regional political power broker he had become. Who wanted to be bought out? Who wanted obscurity? But the acquisitive giant held the high cards. The client company was public, and other large shareholders, unconnected to the family, favored the deal. The majority of the board's members were ready to sign on the dotted line. The farm equipment scion turned to the consultancy. Make it stop, he pleaded. Whatever it takes. The senior partners called in Scott, described the mission for DARK DAY, and Scott made the contact.

DARK DAY did what was asked. A video showed the ex-girlfriend buying and then injecting heroin. Scott was nauseated by the scene of her wrapping a dirty rubber hose around her emaciated upper arm to highlight a vein and then stabbing the needle into it. Luckily, he saw it alone, standing in his office in front of his computer. He fell back into his chair. Memories of his dead brother, Freddie, came rushing back. The poor woman said to the camera that she didn't know was there—she thought she was talking with a dealer filling in for her regular source—that the acquiring CEO was the reason for her ruin. She'd used drugs before, she said, but when she was unceremoniously dumped by the man she thought was her avenue to a better life, she fully succumbed. What was the point, she said plaintively to the fake dealer. Nothing good was going to happen for her now.

The senior partners were pleased with the work done by DARK DAY. A private investigator was hired to contact the CEO set on the takeover and inform him she had heard that a video existed featuring this scandalous scene starring his ex-girlfriend. It would be a shame if it became public. There was a way out, the investigator said. Drop the takeover effort—or else.

The private detective was technically hired by an obscure company that was nothing more than a post office box and would be hard to trace back to the consulting firm. Even if the firm were somehow connected, the partners felt confident they'd be protected, because they worked with PIs who they believed would go to prison before revealing the name of a client. You could never be totally sure, of course, when dealing with human beings. Scott often lamented that in his business dealings; human weakness and irrationality were the wild cards that too often prevented plans from succeeding. It would be easier to deal with intelligent machines. This was another example. The farm equipment manufacturer had a good price on the table. It was the leader's ego that kept the deal from being consummated. But he was the consultancy's client. The firm thrived because the people who paid them knew they would do anything for a client. On the other side, the CEO wouldn't have been in the spot he was in if he hadn't had a penchant for adulterous affairs with troubled women whom he carelessly discarded.

The takeover attempt was abandoned.

Scott was told at the time of his involvement with DARK DAY to dispose of the burner phone he'd used to contact the murky entity. The DARK DAY number given to him was written in pen on a plain piece of paper. Scott was to rip that up and distribute its contents in different waste baskets around the office. But Scott didn't throw the phone number out right away. Even after he had used it, he studied it and studied it until he knew the digits as well as he knew his Social Security number. He had no practical reason to do this, but the very existence of the firm's relationship with DARK DAY and his direct involvement told Scott he needed to have pertinent information to trade with the authorities in case things went south and the firm's questionable doings were someday exposed. Knowing by heart the contact number for DARK DAY seemed like a wise act of self-preservation. Once he had memorized the numbers beyond fear of forgetting, Scott ripped up the paper, as instructed.

Now on leave from his job and no longer representing the company where he had worked for thirty-plus years, Scott bought a new, cheap phone. He sprang the entity's phone number free from his memory. The vague reply at the other end told him the number was still in use. DARK DAY lived. He was given the name of an Italian restaurant on Staten Island. He would be met there at 7:00 p.m. in two days. He was told to check the directions on an internet-connected computer at a public library (not the one in his town), write them down on paper, and destroy the paper after they were used. No Google Maps on his phone.

Scott didn't think the middle-aged man who sat across from him at the small corner table in the back of the dimly lit restaurant was the same one he had encountered in the New Jersey diner years earlier. It was hard to know for sure. They both seemed as unremarkable as possible.

"Let me start by saying this is personal. It's not the firm's business. It's mine," Scott said.

"That's most unusual," the man said, without looking up from his menu.

"I know. I realize that. It's just that my personal situation . . ."

"We know all about your personal situation," the man said flatly.

"Good, that makes things easier."

"I will have to get clearance before we can proceed on a personal basis."

"That's fine. What I am after now is simple, way below the kinds of things you are used to accomplishing."

"Best to leave us be the judge of that."

The man held up his hand, cutting off conversation. A waiter hovered. The man ordered and looked at Scott, who hadn't even thought about the menu. He was momentarily flustered, then, remembering they were in an Italian restaurant, asked for veal scallopini. It wasn't until the food arrived and they each took a few bites that the man motioned in a way that told Scott it was now reasonable for him to get to the substance of his request.

"I need the contact information for two people: email and home addresses, cell phone numbers, and work addresses. That's all. I've done my own searching, and I've come up empty."

Scott spoke the names Justin and Emily Skilbahl. The man made no move to record the names, but he nodded.

"I may need other, more complex services in the future," Scott added, hoping that the promise of more adventurous and lucrative work would entice DARK DAY into taking on such a mundane task.

Assuming he received approval for the job, the man said, they would meet again in three days at a restaurant in Forest Hills. He spoke only the name. He told Scott to look up the address and directions on a computer that couldn't be connected to him. Scott nodded and said he now knew the drill. If DARK DAY declined the job, someone would let Scott know.

"Since this is my business, not the firm's, how will I arrange paying you?"

The man placed both hands on the white linen tablecloth. They were smooth, medium-sized hands. Nothing noteworthy about them.

"We'll worry about that another time."

"Also," the man added, removing some bills from his wallet, "I'll pay the check."

– 30 –

Something physical afflicted Scott as he drove home from his dinner with the man from DARK DAY. It started as a shoulder ache, and Scott thought perhaps it had been triggered by his posture in the driver's seat. But he was sitting the same way he always sat. The seat hadn't been adjusted, nor the steering wheel. He rearranged himself anyway. Slid forward in the seat, then used the lever on the left side to recline the seat. That didn't help. Scott didn't like driving in such a reclining position, so he shifted back to upright. Was it now straighter than his preferred position? It was difficult to tell. He shouldn't have moved it in the first place. The pain in his shoulder subsided after a few minutes, only to be replaced by what felt like an internal thumping in his left bicep. Scott was acutely aware of any sensation in his left arm. That could signal a heart attack. He was in the age range now when such thoughts weren't pure paranoia. Lord knows he had enough stress. But that was debunked, wasn't it? Didn't he read that? That stress actually had nothing to do with heart attacks? Or maybe it was that stress wasn't the primary cause. No, stress was still a killer, right? He couldn't remember. He was distracted by the pain in his left arm. "Not tonight," he whispered in the quiet car. "I'm not going down tonight. Not in the middle of all of this."

The pain in his arm stopped without Scott noticing right away. When he finally did note he was feeling better, Scott thanked a God he didn't believe in. As quickly as the panic had arisen—the fear that his life might end then and there—it dissipated just as swiftly once his arm stopped signaling discomfort.

He remembered a day in the office when he and his best work friend, Parker Frontas, were still relatively junior and DARK DAY was just a rumor that wafted around up-and-comers like Parker and himself. Scott was dismissive of talk that the consultancy sometimes teamed up with a mysterious organization that operated outside the law. Parker thought it a realistic possibility.

"It's always win first here," Parker said, "whatever it takes."

They sat next to each other in a row of cookie-cutter offices. One day, Parker walked into Scott's space and said: "I've been thinking for a while about getting out of here, putting out my own shingle. I'd love for you to join me."

It was the last thing he had expected to come out of Parker's mouth. "I don't know," Scott said slowly. "I've got a daughter and a wife who doesn't earn anything and a pretty big mortgage."

"It's a matter of faith, Scott. You're a confident guy. And bottom-floor opportunities don't come around every day."

No doubt, Scott thought. It was attractive. He enjoyed spending time with Parker and admired his smarts and work ethic. The upside was potentially huge. But it could also quickly crash and burn. That would leave him where exactly? Having wasted all the years at the consultancy, working hard, weekends and evenings, catching the eye of the people who mattered. All for nothing? Parker said Scott was confident. Yes, he was. Confident, self-assured, whatever term you wanted to use. How else would he have gotten to where he was? All accomplished without the built-in advantages of Parker Frontas. He liked Parker, liked him very much. But Parker seemed unaware of the chasm between them based on where they had started in life. Parker grew up in an affluent Connecticut town. His father was a hedge fund veteran. Parker went to such-and-such private day school, followed by Yale, like his father and grandfather before him. He wasn't a state school guy like Scott. The way Scott saw it, Parker could afford to take a flier on starting his own business. Scott didn't have that luxury. He had to be practical, and build on what he had started.

Parker ran his hand through his thick, dark hair, which he never seemed to comb but always fell nicely into place. He pulled on the collar of his plain, but clearly expensive white shirt.

"I'm tired of how we do business here. Favors. Mutual back-scratching. And then there's that talk always swirling about how we occasionally really cross the line. Employing some mystery firm to carry off illegal stunts when the situation calls for it. What sort of consultants do that? I want to do consulting like it should be. Go in, do the research, and make companies better, stronger, more efficient. Tell them when it makes sense to expand into new areas and when it makes sense not to."

Scott had no problem with the words that came out of Parker's mouth. That's how he would have defined consulting work too. Rational business planning.

"We don't know if any of that talk about a mystery firm is true," Scott said.

"No, we don't," Parker admitted. "But it sure does fit with everything else around here."

The next day, Parker handed in his resignation letter. Scott was truly sorry to see him go. He also worried he'd made a mistake by not joining Parker in his new endeavor. Scott didn't have many friends at work. Almost everyone at his level seemed like a competitor. Parker should have been one too, but Scott never viewed him that way. Parker told Scott to look him up when Scott finally had enough of the place. Scott wished him luck. Now, with the heart attack scare receding from his consciousness, Scott thought about how things would have turned out differently if he had joined Parker all those years ago.

– 3 1 –

Detective Delmore Kerbich was firm. "We need to see you at the station. Today, soon. As soon as you can."

"Are you going to arrest me? Should I bring a lawyer?" Scott attempted to sound playful when he said that, but the detective's words alarmed him.

"Not planning to. If we change our minds, you'll be able to call your lawyer."

Scott was not at all relieved by the response. There was no hint of humor in the police detective's delivery. "I can be there in a couple hours," he said.

Scott was ushered into a small, windowless interview room and informed by a uniformed cop the session would be recorded. A video camera above the door stared menacingly at him. Fifteen minutes passed before Kerbich entered. It was like waiting for a doctor. Probably some psychological ploy taught in police school. Make the suspect sweat. The delay was unnecessary, Scott thought. If you are sitting by yourself in a plastic chair in an interview room in a precinct house, the police already hold quite a tactical advantage. Kerbich's chair didn't seem much better than his. The detective wore a not-bought-this-decade brown sports jacket over a white shirt, but no tie. Formal. He looked even thinner than at their last encounter. The detective tossed a glossy eight-by-ten photo onto the coffee-stained table that sat between them. It showed Mickey Genz, mouth agape, eyes wide open. Genz was propped against the side of what looked like a bed. Blood trickled from the side of his mouth.

"Oh my God," Scott whispered.

"So you know him?"

Scott considered for a second. "Yes, yes, I do. Mickey Genz."

"And what was your relationship with Mr. Genz?"

"Was, was. What do you mean was?"

"Isn't it clear from the picture?" Kerbich asked, with a sing-song lilt that contrasted horribly with the photograph. "Mr. Genz is dead. Very dead."

"Oh, no . . ."

"Oh, yes, discovered this way last night by a friend who was unsuccessfully trying to reach him for a couple days. The friend got the landlord to unlock the door. Landlord went with him, so they found the body together. Coroner says it's homicide."

Scott took a deep breath. He'd prepared on the drive into the city to go over familiar ground with Kerbich. Questions about the holes in his story. Who could vouch that Scott was in his office in the late afternoon of the day of Ed Blaus's murder? No one. His assistant, Kyle, wasn't around after 3:30. He'd had no late afternoon meetings scheduled. Kerbich had visited his office, as promised. Kyle filled Scott in afterward. The police looked around Scott's office and Kerbich walked the short route from there to the bank of elevators, Kyle reported. Kerbich noted to one of his colleagues that there were no security cameras between the two points.

"Here's the interesting thing. Your guy Genz was apparently a note writer. You know, reminders. But of a particular kind. He wrote things on Post-its and stuck them around his room. Not things like 'pick up toothpaste' or 'call Mom.' They were little bursts of commentary. Almost small poems. Most of them were about you, and none of them complimentary." Kerbich looked down at his notebook. 'Fuck Morgan. Get him to pay.' 'Don't let him get away with it.' 'That goddamn bastard.' 'Smart-ass fucker.' '200 thousand, nothing less.'"

Scott didn't say anything.

"Is that last one a haiku? I forget what constitutes one. My father would have known." Kerbich looked lost for a minute. Then he recovered himself. "Anyway, whatever their literary pedigree, these are odd notes, wouldn't you agree? It was like he was revving himself up for an encounter with you. Sort of a pep talk. Would you care to elaborate?"

"He tried to blackmail me," Scott said softly, forcing himself to focus. The stakes were too high to be thrown by this. "I wouldn't allow it."

"Blackmail? How interesting. Was this serious crime, this significant felony, something you reported to the police?"

Scott shook his head. He wondered whether he should simply fill the detective in on the full extent of his dealings with Mickey Genz. He couldn't see a significant downside. Not immediately. He would have done exactly that if Genz had followed through with his threat and gone to the cops. He remembered from many business negotiations over the years that when someone surprised you with a big new piece of information, the best thing to do was call it a day, delay the talks, use any pretense, no matter how thin, to buy time, to break things off. The key was to get some time to think. Because your adversary just revealed an informational advantage that changed the shape and dimensions of the playing field. But Scott couldn't ask to come back tomorrow. He did request water. That gave him a small break. He had to decide how to proceed. He talked.

"We grew up together. I mean not just the two of us, but in the same neighborhood. Lots of kids, you know. Well, it had been decades since we'd been in touch, but once my daughter introduced us to Ed Blaus, I conducted some research. Mickey Genz helped with that."

"Given his rap sheet, small-time but stretched over a good number of years, Genz doesn't seem like the sort of person with whom an upstanding citizen of Scarsdale would pal around."

"There was no palling around. It was a practical arrangement. That's like me saying I'm surprised an erudite man like yourself hangs around with the informants I am sure you pay to help you on cases. I imagine they aren't called stool pigeons anymore."

"They are not. What did Genz do for you and why did he think it was worth $200,000?"

"I paid him $5,000 for information. I didn't want Blaus involved with my daughter. That's not news. Genz, who never left the neighborhood, found out some stuff about Blaus's family for me, from the time when Ed Blaus was growing up."

"Dirt."

"Yes, I was looking for dirt. As I'm sure you've discovered, it's not very difficult to find dirt about Ed Blaus."

"You speak so poorly of the dead."

"Oh, please."

Delmore Kerbich laughed. Scott wanted to stand up, walk around a bit, but figured that would make him look anxious and therefore guilty when the video was played for an audience somehow, somewhere. So he stayed seated, and he talked some more. He detailed finding out about the existence of Ed Blaus's brother from Genz and then later—not from Genz—about the raw deal Ed had sprung on Michael. He said that after Blaus was killed, Genz thought he could blackmail Scott for $200,000 by threatening to expose to the police the existence of Scott's earlier investigation into Blaus. Scott said he'd told Genz no, and that was that.

"You're not trying to pin Blaus's murder on his brother, are you?" Kerbich asked. He pushed back in his chair, two legs coming off the ground.

"That's outrageous. I don't have to pin anything on anybody. That's your job. The point of the story of Blaus's brother is to show yet again what a louse Blaus was. Lots of people had good reason to hate him."

"Yeah, yeah. We also found out about the brother and how Ed placed him in an institution. We went to talk with him and the people at the group home he moved to years ago. No need for you to worry about him. He's cleared. He's doing fine."

Kerbich consulted his notes.

"Here it is," he said. "In addition to Michael, we spoke with JoAnne Pesto, one of the supervisors there. She's particularly fond of Michael. She says that it was hard telling Michael about Ed's death, but he seems beyond it now. As a matter of fact, she says he's recently come out of his shell. He joined the residents' advisory board, which talks with management about issues such as what's on the dinner menu, and she says she's seen him hanging around in the social room after dinner with a few other residents, something he'd not done before."

"That's good, I'm glad," Scott said. He felt like he knew Michael Blaus, though he'd never met the man.

The two looked at each other as if they were sitting on opposite sides of a chessboard. Scott reminded himself that every word he said would be evaluated, even twisted, into Kerbich's version of events. After a time, Kerbich spoke. "Do you have any more private investigations going on that I should know about?"

"No," Scott said quickly. "I can't imagine you seriously believe I had anything to do with Mickey's death. I have no motive there."

"Blackmail shows up as a reason in a lot of murders."

"It was dumb blackmail, really. I already told you I rebuffed him. And now everything the poor guy was trying to hold over my head has been placed at your disposal. That's why I told him it wouldn't work. You already have what he had on me. Is it surprising I paid $5,000 for information about Blaus? That I didn't like Blaus and believed that he was wrong for my daughter in every way?"

"Did you tell your daughter about Blaus and the brother?"

"No."

"Why not?"

Why not? What a question. One Scott had wrestled with before everything blew up. Because it could backfire. Because she might have still sided with Blaus. Because she might have hated Scott for spying, for always thinking he knew what was best for all of them. Because when it came down to it, Scott couldn't shake the idea that Blaus hadn't treated his brother any worse than he had treated his own sibling.

"Before I could say anything, the affair between Blaus and my wife became known to my daughter. Soon after that he was murdered. The facts about Blaus's brother no longer mattered."

"I expect forensics to soon tell us more about the cause of death for Genz. We already know he took a beating before he died. Couple of busted knees and various contusions. In the meantime, you stay put. I could have the DA move to confiscate your passport, so keep that in mind."

Scott nodded. He rose slowly.

"I don't know what it is, Morgan. People you have a beef with have a habit of turning up dead. It's not a good thing."

"Don't I know it," Scott said wearily. He walked out the door.

– 3 2 –

Scott paced up and down the residential street in Queens. It was 5:30 p.m. and still light. Parked cars filled both sides of the street. It had taken him forever to find a spot for his own car. He thought walking would make him look less conspicuous than huddling in the doorway of the apartment building where, he had learned, Emily Skilbahl lived. Pedestrian traffic was sparse, punctuated by small bursts of activity that Scott attributed to the arrival of another subway train at a nearby station, disgorging residents returning from offices in Manhattan. Then he spotted a thin, frail-looking woman in a long blue coat approaching alone from Astoria Boulevard, the busy street that ran through a chunk of the borough. Her blond hair was twisted into a knot atop her head. She looked lost in her own thoughts, her mouth silently forming the words of an internal conversation. Her left side was pulled down by the weight of a reusable grocery bag slung over her shoulder. Scott crossed the street and came up swiftly behind her.

"Don't be scared," he whispered huskily as he matched her step for step. "I'm Scott Morgan. We need to talk about Ed Blaus."

She looked up at him wide-eyed, but said nothing. In the apartment building vestibule, she turned on him.

"What's the idea? What makes you think you can come up and surprise me on the street like that?"

"I didn't have a choice. The police are trying to pin Ed Blaus's murder on me. Or worse, my daughter. You have a son, you can understand how that feels. All I want to do is talk. I have to get to the bottom of things."

Emily Skilbahl looked directly at his face. He wondered what she found there.

"All right," she said. "You can come up for a few minutes." Once they were inside the apartment, she motioned to a seat at the kitchen table. She unpacked her groceries and hung up her light coat.

"Do you want something to drink?"

"A glass of water, thanks," Scott said. When she placed the glass on the table, he asked, "Would you sit down?"

"I think I'll stand. You still make me nervous." He didn't think she looked nervous.

"Not my intention, though I can see how my suddenly appearing like that . . . What else could I do? You didn't answer my emails or my phone calls."

"You could have stopped trying." She smiled at that, making the lines near her eyes crinkle. Scott thought she looked sad, despite the smile. He studied the elegance of her features, her narrow nose and soft blue eyes. He pictured her decades younger, cavorting in Manhattan restaurants and clubs with a young, dashing Ed Blaus.

"That's just it. I can't. Not until this is put to rest."

"Will it ever be?"

"Would you tell me something about yourself and how you met Ed Blaus?"

"Oh, God. Ancient history. Barely remembered."

Scott doubted that last part was true.

"I was in my late twenties. Loved New York back then, like most young transplants do. He was a bit older. We met at a party. Started dating. His marriage was over. I was never quite sure if we were truly exclusive, despite what he told me. Ed had this man-about-town thing; women were always circling around him. He was still much in demand as a literary figure. He told me it was just him and me. No one else. Then I got pregnant, accidentally. That's when I saw the other side of Ed."

"Other side?"

"The charm, the cleverness, it all disappeared. He said, 'That's on you. Take care of it.' Not 'Have you thought about having an abortion?' Not 'It's your choice and I'll support whatever you decide.' Not 'That's wonderful news.' No, he said, 'That's on you. Take care of it.' I was considering an abortion, going back and forth, but when Ed said that, with absolute coldness in his eyes and in his voice, well, it settled things for me. I was determined to have the child. I'd like to think I was going to have the baby in any event. I guess I should thank him for that. For sealing my decision." She tried to laugh, but no sound came out. Scott shook his head and again indicated the seat on the other side of the small table. This time, Emily sat down.

"When I told him I was going to have the baby, Ed accused me of getting pregnant on purpose, of tricking him so that I could get him to marry me. That wasn't true. Or that the father was someone other than him. Also not true. He became the outraged one, the one who had been wronged. Needless to say, he dropped me then and there."

"He denied he was the father, so you had to go to court," Scott continued.

"Yes, it was the last thing I wanted. The publicity. The photographers and the reporters yelling questions at me when I tried to get to the courthouse or get out. My family's in western Nebraska. They're quite conservative. When they found out I was single and pregnant, they closed ranks and shut their doors. I was alone. I didn't know how I was going to take care of a baby on my own, so I went to court."

"Did Ed come through, once he lost the case?"

"Not really. He often claimed poverty, and a lot of the time I think he was actually broke, or close to it. He never followed up with anything commercially worthwhile after *A View from Below*. But he felt the need to maintain the lifestyle of a successful author. He taught some, and started traveling around to do that."

"And his relationship with Justin?"

"Close to zero. That was the most heartbreaking part of it. The way he ignored Justin. You could see the look in the boy's eyes when Ed would call at the last minute to break off an appointment to see him. Those eyes said it all. 'What did I do? Why doesn't he love me?' Heartbreaking."

"Indeed." *What an absolute bastard*, Scott thought.

"So now you know my sad story. The one thing I'll never regret is having Justin."

"Though, of course, having a child changed your life."

"No more party lifestyle, you mean?" Emily laughed. "Yes, for sure. I found a nine-to-five, moved to Queens. Stopped keeping up with friends, or they stopped keeping up with me. Not too many men are interested in being with a woman tied down by a child, especially a woman who sues for support."

"I find that hard to imagine," Scott said. "I mean the lack of male interest."

"I'm past the point of being influenced by flattery, Mr. Morgan."

"Scott."

"Scott."

"Have you spoken with Detective Kerbich?"

"Oh, yes, a couple of times," Emily said. "Quite a fellow. Doesn't seem like a policeman. More like, I don't know, a comedian or something."

"May I ask what he was most interested in knowing?"

"It seemed like the basics. You know, what we just went over, how I met Ed, all that. He did ask if I knew you or your daughter or your, uh, wife. Sorry about that situation."

Scott put up his hand as a signal not to worry about mentioning it. "Strange things happen in long marriages. Or any marriages, I suppose." There was an awkward silence, during which Scott studied his empty water glass. "I just know this from watching television shows, so maybe they don't do this in real life, but did Kerbich ask where you were at the time of the murder?"

"Very good," Emily said. "You are quite the investigator yourself. Yes, he did ask me for my whereabouts. I think that was the word he used: 'whereabouts.' I took a few days off that week—including the day of Ed's murder—to help with this group project I'm involved in. We're restoring this beautiful old Greek Orthodox Church in the neighborhood."

"You know something about construction?"

Emily laughed, this time audibly. He liked the sound of it. "I know how to carry things and mix plaster and the like. We're the volunteer work staff. The professionals tell us what to do. I'm not even of that faith, I'm Lutheran, but I do care about preservation, and I took a couple architecture classes in college."

"It's very good of you."

Emily shrugged her shoulders.

"Did you keep up with Blaus at all in recent years?"

Emily hesitated. "No," she said. "Once Justin became a teenager, he mostly handled contact with Ed. Not that it was very often. I thought it was best for the child to deal directly with his father, rather than through me. I thought it would help their relationship. That it would be harder to ignore Justin if the messages and the phone calls were from him. I was wrong there. When Justin turned eighteen, child support payments stopped, so I had no good reason to be in touch with Ed after that."

"I'd also like to talk with Justin," Scott said. "Would you put in a word for me?"

Emily frowned. "I don't see why you need to speak with him."

"I'm just trying to puzzle all this out. Like I said in the lobby, I'm on the line here, as is my daughter."

"My son doesn't have any information that would help you."

"I don't expect so," Scott said. "But you never know. Something that seems unimportant might mean something to me, given the other information I've gathered. I do need to talk with everyone who knew Blaus well. I'd like your help getting Justin to talk. I don't want to show up unannounced on his doorstep, like I did with you."

Emily considered. "Okay, come back in two days. That's Justin's day off. Six o'clock. We'll call him together. It will be better that way. I'll let him know."

"Thank you."

The conversation was clearly over, but Scott felt a strong urge to stay. He spent so much time alone. There was something alluring about Emily. She was funny and sad and really quite beautiful, enhanced by, rather than despite, the wear and tear and worry etched on her face. Her light blue eyes, he imagined, were once bluer, but this current hue was more unusual, and her eyes paired wonderfully with her straw-colored hair, peppered with strands of gray-white. He had no one waiting for him anywhere. He sensed Emily wanted him to remain, but he didn't trust his own instinct. What did he know about what the woman was thinking? He hadn't even known what was going through the mind of his wife before she betrayed him. He was not good at reading intimate signals, that seemed a given, though sitting across a negotiating table from a business adversary or potential client he was as astute as the best poker players. What a contrast to his love life. And what if he was correct that Emily also felt some spark? What good would come of any entanglement with a murder charge hanging over his head? Especially with a person also in Ed Blaus's circle. *Keep your eye on the goal*, Scott told himself. *Move forward, don't be distracted.*

He felt his jacket, draped over the chair, rubbing against his back. He should reach for it, stand up, and leave. But he didn't move.

"Could I have a refill on the water?" he asked.

Emily picked up the glass, ran it under a water spigot inside the refrigerator, and brought it back to him. "I'm going to make a simple dinner. Pasta and something, I haven't decided what. Would you like to stay and join me?"

"I'd like that," Scott said, "very much."

– 3 3 –

Two days later, as planned, Emily put her cell phone on the kitchen table and hit the speaker button. She selected Justin's name from the recently called list. Once again Scott was sitting at the table, feeling a comfort and familiarity out of proportion to the short amount of time he'd spent there.

"Hello," Justin croaked.

"Hello, dear," Emily said. "I'm here with Scott, Scott Morgan."

Justin emitted a sound that was hard to categorize. It was not a happy sound.

"Hello," Scott said.

"I'm gonna make one thing clear from the start," Justin said. "I don't want to be on this call. I don't want to talk to you, Scott. I'm doing it because my mom asked me to, but I think she is being naïve."

Scott said he understood, admitted he had no real standing to make inquiries, but explained he was doing so because he and his daughter were on the hot seat with Kerbich and the police department.

"So, you're trying to get off and get somebody else on that hot seat," Justin said.

Scott's gaze locked on Emily, whose eyes showed concern. He smiled in an attempt to reassure her. "The idea is to understand everyone's relationship with Ed Blaus and hope that leads us and the police to the facts of what happened the day he was killed. All of us who had nothing to do with Ed's death should share that goal, and it's in all of our interest to get to the truth."

"It seems my interest is doing just fine, better than yours."

No doubt, Scott thought, but he did not respond. Instead, he asked about Justin's recent dealings with Blaus. Sporadic, Justin said. He mentioned thinking about changing his last name to Blaus and said he had planned to ask Ed about it. He characterized it as a passing thought that might help his struggling acting career. "What did Ed have to say about that?" Scott asked.

"That's just it. I never got to ask him."

After the initial decision, Justin said, he'd started weighing the potential disadvantages of a name change. It would have meant hassles with his driver's license and passport. At the same time, it might not do him any practical good. He'd already established himself as Skilbahl among casting directors. His pictures and résumé used that last name. If he took on Blaus, he'd have to start again from zero. And who knew of Ed Blaus now? Maybe a few literary old-timers and MFA students. No one who had anything to do with New York theater or film or television or commercials. So what was the point? He kept going back and forth on whether to approach Ed, he said. Then Blaus was killed before he had the chance.

Emily avoided Scott's eyes as Justin spoke.

"How would you characterize your relationship with your father?" Scott asked.

"Nothing much," Justin said. "My mom's the only person who has been there for me." Emily's eyes watered, and she moved a hand toward them.

After a short silence, Justin's tone changed.

"Why do I need to keep answering these questions?" he asked with more than a tinge of anger. "You're not a cop. What are you, some big-shot business guy? That doesn't give you any right . . ."

"Justin, please," Emily cut in. "Scott's just trying to get a full picture of things. There's no harm in telling him what you've already told the police."

Scott hurried through his remaining questions, believing the young man might at any point end the phone call. The day of the murder was a day off for Justin. During the key late afternoon hours, Justin was watching a film, alone, at a movie house in the Village. He'd paid cash. Justin returned home, he said, around eight.

"I don't know if that was the right thing," Emily said to Scott after the call.

"Well, thank you for arranging it."

"I could tell Justin was unhappy and, uh, uncertain about you. Is he right that I should be suspicious of you?"

Scott touched her shoulder. It was the first time he'd made physical contact. He figured Justin's lack of a solid alibi worried Emily, as it would Scott if Justin were his son.

"Hey," Scott said. "Can I take you out to dinner? I'm sure you know some terrific neighborhood spots."

Emily flashed her careworn smile, the expression Scott found most endearing about her, and assented.

— 3 4 —

It had been five months since Ed Blaus was stabbed to death in the apartment he'd shared with her daughter and where she'd spent any number of wine-drenched afternoons in sexual dalliances with Ed when Meredith Morgan decided she would get in touch with Sarah, regardless of the consequences. How much more hurt could Sarah pour on her after the self-flagellation Meredith had engaged in while holed up with her sister in western Connecticut? The majority of the outrage on social media was aimed squarely at Meredith. She tried not to look, but some days, when her self-loathing was especially strong, she read. The most hurtful comments stayed with her long after she saw them. Women who said they were of similar age talked as if she was the Devil incarnate, making it sound like Meredith had done something much worse than simply conduct an affair with Ed. People of various ages accused her of killing Ed because he had dumped her— if she couldn't have him, no one, including Sarah, would. Why hadn't the police arrested her? It was plain as day. Women and men younger than Meredith said she was desperate and insecure and latched on to her daughter's man because her own life was empty. Meredith's sister tried to get her to stop looking. On particularly bad days, Meredith felt she deserved all of it, even the most twisted, rancorous, sickening posts, those that wished or threatened heinous violence upon her or simply told her to kill herself. Why not? She'd lost the love of her only child. Her marriage, already fragile and mired in monotony, was now over. Her circle of friends was gone. She feared Scott's wrath. Not violence, or cruel words, that was not the Scott she knew. It was his systematic, calculating cleverness that worried her.

Today was different. Today was going to be about Sarah and

whatever it took to get her daughter onto the path of forgiveness, no matter the length of that road. Meredith's texts to Sarah had gone unanswered. Sarah's personal email address had changed. Email missives from Meredith bounced back. Meredith hit Sarah's cell phone number. She'd done it so many times before, but today the plan was to not give up, to keep calling until Sarah picked up. It was a Saturday morning, so work wouldn't be an issue. She would call all day. On the tenth try, Sarah answered.

"You're lucky I didn't just block you."

"Thank you," Meredith whispered. She was determined not to cry, but simply hearing her daughter's voice just about destroyed her resolve.

"I can't imagine I have anything to say to you."

"Then just listen, please," Meredith begged. "Just let me say how so, so, so incredibly sorry I am for what I did. To you."

"You should be," Sarah said, though the starch that had been evident in her first words seemed to have diminished. "You should be."

"Darling, darling. I love you so much. You are my child. I gave birth to you."

"Then why?" Sarah asked. Both women started to cry.

"I wish I knew. Because I'm selfish. And maybe, if I'm honest, jealous of you and your youth and, well . . . there is no excuse."

"No, there isn't."

The two women then talked of less explosive matters. Sarah asked what Meredith's living arrangements were like. Meredith praised her sister Carole for having taken her in, no questions asked even during those horrendous early days when television cameras set up on Carole's lawn once word got out of where Meredith was staying. "She's also lonely, so maybe I am doing her some good by being here," Meredith said of her older sister, whose grown children both lived out West. "I can't stay here forever, though I also can't imagine what to do next."

"Have you spoken with Dad?" Sarah asked.

"Not recently, and I'm pretty sure he would refuse to talk to me. He's a lot colder than you."

"Don't start criticizing Dad to me," Sarah said. "He's been a big comfort in all this. Totally supportive, especially after you, well, to put it politely, disappeared from the scene."

"That's good. I am glad you have had someone to lean on," Meredith said.

"Even I have to admit Dad was right about Ed. He said from the start he didn't trust Ed and that he was wrong for me."

The conversation turned to the case, though neither woman used the word "murder." "Have you talked to that funny police detective again?" Meredith asked.

"Of course. It's like I'm their go-to person to interview over and over when they're stuck, and they do seem stuck. Though I wouldn't call him funny. He can be likable, but also pretty scary when he wants to be. I mean, he's the opposite of a tough-talking cop, but he has a way of implying darkness, hinting at some piece of information he has that he won't tell you about. Never coming out and saying, but I think he knows more. I am glad Josie, my lawyer, sits in on the interviews."

"I didn't mean funny like humorous. I meant peculiar. Kerbich is a peculiar man. I don't know how he wound up on the police force. I mean he'd seem more appropriate at the reference desk at the library."

"I wouldn't underestimate him."

"I wonder what Kerbich thinks of your father. To me, he's the logical suspect."

"Mom, that's a terrible thing to say. I just got through telling you how good Dad has been."

"The two things completely go together. You say your father has never been more supportive. From the start he wanted to protect you from big, bad Ed. Would go to any lengths to do it. Then when he found out about me and Ed on top of that . . . "

"Mom, you can't be serious. You can't possibly think Dad would kill someone."

"To be honest, for as long as I've known him, I don't know what Scott is capable of or not. There are parts of him that are foreign to me, even now."

– 35 –

The fish dinner they had a few blocks from Emily's apartment was delicious. Scott wasn't sure if it was the couple of glasses of wine, but sitting across from Emily he started experiencing feelings that had lain dormant for years. His breath quickened. He was content to sit silently, with no desire to talk, or get whatever point he was trying to make across to whomever was accompanying him, an impulse that seemed always to be with him. Not now. He was happy to sit back and swirl the remaining wine in his glass and look at and listen to Emily. Mostly look. Her face was naturally beautiful, somehow rendered even more striking by the deep lines etched across her forehead and softer creases elsewhere on her face that spoke of the passing years, testifying to the dashed hopes of the once-young woman who had made her way to the big city in pursuit of her dreams. It contrasted with Meredith and the women in their circle of friends, who regularly fretted about aging. Some paid for surgery to try to do something about it. He surmised Emily cared nothing about the things Meredith focused on, that Emily was rooted in a world he had lost touch with since he'd become wealthy and moved to the suburbs. The real world. That's where her beauty emanated from. It was authentic beauty, and in Scott's eyes, it made her desirable.

Emily's neighborhood, with its squat apartment buildings and row houses, reminded him of the Brooklyn of his youth. When she invited him back to her apartment after dinner, he accepted. The night they spent together filled Scott with physical sensations that temporarily vanquished his ever-churning worries. His brain was silenced for once. The intensity was such that when they finished and he lay on his back, he was afraid he might cry and, if he started, wouldn't be able to stop the tears. But he held back. He reasserted control. Then he fell asleep, heavily. The next thing he knew, Emily was gently shaking his shoulder.

"I have to go to work," she said. "The door will lock when you close it behind you. No rush."

— 36 —

On a drive back to his house one Sunday evening, more than a month after he and Emily had begun their relationship, Scott bathed in the warmth of his feelings for her. Another happy weekend had been spent in her company. But with each passing mile, harsher realities intruded on his contentment. Now that he'd come to know Emily and Justin, he believed he had covered the key players Detective Kerbich had interviewed about the murder of Ed Blaus. He knew what every one of those people was doing on the day of Blaus's murder. The time to act was now. To make sure the person arrested for the murder was not himself or a member of his family. His brutal calculation came down to this: someone else would have to take the fall. Justin Skilbahl had been right when he accused Scott of looking for a scapegoat. And the person who best fit that role was the very person who'd called Scott out on his true motive: Justin.

Scott and Emily had brunched earlier that day in a neighborhood place that had recently reinvented itself, with fancy drinks and splashy names for the pancakes and eggs Benedict, in order to better attract the Manhattan transplants in the area who'd fled the island's high prices. He and Emily sat smiling at each other over Bloody Marys. He was happy. Emily seemed happy too. They'd spent another lovely night together. They spoke idly as they waited for their food, and something in that meandering conversation triggered Emily to tell Scott the real story of Justin and his plan to change his last name.

"That time we talked with Justin on the phone, it was curious to me, because he's usually so honest, blunt, really," Emily said.

"What do you mean?"

"He told you he never asked Ed about the name change. That

he had second thoughts and then Ed was killed, so he never got the chance."

"That's not true?"

"Oh, he might have had second thoughts. I told him from the start it was a terrible idea. But he did talk to Ed. He told me he did."

"And?"

"Ed rejected him, as always. Told him not to do it, not to take the Blaus name, that it wouldn't bring them any closer. Terrible."

"Terrible," Scott repeated. "I imagine Justin was upset."

"Devastated."

That sealed things for Scott. "Devastated." Justin was devastated by Blaus's latest rejection. That's what he needed. Scott already knew Justin didn't have a strong alibi for the day Blaus was killed. He knew the son harbored a lifelong antipathy toward his father, who by any measure had treated him poorly. But there had been no catalyst. Why, after a lifetime of neglect, would Justin pick now to kill his father? It didn't make sense. But now it did. This was new. This was motive: one final, intimate rejection that had pushed Justin over the edge. How much could the young man stand? Blaus was engaging in psychological torture. After this final insult, Justin cracked. This story made sense to Scott.

But could he do it? Had his values been so twisted by his many years in the shark-infested business world that he would frame an innocent person? It was a horrible thought. He countered by telling himself he had no choice. That if Justin didn't take the fall, he or Sarah would. Then a more chilling idea occurred to him. Maybe this was who Scott was all along, even before he went to work for the firm. After all, hadn't he ignored his own brother's cries for help?

He pictured Emily receiving news of Justin's arrest. Saw her thin, pale hand dropping the phone as she absorbed the message. How could he do this to her? What sort of monster had he become? What would she think if at this very moment she knew Scott— the man who'd become her lover—was plotting to take away her only child? Set him up for murder after she had confided in him? All to protect himself and his daughter. His family above her family. The call of us, not them.

The key, if he were to do it, would be to keep her from knowing, ever. But how could he go on, even if not discovered? How could he live with his actions? He thought of himself as tough, rational, dismissive of emotion as a hindrance in business as in life. But this. This hideous act was levels beneath anything he'd ever done.

He thought of Sarah and the worry he found harder and harder to suppress that she could be arrested for the murder of Ed Blaus. For Sarah, then. The dreadful truth was that for Sarah, he would do whatever was necessary, regardless of the innocent lives he might destroy—even if it meant betraying a woman he believed he was beginning to love.

This time, he wouldn't fail. Like he did with Freddie.

—37—

Five days later, Scott met the same representative from DARK DAY, but at a different restaurant, this one tucked away in a small town in Rockland County, a few exits past the Mario Cuomo Bridge. The man was already there, in a secluded booth, when Scott arrived, even though Scott was ten minutes early.

"Let's order first," the man said by way of a greeting.

Scott wasn't hungry, but he understood the protocol. The idea was not to do anything—no matter how small—that might call attention, that might help the waitress remember them a week from now or six months from now if anyone came around asking questions. Sitting in a restaurant and only sipping a lukewarm glass of water was the kind of thing to avoid.

Scott ordered a hamburger.

"This is still personal business," Scott said, wanting there to be no misunderstanding about the big ask to come.

"Aware," the man said, "since the request didn't come through your usual corporate channels. We checked, just to make sure you are still in good standing with your company. If not, we couldn't continue to work with you—conflict of interest. It is understood that you are currently on leave. But our expectation and your company's expectation is that at some point you will return. Once your personal business is concluded. That is a condition you must accept for us to continue to work on your personal matters. Your company has given its okay."

Scott nodded. He pushed his fork around the Formica, just to have something to do with his hands. He noticed a couple of brownish stains on the table top.

"I really appreciate the forbearance," he said, feeling like a penitent. "As far as payment . . ."

The man cut him off.

"First, tell me the requirement. We will decide if we can accommodate it. If it is a go, we will charge you a fee. We have a good sense of your net worth and see no value in making claims on a person he can't fulfill. That's bad business."

"I agree," Scott said.

It was one of the few times in his adult life he saw no possibility of negotiation. He had zero leverage with DARK DAY or with his employer. They could dispose of him, but he couldn't walk away. He knew too many secrets, was in too deep. Was it worth it? He needed to stop asking himself that question. A path of action was chosen. There was no turning back. He looked past the bland man to a poorly executed painting of three juggling, melancholy-looking clowns that hung on the wall behind him.

"I am not aware precisely of where the police are in the investigation of the murder of Ed Blaus," Scott began.

"Or imprecisely, I imagine."

"True enough."

"The policeman leading the investigation, Detective Delmore Kerbich, he is unapproachable. Just so you know," the man said. His intonation was flat.

"I figured as much, but that's not where I was going."

Scott summarized what he knew: he and Sarah were the main suspects, perhaps his estranged wife, Meredith, too. They all had motive; they all had opportunity.

"Did you kill Ed Blaus?" the man asked.

"No," Scott said sharply, surprised by the question.

"Have you asked your daughter if she did?"

"I have not," Scott said.

The man shifted slightly in his seat. He winced. It was the first time Scott had seen anything but a bland, poker face on his dining companion.

"Sorry," he said, "That was unprofessional. Personal curiosity, which has no place here. Those questions have no bearing on whether or not we accept the assignment."

"Understood," Scott said.

Scott found it increasingly difficult to swallow each bite of hamburger, though there was nothing wrong with it. He didn't want to do anything out of the ordinary, so he forced himself to keep chewing. He was grateful to take a break between bites to describe what he now wanted.

He shared everything he knew about Justin Skilbahl: his inability to provide a strong alibi for the late afternoon of the murder and his difficult relationship with his father, culminating in Blaus's rebuff of Justin's request to take on his last name.

"Oh, yes," Scott said, "one more thing. When I spoke to Justin on the phone with his mother present, he said he never wound up asking Blaus about the name change. Didn't get around to it before Blaus was killed. That was the opposite of what Emily told me."

"Emily?"

"Emily Skilbahl, Justin's mother."

The man nodded. "We'll be in touch."

– 38 –

Scott believed his big house's silence—except for old-age creaks—was the reason his dreams remained so vivid, even after he'd risen, showered, and headed to the kitchen for coffee. In the pre-Ed Blaus era, Scott rarely remembered his dreams. Sometimes, the stresses of work had manifested themselves in twisted forms. He knew this because they and the odd juxtapositions they assumed would remain in his consciousness when his alarm rang at six, but they would dissipate almost immediately. Now, even with the investigation hanging over him, sleep was not hard to come by. The difference was that slumber induced lengthy, surreal scenes that stuck with him the next day. He might be on the run from would-be assassins, armed men with blank faces. Once he was trapped in a labyrinth in a building somewhere underground. It resembled the offices of his firm, which in reality sat midway up a skyscraper. He was searching for Detective Kerbich; he had important information to deliver. When he found Kerbich, the policeman morphed into a giant, hideous creature, oozing toxic fluids. Scott shielded his eyes from the horror. When he awoke, one arm was slung across his face. He was breathing hard and relieved to find he was in his familiar bed, though the empty space on the other side still taunted him. It was 3:00 a.m. Scott was reluctant to fall back asleep, certain it would mean another fantasy assaulting his senses. He tried to rest without sleeping, eyes closed, breathing evenly.

When Scott next looked at his phone, charging on the nightstand, it was 3:38. *Okay,* he said silently, *rest, breathe, just breathe.* And in this way, he did for a time avoid more dreams, but his mind refused to shut off. Instead he remembered his father calling him while he was at college. Sophomore year. The call, to the landline in his dorm room, seemed to have come from another planet. It was late; Scott had just come back from a fraternity get-together. It was Thursday night, and his first Friday class was not until noon. He could let loose on Thursday nights, and he did. He greeted the unexpected call too jauntily, happily high and comfortable in his college world. His father's unfamiliar articulations, bordering on an extended moan, killed that pleasantness fast and fully. Freddie was gone. They didn't know where. He hadn't returned home for two nights. For all the school trouble and obvious signs of drug use, this had not happened before. Scott remembered his first thoughts: *This can't be true. Freddie's still in high school. He can't be that far gone.*

Scott asked his father if he'd called the police.

"No, I'm afraid."

"Of what?"

"That they'll arrest him if they find him. Or . . . " He stopped talking.

Or, Scott filled in, *they'll find him dead.* Scott told his father he would catch the first bus in the morning. Bleary-eyed and back in Brooklyn late that Friday afternoon, Scott went first to the schoolyard a few blocks from the family apartment. The March wind chilled him through his too-thin, university sweatshirt. The sun was just about gone, but teenagers were out. A group of boys huddled ominously in a far corner. Scott looked to other areas of the schoolyard and recognized a couple of boys who'd once been friendly with Freddie. They were skateboarders clacking up and down benches set close by the high fencing that surrounded the place. The boys proceeded down the winding incline of an entrance for wheelchairs. Freddie had given up skateboarding and moved out of the group, into something that was now drowning him. Scott asked if they'd seen Freddie. They shook their heads.

"Where do the dopers hang out?" Scott asked.

One of the boys laughed. "Dopers? Come on."

"Listen, asshole," Scott said, and he pushed the slender youth's shoulder, sending him stumbling backward so that he almost tripped over his skateboard. "Freddie's missing. I don't need any bullshit from you."

"All right," the boy said, trying to sound tough but failing. "Keep your fucking hands off."

Night was fully on by the time Scott had information about where he might find the kind of young people he had in mind. Scott borrowed his parents' car. He found a parking spot across the street from the boardwalk. Mist seeped in from the Atlantic Ocean. No one seemed to be around. Scott wasn't positive this was the spot. It had been a long while since he'd been at the beach.

A single dim streetlight illuminated the sandy stairs that led to the boardwalk. Scott took them, traversing to the other side and descending another set of steps onto the beach. The waves were louder now as they crashed against the shore and receded, crashed and receded. It was a show performed for Scott alone, it seemed. He turned his back on the beach and the ocean, bent at the neck, and made his way under the boardwalk. The space wasn't quite high enough for him to stand upright. The sturdy posts that held the boardwalk upright reeked of dried urine. Scott mumbled obscenities for want of a flashlight.

He moved clumsily from post to post, his sneakers filling with sand, guided only by the weak shafts of light sneaking in between the boardwalk's wooden planks. He was moving in the direction of Coney Island, his pace hampered by the dim lighting and the drudgery of traipsing along the sand.

Maybe he hadn't started in the correct spot. Maybe he was headed in the wrong direction. These doubts nagged at him as he barely avoided stepping on a syringe half submerged in the sand, needle pointing skyward. He cursed and scraped the top of his head against the boardwalk undergirding as he skipped to the right.

A voice emerged from the darkness. It came from ahead and to the left, closer to the beach. It was a girl. Hard to say what age, though young. He came upon her lying on her stomach in the sand, face turned sideways, toward the water. She wore a blue windbreaker. Was she talking? He moved cautiously, eyes alighting on the wet, sand-encrusted Converse sneakers covering her tiny feet.

A child's feet, Scott thought.

The torn hems of her jeans were wet and sandy. Her hair was matted. Scott bent over to listen more closely. She was snoring. He saw, a couple feet from her, a blue bandana dotted with red.

Blood, he thought. *Probably what she'd used to find a vein when shooting up.* He saw her back rise and fall. He heard the snores, softer now. She was alive. He moved on. More discarded needles. This must be the gathering place.

A couple hundred yards from the girl, propped up against one the posts, was his brother. Freddie was wearing a green winter jacket, one Scott recognized as a birthday present from their parents a couple years back. The lanky Freddie had had a late growth spurt, and now the coat's arms didn't cover his wrists. Like the girl's, his sneakers and pants bottoms were wet and covered with sand. Freddie's hair was long, pulled behind his ears. He hadn't shaved in who knew how long, but his beard wasn't full, leaving blotches of nearly clear skin along his jaw.

When he got close enough, Scott could hear Freddie breathing. Thank God.

That wave of relief was followed almost instantly by disgust. What the fuck? Who does this to himself? Who was his younger brother? What had become of him in the two years Scott had been at college? Where was any shred of self-respect?

Scott bent down and sniffed a foulness he couldn't identify. Sweat and grime and what else? Had Freddie pissed his pants? Great. Perfect. Scott nudged Freddie's shoulder with his foot. Freddie grunted. Scott nudged him again, harder this time. Freddie's eyes opened. Glassy, unfocused. Scott crouched next to Freddie, trying to ignore the smell. He put a hand on Freddie's shoulder, shook him some more. "Hey, it's me." Freddie looked at him. It took a while, but recognition finally registered. Freddie started to cry, quietly, tears running down his face. He made no effort to wipe them. "Hey, hey," Scott said. "We don't need that. Let's get you out of here. Can you stand up?"

Freddie nodded. But he couldn't. Scott lifted him. His brother, always thin, now seemed almost weightless. Freddie's jeans sagged, exposing pale skin around his hips. "Okay," Scott said, "put your arm around me." Freddie did. And like that they slowly emerged from under the boardwalk. The mist had turned to steady rain as they found the nearest set of steps. Freddie was moving better on his own steam, and Scott released him to walk alone. Then he remembered the girl.

"Hey, do you know that girl who passed out down there? We ought to let her family know. It's dangerous for her to be lying there, exposed."

Freddie shook his head. "Just Lily," he said. "Nothing else."

"Nothing at all?" Freddie shook his head again.

When Scott got Freddie folded into the front passenger seat of their parents' car, he locked the door and went looking for a pay phone. He told the 911 operator what he knew about the girl's condition and location. When the operator asked for his name, Scott hung up. He trotted back to the car. Freddie had dozed off. On the drive back to their parents' apartment, with a snoozing Freddie beside him, Scott thought about the game he and Freddie had played when they were kids sharing a bedroom. Freddie must have been about six, which meant Scott was nine. Freddie was going through a phase when he was convinced an evil red dragon was hiding under his bed. The dragon had the ability to make itself invisible until the bedroom lights went out. Once that happened, Freddie could see it breathing fire under there, ready to emerge and attack. No one else could see the dragon. Only Freddie and only in the dark. Scott came up with a plan. He turned into Uncle Buster, their invented long-lost uncle who had arrived in the Brooklyn apartment after years in some faraway place, where he'd specialized in fighting and taming dragons. Uncle Buster was world famous for that. When their mother insisted it was time for lights out, Freddie would peer under his bed. He saw the evil dragon, about to cause mayhem.

"Uncle Buster," he'd say, "The dragon's getting ready to breathe fire."

"Is he?" Scott would reply as Uncle Buster, puffing out his chest. "We'll see about that." He'd get up from his own bed at the far end of the room, come over, and get on all fours to look under Freddie's bed. "Hey, dragon," he'd say, "this is Uncle Buster. You better go to sleep or Uncle Buster is going to have to kick your butt." He'd then tell Freddie the dragon had gone back to sleep; there was nothing to worry about. Freddie would nod. That did the trick. Soon, both boys were slumbering.

Histrionics greeted Scott's arrival with Freddie. Their mother wailed; their father thanked God, loudly and repeatedly. He and Scott helped Freddie undress and pushed and prodded him into a warm bath. Their mother took his clothes and thrust them into a plastic garbage bag. They were too far gone for laundering. They eased Freddie into a fresh set of pajamas and put him to bed. The same bed in the same room where not that many years earlier he'd worried about a dragon waiting for the lights to go out. A dragon kept in check only by the nightly ministrations of brave Uncle Buster. With Freddie in bed, Scott sat with his parents on the plastic-covered couch in the living room.

"What happens now?" Scott asked.

"We'll get some food into him in the morning," his mother said. "We'll take him to the doctor."

"I'll have a good talk with him," Scott's father said. "He's got to stop this."

Scott thought, *These people don't have a clue. They don't know what they're up against. Have a good talk with him. Take him to the pediatrician. My God.* But Scott said nothing. He had no better ideas. His mother put a spare sheet over the couch. He had no interest in sleeping in the bedroom he and Freddie shared all those years. She got Scott a pillow and a blanket from the linen closet. His parents silently wandered off to their own bedroom while Scott settled uncomfortably on the couch. The next morning, Scott got up before Freddie and told his parents he had to get back to school as soon as possible; there were group assignments he'd already put off to embark on this emergency mission to Brooklyn. The classmates who had been penalized by his quick departure couldn't be disadvantaged further. It was a lie. He needed to get out of the apartment, away from his parents, away from Freddie. His life, his new life, awaited him back at school. Out of the neighborhood, out of Brooklyn. His parents thanked him again for coming down to help. "You saved your brother," his mother said, crying.

Saved indeed, Scott thought as he drifted back to the reality of his fifty-eight-year-old self in the early hours of another day in his Scarsdale house. After that, Freddie had just gotten worse. It wasn't a direct descent. He'd straighten out for a while, even go back to school for a few weeks, attend group counseling for drug users organized by the high school or one of the churches or community centers. Then he'd start using again. Private rehab centers were too expensive. Their parents put him on a waiting list for public facilities. The list seemed endless.

After a couple of years of that, Scott delivered his tough-love advice. His parents shouldn't put up with the constant worry, Freddie's stealing from them, his more frequent disappearances. Cut him off, Scott said. Make him realize finally that he had to stand up for himself, reach out to them if he was truly ready for their help. Fine advice, sure. People had written books about it. He knew now that his approach was also the perfect cover to allow him to avoid the familial nightmare Freddie had created.

He did not want to go back to Brooklyn. A clean start beckoned as graduation approached. Scott understood now that only he could have made a difference for Freddie. He would have known, even then, how to work the angles, to get Freddie into a treatment facility, where he'd at least have a chance of getting clean. Even if it meant taking out loans. Scott knew his parents weren't capable of getting that done. They were too passive. They'd wait forever until Freddie's name came up for a place in a public program. Except it never would. Other people would use whatever connections and influence they had to get their own relatives into treatment before Freddie. His brother would forever be on a list. Scott could have made a difference. And he didn't. He instead told his parents to throw Freddie out of the apartment. To shut him out. Scott's parents listened to him; why wouldn't they? Scott was their golden son, about to graduate with a degree in business. Who else should they listen to when they were fortunate enough to have such a smart and talented son? One who knew early on how to navigate in the world. They took Scott's advice, as much as it hurt them to do so. They turned their backs on their other, suffering son. Soon enough, Freddie was dead of an overdose.

Scott rose from bed. It wasn't yet dawn. He got in the shower and turned the water to its hottest temperature.

−39−

Scott's phone buzzed; Josie Horvitz, the lawyer he had hired for Sarah, was calling.

She sounded out of breath. "Walking to my Uber driver, who's waiting in the wrong place," she started. "We just got done with another session with Kerbich and I wanted to fill you in pronto."

"Where's Sarah?"

"She said she wanted to walk for a bit. She didn't want the ride I offered."

"Sounds bad."

"Well, I'd call it new information. Sarah didn't leave the office on the day of the murder when she said she did. The police are now aware."

"What?"

"Surprised me too. I'd had more than one of the lawyer talks with her—you know, I'm the one you can trust, I'm the one able to keep your confidence, but you have to be honest with me. I guess it didn't stick."

"What exactly do they know?" Scott felt his knees sag. He looked around the kitchen for a chair. He sat. The phone trembled in his hand.

"That she left the office the day of the murder at 5:08 p.m., not 6:30-ish, like she said. Oh, I'm at the car, finally. Wait."

Scott heard Josie give her name to the driver, close a car door, and rustle around. "I'll be circumspect in what I say now. Will send you a fuller report later."

"Is this terrible? I mean it is terrible. How terrible is it?"

"Not helpful, for sure. Once they revealed their hand, I told her not to answer anything else. Delmore came at her from a bunch of different angles, hot and cold, ended with threats about how she was making things worse for herself by not cooperating. That comment made her cry."

Scott felt a sharp pain in his side. "Oh, geez," he said. He suddenly wanted to get off the phone. "All right, send me your report as soon as you can. I'll call you if I have questions."

Josie Horvitz's email showed up a couple of hours later. She was to the point. Scott was impressed all over again with the young lawyer. He was thankful Josie had kept his daughter's reactions to the ordeal to a minimum. The pain in his side that developed at hearing about Sarah's distress had dulled but not disappeared. The report read:

"Detective Delmore Kerbich stated police have badge swipe data from Sarah's office building that contradicts her earlier statements to the police. He wouldn't say how long they have had this information or why they are revealing it now. When I pursued questions in this area, Kerbich said he would ask the questions. He said entry and departure data from Sarah's office building can be reliably linked to individual badge numbers. There is no chance of a misidentification, he said. On the day of the murder, Sarah's badge swiped out at 5:08 p.m., with no data showing reentry that day. She had previously stated she left around 6:30 p.m. Kerbich repeated that the coroner put the time of death as anywhere from 3:30 p.m. to 6:00, maybe 6:15 p.m. He noted that by leaving at 5:08 she could have been home in plenty of time to kill Blaus. If the subway is running well, it only takes about twenty to twenty-five minutes to get back to the apartment, he said. At this point, I raised a couple of objections to Kerbich's statements and conclusions. For one thing, the swipe in and out times were based on Sarah's badge, which is a significant distinction from Sarah herself. I also objected to Kerbich's time frame about how long it takes to get from Sarah's office to her apartment. What did he mean specifically by twenty to twenty-five minutes if the subway was running well? Define running well. I reminded him that he was a police detective and not an expert on intra-Manhattan travel. Kerbich ignored my objections. He said I could raise objections in court. They didn't mean anything in a police interview room.

"I advised Sarah at that point not to answer any of Kerbich's subsequent questions. They included, but were not limited to, why did you lie about the time you left? What did you do after you left work at 5:08 p.m.? Did you encounter Ed Blaus alive in the apartment that day? Did you kill Ed Blaus? As I noted earlier, Kerbich occasionally issued threats about things going harder for Sarah if she didn't cooperate. He said the police would on their own get the answers to the questions he asked, even if Sarah didn't respond. When he seemed to run out of inquiries and threatening statements, I asked if we could go and he said yes, but Sarah should not leave the city. This was informal, not a court order, but my advice to Sarah was to heed those restrictions, not to travel any great distance and certainly not out of the country. I told her visiting you in Westchester was perfectly fine."

Scott texted Sarah and asked for a call. He got no response. Later, he tried again with a more urgent message. His phone buzzed. Sarah sounded sleepy. It was 6:00 p.m.

"Have you taken something?" he asked.

"Ambien, that's all."

"Not too much, right? And don't mix it with anything you shouldn't."

"All right," Sarah muttered, her voice flat. She said she was out of commission for the evening, couldn't handle any more talk, more questions. She was alone in her friend's apartment. The friend was off on a two-week business trip/vacation combo.

They met the next night at a French restaurant near where Sarah was staying. She wore dark glasses. Scott wasn't sure if they were in service of guaranteeing anonymity or hiding eyes that would have betrayed the excessive use of prescription drugs.

"I know this is a lot to handle," Scott said as softly as he could manage. He determined on the drive down he would not ask why she lied about when she left work on the day of the murder. He would not scold her or point out how lying had made things much worse, that it focused police attention on her even beyond the harsh spotlight that already existed. Imitating the DARK DAY man, he said they needed to order food and drink, to be as inconspicuous as possible. Sarah nodded.

Scott said, "Let's just talk. Just talk, no big deal, okay? If you left work a little after five, what could you have done after that to still get to the apartment just before seven? That was the time you told the police you arrived home, right?"

She nodded. "It was a nice day," Sarah said. "I could have walked back, rather than take the subway."

"Have you walked it before? How long does that take?"

"About forty-five minutes, maybe an hour."

"Okay, an hour," Scott repeated. He noted that neither of them had touched the food the waiter set down in front of them. He poked at his fish and indicated Sarah should take up her utensils. She forked up a few greens and placed them in her mouth, which had opened in slow motion, like a yawn. "That's good," he said, "I like an hour." With the new, police-confirmed departure time from the office, a leisurely walk home put her arrival at the apartment as late as about 6:10, near the outer limit of the coroner's time-of-death zone. Still, too close for comfort. Scott wondered aloud if there was anything that might have happened on the walk that further delayed her arrival.

"Could you have stopped somewhere to buy something?"

"Not that I remember."

"If you did, there would be a credit card record, which is easily traceable. You never use cash, right?"

"Right."

"A drink with a friend?"

"Uh, no."

That wouldn't work, Scott thought. *It would require a friend's testimony and a credit card charge for the drinks.*

"It's an hour if you walked slowly but directly, right?" Scott asked rhetorically. "But if you window-shopped along the way, maybe even stopped into a store to look at a few things but didn't buy that day, well, that would change the timeline and stretch it considerably."

"Considerably," Sarah repeated, rather dreamily. "That's a nice word. It makes you sound very, I don't know, smart."

He clearly did not have a partner who was 100 percent focused. He wondered again what she was on. She smiled vapidly at him. The walk and window-shopping sounded better and better to Scott. Less than optimal, but the best of a bad situation. That was their mantra at work. Companies paid them to take less-than-optimal situations and make them into something acceptable, maybe more. At work, there were all sorts of specialists internally and externally to consult with on any kind of problem. There was no one he could talk to about this.

He needed DARK DAY to come through now more than ever. No

doubt the new information made Sarah Kerbich's prime suspect, if she wasn't already. There was little physical evidence. The murder weapon had not been found. But the pressure for an arrest was still immense—the investigation had already dragged on for many months—and Sarah's lie and the fact that she had discovered the body put her front and center. He wondered if she might be arrested today, tomorrow, or the next day. *Come on DARK DAY, come on.*

Scott knew asking for a progress report was strictly out of bounds, a cardinal sin that would prompt the group to drop him as a client. It would also redound negatively on his company's relationship with DARK DAY. Since he was out on an open-ended leave, pissing off his employer was the last thing he wanted to do. He needed for him and his family to be cleared of the scandal if he was to make his way back into the consultancy's good graces. He understood the reasons for DARK DAY's policies. They wanted to keep contact with clients to a minimum. Every extra communication was another chance to get caught, another line hanging out there for someone, sometime to discover. There would be a result when there was a result. No time frame offered. No tidy, printed executive summary at the end. That's how they kept everyone involved as safe as possible from the prying eyes of the authorities and the press. If they accepted a job, they would complete it. There was no doubt about that. You would find out the result when they wanted you to. So, Scott reminded himself, there was nothing to do but shut up and wait.

– 40 –

Scott's phone buzzed; this time it was Emily. They were spending most evenings together now, and Scott couldn't remember when he'd been so happy to simply exist in the same room as another human being. At least when he was able to suppress the knowledge that he'd set in motion a plan to trap Justin, her only child, in a murder investigation that could send him to prison for the rest of his life. That proved easier than he had imagined, which was a relief in one way but disconcerting in another. Again Scott was forced to confront his own values as a human being. Who could do such a thing, let alone not be traumatized by it? It helped that nothing had actually happened. It was still abstract. But he knew there was a time limit.

"Hi, honey," he said into his phone.

"Scott, I don't know what to do. I think they are going to arrest Justin for killing Ed."

"What do you mean?"

"They had him down at the station. Kerbich and some other cops. They told him a witness has come forward to say Justin admitted killing Ed. They told him they could help him with a lesser charge if he made a full confession."

"That's crazy. What did he do?"

"He freaked out. He said he stood up from the chair and said he didn't kill anyone and he wasn't going to confess to something he didn't do."

"But they didn't arrest him?"

"No. They told him to stay close."

Just what they had told Scott. Just what they had told Sarah when they caught her in the lie about when she had left the office the day of the murder. That was more than a month ago, and Sarah hadn't heard from the police since. She was not doing well with the uncertainty.

"Okay, hold on, don't panic. I'll get in the car and head down."

"I was at the office when he called," Emily said. "I'm heading home now. I'll get there before you."

Scott got down to business as soon as he walked in.

"You need to get him a good criminal defense attorney," he said.

Emily began to protest, but Scott raised his hand. "Don't concern yourself about the cost. I'll pay."

"I can't let you."

"Of course you can and you will."

Scott's tone brooked no comeback. He sat at the kitchen table.

"Once you have the lawyer, he or she can try to figure out what exactly the police have, talk to Justin and strategize from there."

Emily asked if Scott could suggest a specific lawyer or law firm. Not wanting to connect with any of the attorneys his company used or anyone in the orbit of Sarah's attorney, Josie Horvitz, he demurred.

"Let's do some Googling," he said.

Emily's already pale complexion had turned ghostly. He stood up and approached her standing at the stove, wrapping his arms around her.

"Don't worry, it's going to be okay," he said.

Emily sniffled into the left side of Scott's chest.

"I don't know what I would do without you."

Scott stared straight ahead, at the kitchen window. Odd, but he never before had noticed how dirty it was.

The next night, Scott was on City Island at a seafood restaurant. He'd spoken to Emily just before getting into his car to drive there. She was disappointed he wasn't coming to see her. He told her the dinner was with an important client seeking advice about a business issue. They'd worked successfully with Scott in the past, so only Scott would do. Yes, the client was informed Scott was on leave, but that's the way some clients are: their needs are the only ones they acknowledge. He told Emily it was in his self-interest to go ahead with the dinner. His partners appreciated it, and it helped reinforce Scott's value to the firm. He'd been away from work a long time. It would be easy enough for them to think the place ran just as well without him.

The lawyer Emily hired with Scott's money was capable and

reassuring. He'd already talked with Justin at length and sniffed around Kerbich. Not much was gained on that front, but the lawyer said that if the police had more than this one witness (unless the witness had a tape, it was his word against Justin's denial that the conversation had ever happened), they would have arrested Justin. The fact that Justin was walking around, going to work, was a good sign. A very good sign.

At the restaurant, Scott ordered the halibut. This time he didn't have to be told to act natural. Scott wondered how the DARK DAY contact always managed to get restaurant tables that were noticeably apart from other diners, even when the restaurants were nearly full. Scott figured they sent scouts to every restaurant in the tristate region and noted those with a more secluded table or two. They never asked to meet at a Manhattan restaurant. Any spot in the heart of the city was probably too conspicuous, though Scott never asked for the rationale behind the group's rendezvous choices. If he were to ask, he presumed, he wouldn't get a substantive answer.

After stiff pleasantries and the arrival of their food, the DARK DAY man, the same contact Scott had met throughout, began to bring Scott up to date.

"Interrupt me a few times with a question or a comment," he said, "so if anyone is paying attention to us, it looks like we're having a real conversation, not me conducting a monologue."

After research and evaluation, the group had discovered that one of Justin's roommates—technically a former roommate, since he had moved out of the shared apartment a few weeks after the murder—had a vulnerability that could be exploited. His name was Steve Smither, twenty-seven years old, raised on Long Island. He had a low-level job at a bank in Midtown. He also sold drugs on the side. Cocaine mainly. An important income supplement. The connection who kept Smither supplied had spent time inside, but he was still a step or two removed from the real guys.

"By real guys you mean?" Scott interrupted as instructed.

"Those who import and distribute at scale. Who are tied to the big syndicates here and south of the border."

Scott nodded. Just typical dinner conversation.

"Anyway, perhaps unknown, perhaps known to Steve Smither, his connection started receiving, and selling to him, cocaine laced with fentanyl. It lowers the cost of the product. The problem is it's deadly."

"I think I read that somewhere, about all the fentanyl overdoses."

"I'm sure you have," the DARK DAY man continued. "Anyway, it's hard to know how much lacing is too much lacing and who knows who's doing what within these syndicates and for what reasons?"

Smither had received a delivery of cocaine with a high percentage of fentanyl.

"One of Smither's customers had to be hospitalized. Smither knew about that, because the guy told him what happened. The buyer was understandably outraged. He threatened to report Smither to the cops. But he didn't. He just stopped buying from him. But one girl, young, twenty-one, a college student, was home on a break and wanted to get high. Someone referred her to Smither. First-time customer. Last time for her. Like I said, that batch had too much fentanyl. Smither kept selling it anyway. She snorted a lot that night, alone. Her parents were out. They came home and she was dead."

"Holy."

"Cops couldn't solve it. Maybe because it wasn't a regular connection. All her friends denied sending her to a dealer."

"But didn't she have to make contact with Smither? Wouldn't that have been on her phone?"

"Smither used burner phones for his dealing. He never has the same number for long. One of his regulars calls to make a buy; Smither says a week from now the number is going to be X. Do not put it in your phone. Write it with a pencil on a piece of paper. A few weeks later there's a new number. The cops found a number they were convinced was the one the girl used to call Smither, but by the time they were on the trail, it led nowhere."

Scott had done his best to make it seem like a conversation, but he suppressed the most obvious question. If the police had come up cold following the evidence in the death of the young woman, how did DARK DAY solve the case? He wasn't sure he wanted to know. DARK DAY could and did resort to methods unavailable to the police if they followed the law. The group's reputation, already strong in Scott's mind, climbed a couple more notches. He asked how Smither reacted when DARK DAY confronted him with the discovery.

"I will say only this: Smither reviewed the situation and several days later marched into the precinct house where the Ed Blaus murder investigation is centered and announced he might have pertinent information. Smither recounted that about two weeks after the murder, he ran into Justin Skilbahl at a downtown dive bar, drinking alone. He asked Justin why he wasn't at his waiter job, and Justin said he called in sick. Smither asked him what was going on. To Smither's observation, Justin was heavily drunk. Justin said he didn't know if he could go on. Smither asked what he meant; he thought Justin was being dramatic about the loss of his father. Justin said he couldn't live with what he'd done. 'Oh, come on,' Smither said, 'whatever it is, it can't be that bad.' He told the police he thought Justin was referring to unkind words he'd had with his father that couldn't be undone now that Ed was dead. 'You don't think murder is so bad?' Justin said. 'Who'd you murder?' Smither asked. 'My father,' Justin said.

"I know," the man continued, "the obvious question Detective Kerbich would ask and did ask: 'Why did you wait so long to come forward? It's been many months since the murder.' Smither told him it was a number of things. At first, he didn't believe Justin. After all, the guy was super drunk, and Smither thought Justin just felt bad about his father having been killed. He said Justin was always overly dramatic. He was an actor, so it was to be expected. At the time, Smither dismissed it. He thought there would soon be an arrest of someone else for the murder, and that would confirm that Justin was just blowing smoke when he said he killed Blaus. Like everyone else, Smither followed the case in the media. There wasn't an arrest. Time kept moving on. People in high places were getting impatient, he read. The cops were stonewalling reporters' questions about what was going on. That all brought back to him the incident in the bar. Could there have been something to that? What Justin said that night? He also remembered that after Ed Blaus rejected Justin's taking Blaus as his last name, they'd sat around with a few other friends at someone's apartment talking about it. Drinking while they did. Didn't Justin say then he'd get even with Blaus? Do something to mess him up? Or was that someone else? Or Justin and someone else? Smither said he couldn't fully recall. But threats were definitely made that evening against Ed Blaus.

"Then he read a news article that reported Sarah Morgan had again been questioned. It quoted an unnamed police official saying she was the primary suspect. Smither said to Kerbich, 'When I read that, I thought I should tell you what I heard from Justin. I couldn't live with myself if he did the murder and this innocent person, this Sarah Morgan, whoever she is, was convicted instead.'"

Nice touch, Scott thought. Not only fingering Justin, but specifically saying he was doing it so an innocent person—the person they were trying to get off the hook—wouldn't be wrongly blamed. It was an admirable execution with a key, less-than-optimal fact, how long it took Smither to come forward with his story. There was no recording or other hard evidence to support Smither's story.

"Smither's got an open-ended commitment to us," the DARK DAY man said. "If he recants or changes his story, he knows we'll pin that girl's death on him."

There was nothing left to say except thank you, so that's what Scott did. He would hear from DARK DAY again when it was time to pay for their services. It would be a large amount, though impossible to know how large. Would it be a month, a year when he next heard? Who knew? It might not be until the investigation into the murder of Ed Blaus was put to rest, so the heat would be lower.

– 41 –

As Scott heard the familiar click of his key opening the front door to his dark, empty house, he wondered if the case would ever be resolved. He was amazed at what DARK DAY had been able to do: locate the drug-selling killer of an unfortunate young woman and turn him into a vehicle to divert attention from his daughter. Still, Steve Smither's story didn't prompt Delmore Kerbich to lead a string of squad cars to Justin Skilbahl's door. It was one man's word against another's. And it wouldn't take much for New York police to discover that Smither's main source of income came from illegal drug sales. That certainly wouldn't help his credibility. Then there was the months-long delay in coming forward. No way Kerbich liked that. There still was, as far as Scott knew, no physical evidence tying anyone to the crime. Smither's story moved Justin into the top tier of suspects, but did it vault Justin ahead of Sarah in Kerbich's eyes? Sarah had the more compelling motive: her live-in lover had cheated on her with her own mother, for God's sakes. What was Justin's motive? That after a lifetime of neglect at the hands of Blaus, he was driven to kill his father because of one last insult: Blaus's refusal to share his last name? Maybe. It had seemed like solid gold to Scott when Emily first told him about Blaus's humiliation of Justin. Less so now. Meanwhile, Sarah had already been caught in a lie, and there was an incriminating timeline they had to work at altering.

Would police accept a stalemate? From Scott's view, it was the best thing that could happen. Sarah would be safe, no matter what had really occurred after she left her office. Justin Skibahl would be safe. The questionable testimony of Smither was all the police had and would ever have, since Scott felt certain the young actor didn't kill his father. Despite his outreach to DARK DAY, no one would have to suffer. Not Justin, not Emily. Not Scott. It was closing in on a year since Ed Blaus had been murdered. Plenty of New York City murders went unsolved. What if no new information was forthcoming and Kerbich couldn't close the case to the satisfaction of the Manhattan district attorney, who would have to prosecute? Could they all live with the lack of resolution? Scott yearned for it. He knew it would be hard on Sarah. Hard on Justin and Emily too. The constant uncertainty. The threat that hung over them. There was no statute of limitations for murder. Still, a stalemate meant no one would go to prison. His conscience would be spared from having committed a monstrous crime: framing an innocent young man for murder. Never mind that he happened to be in love with that young man's mother.

Scott called Josie Horvitz and told her it was his understanding that Sarah still could have gotten to the apartment on the day of the murder when she said she did, even though she'd left the office more than an hour earlier than she'd originally told police.

"She decided to walk home. It was a pleasant day. I checked. It was in the fifties, cloudy but no rain. She stopped at a couple stores, including Blatar's, the women's clothing place. It's on the way. She lingered over a few items, but decided not to buy. Took her time, just in case Blaus was taking longer than he should have to gather his things. She definitely did not want to see him again, so a slow walk back to the apartment makes sense."

"Did Sarah tell you all this?"

"More or less."

"More or less. Okay. Scott, please do me a favor. Let me do the lawyering here. I don't think it's helpful for you to have conversations with Sarah—without me present—about where she was and when on the day of. Understood? You're a man who should know better about these things."

Scott was embarrassed. "You're right. I'm sorry. When I'm with Sarah, all I think about is how to best protect her. I can't sit still. You understand?"

"I understand you are her father and you love her. That's all well and good, but it can be counterproductive."

"What do you think, uh, of the substance of what I laid out, apart from the wisdom of having the conversation in the first place?"

"I think it's interesting," Josie said, "if we ever get to the stage where we have to get into the specifics of her journey home from work. But we are not there yet, and we certainly aren't going to offer up anything for free."

– 42 –

Emily smiled and reviewed the plaster-of-Paris busts and sculptures of sailing ships built into the restaurant walls. "Unusual decor?" she asked. It was another restaurant in Astoria. Scott had found it online. Emily had never been.

"The food is good; that's all that matters," Scott said.

Back at the apartment, Emily was no longer interested in small talk. The shift was abrupt. "What's wrong?" Scott asked.

"What isn't?" she said. "I call Justin at least once every day. Most of the time he doesn't want to talk. When he does, he goes a mile a minute about how he's going to prison, he's certain of it, and how he won't be able to survive there. He'll die there. Either someone will kill him or he'll kill himself. It's just awful. I can barely stand to listen to it. It's breaking my heart."

Scott winced. "Let him speak with the lawyer again, get his take on the situation. Remember he said all the police have is this guy's word against Justin's. There is absolutely nothing else that supports it."

"The lawyer's done what he can to help. He's already said it more than once. He feels good about Justin's chances. The police don't have enough or they would have moved. Okay, I've got it. Justin's got it. But the lawyer can't guarantee anything. You can't guarantee anything. No one knows what that detective, Kerbich, is thinking. Who knows about prosecutors sitting at their desks? To them, Justin Skilbahl doesn't mean a thing, just a name on a computer screen. Less than nothing. Every article says the people with real power want to wrap this thing up. This is New York. No one will care whether or not he actually did it. I'm not that naive girl from the Midwest anymore. Any day they can show up at his apartment and take him away. Don't you understand that?"

"I do understand," Scott said.

"I'm okay for a few minutes at a time; then it all comes back. It's overwhelming, like I'm drowning."

Scott nodded.

Emily waved her hand, as if trying to dispel the gloom. "Did I ever tell you about the funeral? Ed's, I mean."

Scott shook his head. "I never thought about a funeral," he said. "There was his body, which was still in the apartment when I got there after Sarah called. Then the police took it away to the morgue."

"Eventually they released it, but they had trouble figuring out who would take it," Emily said. "Ed had a few cousins his age, but he had nothing to do with them once he became an adult, and I'm sure they wouldn't want anything to do with handling his funeral. His brother can't do it. So, logically, I guess, they turned to Justin."

Scott shook his head sorrowfully. He got up and approached Emily. He softly rubbed both her shoulders.

"Justin asked me what I thought he should do," Emily continued, "I said, 'You've got to claim the body. Whatever he was, he was still your father.' I told Justin to make sure Ed's brother was made aware of the where and when of the funeral. He heard back from the group home; one of the staff said Michael had decided not to attend."

"You're a good woman, Emily," Scott said.

"I don't know. Ed had no assets to speak of. His friend Henry Levitt set up a GoFundMe to help with the costs. They raised a few thousand dollars."

"Was there enough money?"

Emily laughed. "It cost me $4,000 in addition to what was raised. Justin has nothing, though he did do all the work. We had no idea what Ed would have wanted, except, of course, to have lived forever. Justin looked around for the cheapest place to put Ed in the ground, found a cemetery out on Long Island. There was some final irony in my paying for part of Ed's funeral."

"You'll have to pardon me saying this, but it strikes me as the last act of a lifelong con man. Dying with nothing and depending on the kindness of the people he treated so poorly."

Emily described the scene. A windy day, a smattering of Ed's friends in attendance, all older, downtrodden writers. Justin in an ill-fitting suit. Someone associated with the cemetery led a short service. She read Psalm 23—"The Lord is my shepherd"— and talked about ashes to ashes, dust to dust. A few of Ed's friends spoke. Henry was funny and cited some of Ed's tamer foibles. Asked if he had anything to say, Justin declined. Emily had no interest in speaking. Mary Jenseth, Ed's ex-wife, did not attend. Ed's writer friends talked mostly about *A View from Below*. No matter what else Ed had been about or what else had happened in his life—or his death—the speakers always came back to that book, Ed's crowning achievement.

"I got the feeling if you asked any one of those writers if they would rather have Ed's life than their own—one prominent book in exchange for a lifetime filled with professional disappointment, cruelty, and being murdered at age fifty-five—each one of them would have made the trade. Eagerly."

"Pathetic," Scott said.

"I'm not so sure. I think there's something admirable about Ed's friends' dedication, their compulsion to become well-known writers. I wouldn't say pathetic. More like they signed a pact when they were children that said nothing else in the world mattered except writerly success. None of that for you?"

"I guess I got over anything similar once I realized I wasn't going to be good enough to play center field for the Mets. That would have been at about age ten."

Emily stroked Scott's shoulder. "That's what I like about you, no artistic pretensions. You are solid. But when you were younger, you must have had dreams about what you wanted your life to be like?"

Emily's soft touch worked like a narcotic, relaxing Scott. "For me, it was more about getting out of where I was rather than a specific destination."

"I don't follow."

"Don't get me wrong. My parents were good people. They tried, but you know, they weren't cut out to realize the American dream. Too unassertive, too honest, really. So there were always fights about money, so much squabbling. Not just in our apartment, but it was all over the neighborhood. People were always arguing over petty stuff. I played ice hockey a couple of winters. My younger brother wanted to skate too, so my parents said, 'Here, take Scott's skates,' when I was done with them. But he wanted to figure skate, so hockey skates weren't right for him, and anyway my skates were two sizes too big. How was he going to skate when the skates didn't fit? My brother just gave up. He didn't even try them on, though my mother kept urging him. 'Try them. What could hurt? Maybe it will work out.' It must have been a Saturday, because my father was home too. In the winter he walked around the place in one of those old-fashioned sleeveless T-shirts. The apartment was always too hot, overheated. He couldn't get the heat situation adjusted. So he adapted. I remember my mother's expression after Freddie wouldn't even try on my skates. Such utter disappointment. Not toward Freddie, but directed at my father. She didn't have to say a word; her face said it all. He started pulling at his hair, whatever he had left. 'Skates, skates,' he yelled. 'Where am I supposed to get money for all these skates?' So my goal was to never be him, to never have to be on the receiving end of that kind of look because I couldn't afford a second pair of ice skates."

"And it worked, obviously."

"Yeah," Scott chuckled. "Though my daughter was never interested in skating. I bought her a pair of skates anyway. Top of the line. Maybe they got used once."

"You had to have had a goal, though, more than to just get out of your old neighborhood," Emily said.

"Not really," Scott replied. "One time we went out to a wedding at the home of my mother's cousins on Long Island. We didn't see these cousins much. They were older than my parents, and I'd never been to their home before. One of their children was getting married. I was in a state of wonder. Big house, giant backyard where they easily fit more than a hundred people for the wedding. Every house on the block had more than an acre. Big spaces between houses. You're not going to hear your neighbors yelling at each other about burning the rice or why didn't one of the kids go into the hall to put out the garbage. How many times does the kid have to be asked? From down the hallway, I could hear it like they were yelling at *me* to take out the garbage. I put up four fingers. Four times, I'd say to my brother. He's going to have to be asked four times. I was about fourteen when we went to that wedding. Probably wasn't even that special a suburban house, but it seemed like a mansion to me. If I had a goal, that was my goal. To get to a house like that, well separated from the closest neighbor. The rest of it was just figuring out the best way to get there."

Emily leaned her head against his shoulder. He fought to empty his mind of negative thoughts. Whenever he was in Emily's apartment, gloom descended on him, and the same frightening notion penetrated his thoughts: what if Emily found out he was the direct cause of her and Justin's real-life nightmare? But it was more than the fear of being discovered. It was the hideousness of what he'd done with DARK DAY, hitting him full force. Yes, yes, he told himself again and again: he'd done it to protect Sarah. That was paramount. But it wasn't enough. In those moments, he wanted to rush out of the apartment, hop into his car, and drive away—far and fast. Past the house in Scarsdale, north and farther north, Massachusetts, Maine, destination unknown. He knew the fear of being found out was irrational. Only he and DARK DAY were privy, and there was no more locked-solid entity on the face of the planet than DARK DAY. Still, what if he talked in his sleep? Not that he ever knew himself to do that. But now, with the pressure so great and guilt threatening to overwhelm him, would he crack? He simply had to will himself not to, to carry on with everything as normally as possible. It was getting more and more difficult, despite the steely determination he counted as his greatest strength. He needed to persevere.

Weeks passed, and Scott noticed that Emily was becoming increasingly haggard. She stopped applying makeup before going to work. One evening when he came over and Emily was still in her work outfit, Scott noticed a light stain running down the side of her dark skirt. Had that just happened? Had she gone to work like that and not noticed? Not cared?

That night in bed, Emily began to speak, softly but firmly.

"This is all my fault," she said. "A lifetime of punishment for getting involved with Ed. He is evil. Was evil, past tense, but I feel like even from the grave he's attacking us. Poor Justin. How can you be happy in life when your own father makes clear you are nothing to him, an inconvenience, a problem? On top of that, Justin can't make the acting work. He added to his own misery with the last name obsession. That wasn't about getting a leg up in his acting career. That's just what he said. It was because if his name was Blaus, it would finally show the world Justin was truly Ed's son. Not only because a court ordered it. That he had a father and a name to prove it. But Ed couldn't abide that."

Emily had already made clear that there was no longer any use attempting to make things better with a soothing platitude like "It's going to be okay."

"You don't know that. You have no idea, so stop saying things you don't know about," she'd cried one time.

From that point on, Scott stopped uttering automatic reassurances.

"Emily . . ."

"What, wouldn't you feel the same if your daughter went to prison for killing Ed? Wouldn't you do anything to prevent that?"

Scott remained silent.

"So please don't lecture me on how I should behave," Emily said.

— 43 —

Scott and Emily started spending less time with each other. With some regularity now, Emily said she wasn't up to seeing him. He knew that meant Justin's travails weighed so heavily on her that she didn't believe she'd be able to think or talk about anything else. "I wouldn't be very good company," she'd say. After one such call, Scott shut off the single light in the living room and sat. Just sat and tried to meditate, though he had no idea how. Since Meredith had departed to her sister's place (was she still there? He wasn't sure), Scott spent almost all his time in the house in his study, the kitchen, or their bedroom. In the darkened living room, little used even when the family was an ostensibly functioning unit, he felt as if he wasn't even in his own house. He'd come to feel more at home in Emily's modest apartment than in his own spacious residence. That was before Steve Smither had walked into a police precinct to say Justin Skilbahl confessed to the murder of Ed Blaus. Before Emily had begun to break apart due to anxiety about her son. Back when Emily could still crave companionship, tenderness, dare he even think it, another chance at love. All now extinguished. Brutally. By Scott. He had been able to openly breathe in her presence, to laugh, to want her. He had lived so long with emptiness that he had barely even known it existed. Now, as quickly as she had appeared, Emily was fading from his life. Scott felt his old numbness returning. He was the reason for Emily's descent into misery. It had seemed his only choice to divert Kerbich's attention from Sarah. It hadn't been a strong enough ploy to send the police rushing to arrest Justin. Scott was unfamiliar with the internal machinations of the NYPD and the Manhattan prosecutor's office, so he had to assume, like Emily, that an arrest could happen at any time.

But wasn't that true for Sarah too? Maybe even for him?

He couldn't go back to DARK DAY. What was he going to say: thanks for framing someone for murder to get my family off the hook, but, you see, I've fallen for the guy's mom, so I've had a change of heart. Could we just forget about it? Walk it back somehow. Get Smither to withdraw what he told the police. You have the girl's death to hold over his head. He'll have to do whatever you say. Oh, by the way, that's not all I'm asking. Not by a long shot. If Justin Skilbahl is no longer a suspect, please find someone else to pin Ed Blaus's murder on, because that's still my top priority. Just don't make it Justin. Because of his mother. Who really is a wonderful woman who shouldn't be suffering like this.

This talk would never take place. Scott knew that. That's not how things worked. It was totally unprofessional. Unacceptable. DARK DAY would walk away. They'd let Scott's employer know about it. He'd be out at the firm. Then what would he do? How could he help Sarah under those circumstances?

Scott had set events in motion with DARK DAY, and he realized there was nothing he could do now except live with the consequences. It was in the hands of Kerbich and the DA. He wished fervently for a stalemate, that no arrest would be made.

Whatever happened, he'd made the choice to protect Sarah. Above all else. He wasn't going back on that.

At night, in his quiet bedroom, Scott dreamed variations of a scene in which Emily was drowning, typically sloshing around in rolling waves, shipwrecked and near death. Scott approaches frantically in a small motorboat, his own vessel tossed by storm-heightened waves. Emily's head bobs up and down, visible for a few seconds, then gone. She stretches an arm above her head. Or she reaches out to him. He guns the motor. He gets closer. He slows the boat and strains toward her, closer, closer, but not close enough to grab her outstretched hand. Could he reach her if he just leaned out a little more? Is he holding back? The scenarios vary, but Scott never feels her grasp. Sometimes, he too is tossed overboard. Always, at some point, she is gone.

One morning, Scott awoke at 4:30 and realized he'd had the same dream again. He felt his heart pounding. With the dream still vivid in his mind, Scott thought he really didn't try to save Emily. He just pretended. He wearily got up from bed and headed to the shower.

– 4 4 –

The call came from Brian Prining, the lawyer Emily had hired and Scott was paying to represent Justin Skilbahl. Scott thought it odd that Prining was on the line with only him, without Emily. He thought at first there was a problem with billing.

"I'm sorry to be the one to have to inform you," Prining began. Scott put his cell phone on speaker and took a seat at the kitchen table. He was toasting an English muffin for breakfast. He'd slept late after a particularly turbulent night of harrowing dreams. "I'm temporarily representing Emily now. It can't go on if I'm going to continue to represent Justin. There's a conflict. But for now, I'm the attorney for both of them."

"What's happened?" Scott didn't recognize the rasp in his own voice.

"Emily went to see Detective Kerbich early this morning and confessed to the murder of Ed Blaus."

"What! Are you kidding me?"

"I was stunned too," the lawyer said, though his voice was even. "I advised against it, vehemently. But she was determined. It took all my persuasive skills to get her to allow me to be there with her to make sure at least that the rules were followed. But I couldn't do anything about the confession itself."

"What could she possibly say?" Scott protested. "She didn't kill Blaus. You're a lawyer. You know you can't just say you killed someone and the cops say, 'Oh good, that's settled,' and throw you in a cell."

"Yes, certainly," Prining said. His matter-of-fact tone was grating on Scott, whose heart felt like it was on the verge of exploding. He ignored the odor of the smoldering English muffin. "Though Emily did in fact have a reasonable narrative."

"That's crap," Scott yelled at the phone. "How can she have a reasonable narrative if she didn't kill him?"

"You seem convinced of that," Prining said. "Not that I disagree, but I presume your certainty is based on a belief in Emily rather than incontestable evidence of her innocence."

"Tell me what she said to Kerbich."

Emily told police she had become increasingly upset with Ed about his rejection of Justin's desire to change his last name to Blaus. It was the topper to how cruel he'd been to his son ever since Justin was born. What had Justin ever done to deserve it? If he wanted to hate her for proving Blaus's paternity, okay, but why take it out on an innocent child? On the day of the murder, Emily wasn't at work. It was a vacation day, and she was part of a volunteer group restoring a neighborhood church. But that wasn't an all-day commitment. She was done by noon. She took the subway and got off at the Fifty-Third Street station on the East Side. She wanted to gather her thoughts. It was a pleasant day, and she felt like walking. She headed southwest toward Ed Blaus's Chelsea apartment.

"How did she know he lived there?"

"She knew the address from Justin. Ed always provided his current address and phone number to Justin in case of emergency. Emily came up with a rationale about why she needed Ed's address. Something to do with a legal document he had to sign related to their long-ago child support arrangement. She needed to mail it to him so he could sign and have it notarized. That's what Emily said she told Justin to learn the address."

"And it just so happened she went down there on the day he was packing up? If she went any other day for weeks before he wouldn't have been there," Scott said.

"It appears so. A coincidence. I understand your reference to Ed no longer regularly living there to be related to the discovery of the affair between Ed and, uh, your, I assume, ex-wife. That wasn't public knowledge until after Ed Blaus was killed. Emily would have thought he was there every day, since over the time she knew him, he had no regular employment, which was in fact still the case."

"Did she tell the police she went down there with the intention of killing Blaus?"

"No," the lawyer said, "That was one small victory, if you can call it that. At least she didn't admit to premeditation. She said she wanted to confront Blaus, to get him to change his mind. She wanted to make Blaus call Justin and say he wanted Justin to take his last name, that it was a good thing and that it would bring them closer."

"How did she expect to do that?" Scott asked. "He was a renowned bastard. What was her thinking?"

"Kerbich also asked how she foresaw that happening. She said she was planning to bribe him. She didn't have a great deal of savings, but she believed Blaus was always tapped out and perpetually on the hunt for easy dollars. She assumed he would do it for money.

"Emily said she got to the building and rang the buzzer downstairs. She announced herself to Blaus, and he buzzed her up. Once inside, she said he told her to follow him into the bedroom if she had something to say to him. He was busy packing. She said no. He gave in and gestured to the living room. She took a seat on a chair, Ed on the couch.

"Emily, of course, didn't know anything about the events that preceded her visit, the affair and the breakup with your daughter. She found out because Blaus was happy to tell her why he was moving out. He laughed about it, Emily said. Called your, uh, ex-wife and daughter shallow, bourgeois women. He told Emily they didn't have style, like she had. Emily said even looking at him disgusted her. It was clear to her Blaus hadn't changed at all. If anything, he'd gotten worse, the way he went on about people."

"God, was that man disgusting," Scott said. "Whoever did kill him did a service to humanity."

"Please be careful what you say, Mr. Morgan. I am not your attorney and who knows what could be compelled at some later date."

Emily asked Blaus to reconsider allowing Justin to share his name. She noted that Justin didn't need Blaus's permission, that he could go ahead and change his name if he wanted. So let him, Blaus said. But Emily knew Justin wouldn't do it without Blaus's blessing.

"'Since he could do it anyway,' Emily reasoned, 'why not just tell him you want him to change it? Why not do a good deed, make him feel like you are actually acting like a father?'"

He said no. That's when she offered him money.

"'Name your price,'" she said.

Emily said Blaus laughed at her.

"'Since when do you have any money?'" he asked.

"'I do,'" she insisted.

"'Not enough to interest me,'" he said.

Then Blaus started looking Emily up and down.

"'You're still an attractive woman,'" he said, "'considering your age. I'm obviously through here. Maybe we could make another arrangement in exchange for my being nice to the poor, dear boy. We could be a real family again.'"

Blaus's comments, she said, dripped with sarcasm, throwing her into a fit of rage. She said it was of a wholly different nature than any hatred she'd previously experienced toward anyone, even Blaus when he was at his worst, forcing her to court and denying paternity of Justin. The sexual proposition was one thing; that annoyed her, but didn't surprise her. But to mock what he'd done to Justin and her, to blithely talk about being a real family *again* when they of course had never been a family. Blaus was the one who'd all along denied Justin any semblance of belonging. The man was the Devil. After he spoke the words "a real family again," she said, she pulled a knife out of her purse, stood up, and held it like a dagger in her right hand, lifted to shoulder height. Blaus looked scared. He jumped off the couch and ran down the hallway into the bedroom. She followed. He moved to the farthest part of the room, so that the bed was between them. She remembered seeing open suitcases on the bed and shirts stacked on the dresser. That confirmed for her that he wasn't lying about the affair with Meredith and being thrown out of the apartment.

"They stood like that for a few seconds, and then Blaus appeared to regain his composure. He came around the bed and approached Emily. He said, 'Come on, now, you aren't going to do anything with that knife. I know you. Who are you kidding? You literally couldn't hurt a fly. Come on, give me the knife.' He was close now. A foot away. She said she smelled his breath. That's when she said she stabbed him. As he moaned after the first blow, she said she stabbed him again."

Scott was surprised at how plausible the scenario sounded. "Did she say where she stabbed Blaus and how many times?"

"She was vague on that point," Prining said. "She said she was in such a state of fury, unlike anything she'd experienced, she just didn't know." Scott tried to remember which details the police had released to the media. Did they reveal the number and locations of the stabbings? He was pretty certain they'd said only that Blaus died from multiple stab wounds.

"Where did she get the knife that she pulled from her handbag?" Scott asked.

"From a coworker. He said there had been a lot of muggings and such in the subway, and he worried about her safety. It was a pearl-handled, five-inch knife, she said. She said she always carried it in her purse." Scott didn't know anything about such a knife; Emily had never mentioned it to him.

"What did she say she did with the knife? I mean after."

"Wrapped it up in a towel she took from the bathroom and deposited it in a city garbage can about ten blocks from the apartment building."

"Never to be seen again."

"Presumably."

Prining believed the confession alone was strong, but not enough for the district attorney to feel completely comfortable. The cops were, he assumed, trying to corroborate her story. One way or another they were moving forward. It was too big a case, and they had a credible confession. Emily would be charged and arraigned. He hoped for a manslaughter charge, but second-degree murder was more likely.

"Will there be bail?"

"It would be an open question. I could make the case that Emily is not a flight risk, came in on her own volition, and has no prior criminal record. But the thing is, Emily told me not to ask for bail. She doesn't want it. She'll stay in jail."

"That's crazy."

"This is not a woman thinking straight on many fronts," the lawyer said.

Scott asked him to serve as Emily's lawyer for the duration, to drop Justin, since Justin no longer seemed in immediate danger of arrest. He told Prining to suggest another lawyer for Justin. Scott would pay for both. Prining said he'd get Justin and Emily to consent to that arrangement.

"When you speak to Emily about continuing to represent her, tell her I'd like to continue to get updates from you."

"If she agrees, certainly."

Prining was good to his word about keeping Scott informed.

"There's some news," he said in a deadpan update a day later. "It will be all over the place in a few minutes. We received early word. Emily's been charged with first-degree murder. The arraignment is tomorrow morning."

"Oh my God. On the confession alone?"

"No, there's something else, which helps substantiate her story. Video from the security camera hung on the building next door, the one north on Seventh Avenue from where Sarah and Ed lived. It shows Emily walking by in the direction of the Blaus building at about 4:15 p.m."

"What would Emily be doing in the building next door?"

"Not inside. They have a camera trained on the entrance. It extends a few feet to the sidewalk in front."

"I imagine that means they don't have Justin, or Sarah, or Meredith, or me, for that matter, walking past that camera." Scott knew there were no closed circuit cameras in Sarah's apartment building. Something he urged her more than once to complain to the building's management about.

"I wouldn't know," the lawyer replied. "I don't speculate, there's no point in it for an attorney, but since you are all presumed suspects, I believe if any of you were captured on video during the relevant time period the police would have made you aware."

Scott wondered about Sarah. Could it be she really hadn't gotten back to the apartment until the time she originally told the police? Even though she had left the office nearly ninety minutes earlier than she claimed? Could she really have meandered home on foot, in line with the story the two of them discussed, killing time to make sure Blaus was out of the apartment before she arrived? That couldn't be right. At the restaurant he had come up with the best alibi he could think of, and Sarah had played along. Right? Of course that was right. The story of walking home and stopping in a store without buying anything was concocted. His idea. An attempt to mitigate the lie about when she left work that Sarah had told the police. It wasn't a true story, was it? Was he losing his mind? Everything had been fuzzy since he'd been told of Emily's confession. He thought again about the talk he had had with Sarah after the police discovered she had lied about when she left the office the day of the murder. Sarah wasn't at all focused. Was there a chance she meant to tell him she *had* in fact walked home after work? No, that didn't make sense.

"What will Emily plead?"

The normally stoic attorney sighed. "Emily is not an easy client. She's already confessed. She doesn't seem much interested in her fate. I told her it would still be best to plead not guilty, a sign to the prosecutors they still have work to do. It affords me some room and leverage to negotiate."

"Could you get it down to manslaughter?"

"I will not guess at outcomes. A reduced charge to manslaughter, though, would be extraordinary. Second-degree murder is much more likely. Her own confession is in line with second. She clearly did not go to the apartment with the intent of murdering Ed Blaus, and premeditation is essentially what separates first and second. No doubt charging her with first degree sets out their starting point. But this is all difficult step-by-step terrain, and it is wiser not to get ahead of ourselves. Both for you and me."

– 45 –

Scott didn't want anything to eat. He popped a Nespresso capsule into the coffee maker. He thought of the day, ten years earlier, when he had bought it for Meredith's birthday. Meredith. Where was she this morning? What was she doing? Amazing that after all the years together, she slipped out of his consciousness for days at a time. In the early, heady days with Emily, he compared her favorably with Meredith, fantasized about what life would have been like if he'd met Emily when they were both young. In all likelihood she never would have met Ed Blaus. Emily and Scott would have rubbed off on each other, bringing out their respective bests. They would have had more than one child. Maybe he wouldn't have chosen the career he did, the climbing, the stress, the outsize financial reward in return for what? What was that old country song his father used to play on Sunday mornings when he took a few hours out of his week to relax? Why did his father sit in a Brooklyn apartment and listen to country music? That didn't fit. Who knows? The lyrics Scott remembered were about a tough coal miner who owed his soul to the company store. Scott had a lot more money, but wasn't his story the same? He was no coal miner, of course, but he had let himself become just as trapped. He had molded himself to fit the job. If he'd met Emily earlier, it could have been different. They would have worked it out. And Emily would have stayed lighthearted with him. Undamaged by Blaus, she could have been whoever she wanted to be. Meredith. Where was Meredith? Did Meredith see what she had unleashed because of her affair with Ed Blaus? Did she understand at all the damage she'd done?

Scott knew it was too easy to blame Emily's downfall on Meredith. His wife of thirty years had no knowledge of DARK DAY and the damnable request Scott had made of that group. His framing Justin had essentially destroyed his mother. But Scott never imagined Emily would take this further step and confess to murdering Ed. He had no right to talk about Meredith causing damage. His actions, and his alone, had led directly to Emily sitting in a jail cell.

Scott held his coffee mug as he paced back and forth in his den. He knew the lines, crevices, and swirls in the polished wood floor well enough, but head down, he studied them again. Emily's arraignment was about to start. He dearly wished to be there, to sit in the courtroom and have her turn her placid, ethereal face toward him for support. He would nod gravely, indicating nothing more than he was there, that he would always be there, even when he had nothing to offer except his presence. But it was impossible to be in that courtroom. No one knew about their relationship, and he was intent on keeping it that way. He thought for a moment that perhaps his presence wouldn't be that out of bounds, since he was central to the case. But he quickly realized it would be impossible. The reporters would come up with a storyline to involve him: that he was there to see justice done or to see his family name cleared. Something that would position him in opposition to Emily, that would say or at least imply he was happy she was in the dock, that she would get what was coming to her after all she had put his family through by casting suspicion on them. How could he bear to sit in the courtroom in any case? Looking at Emily and knowing he'd caused her tragedy.

Just hours after the hearing was scheduled to begin, attorney Prining was on the phone. "No bail. We didn't ask. Our plea of not guilty was entered," he said.

"I'd like to visit Emily. But I don't want it to become fodder for the media," Scott said. "Uh, you see, no one understands our relationship, which is best for all involved. Is there something you can do?"

"I can get you on a visitor list, but it is technically a public document. Not that anyone would know unless one of the guards was the type who wanted to leak it to the press."

"I'll take the chance," Scott said.

The following day, Scott sat nervously at the divider that separated inmates from visitors. He saw Emily turn the corner and walk toward him, the familiar sad smile spreading across her face. Her hair was grayer, and she looked thinner.

"How are you?" Scott asked.

Emily shrugged and indicated her surroundings. The visitor center was loud. At the next station, a grandmother tried to corral two squirming youngsters while simultaneously shouting in conversation with her prisoner daughter across the partition. "They're fine, they're fine," the grandmother screamed in response to the mother's complaint about how the little girl was dressed.

"It's like this all the time," Emily said evenly. "Noise even at night. It's so hard to sleep. Otherwise, less terrible than I expected."

"Has Justin been to see you?"

Emily nodded. Her hands were folded primly on her lap. "I told him not to come, but he does. I'd rather he not see me in here."

"It's good," Scott said. "You need to see him, to see people as much as possible."

Emily was silent.

"You didn't have to confess," Scott said. "They hadn't arrested Justin."

Emily lowered her voice, which already was just above a whisper. "I confessed because I killed Ed," she said. Scott wondered if Emily thought they were being secretly recorded. Something about his expression, combining skepticism with pain, seemed to spur her on. "The possibility of Justin's arrest just hung there. 'Limbo,' that's the word. Ever since that roommate came forward with the lie about Justin admitting he killed his father. I couldn't live with it. You saw that. Limbo. Maybe forever, or maybe one day he'd be taken away. It was just impossible. I am breathing a lot better now."

He asked Emily about the day of the murder. "Still playing at being the detective, I see. Like the day we met when you suddenly showed up on my street. No need any more. This case is closed."

Scott asked whether Blaus's suitcases had been open when he fled into the bedroom and she followed. Prining had said that was part of Emily's confession, but he wanted to hear it from her. "At least one was," she said. "It was open on the bed. Maybe two? Probably two. Obviously, I wasn't concentrating on that, but when I first came in, he stood on the other side of the bed, putting it between us. The suitcases stood out to me for a moment. They were separating us."

Any lingering confusion in Scott's mind about whether Emily actually killed Ed Blaus disappeared. Delmore Kerbich had already been questioning Sarah when Scott got to the apartment the day of the murder. Kerbich, he found out later from Josie Horvitz, who'd obtained a transcript of the interview, had asked Sarah if the suitcases were closed and lined up against the wall outside the bedroom when she returned to the apartment. Scott saw them standing that way. Sarah said they were in that spot and that she hadn't touched them. No way Kerbich had missed the discrepancy between that and what Emily had said in her confession about open suitcases on the bed. Unless he surmised that Emily had killed Blaus and then decided to finish his packing. Absurd. Scott figured Kerbich decided not to let the contradiction get in the way of an arrest in a case that put the whole department under the gun. Blaus's murder was now more than a year old. Kerbich had a confession. He had video of Emily at the scene at the right time. He had a woman who he must have sensed was more than prepared to take the fall.

"Do you want to tell me what really happened that day when you went to see Blaus?"

"You can read my confession," she said evenly. "It's all there."

"Emily, come on."

"I mean it."

"I believe your confession is accurate up to a point," Scott said. "You went there to try to get Blaus to change his mind about Justin changing his name. He refused and said revolting things to you. At some juncture, you were in a position to see him packing, to see the still-open suitcases. When you realized you couldn't convince him to do what you wanted, you left. Blaus was very much alive."

Emily didn't respond.

Scott switched gears. "Does Kerbich have more questions for you?" he asked.

"No. I think I am done with Delmore. When I came in that day to the police station, he asked me to call him that." She laughed and touched her hair with her right hand. "I guess when you are confessing a murder to someone, you can be on a first-name basis."

Scott sighed. "I hate so much seeing you in this place."

"It doesn't matter," Emily said, her tone indicating a desire to end the visit. "Justin has his life ahead of him. I've had mine."

Yes, Justin had the bulk of his life ahead of him. So did Sarah. Even so, Scott wanted to protest. But he kept his mouth shut. He had no right to say a word. Scott was the one who had created the circumstances that put Emily in this spot. He knew that all too well. He imagined it would stay with him forever. He pressed his hand against the hard plastic separator. Emily did the same.

"Keep an eye on Justin, will you?" she said.

Scott nodded.

– 46 –

Brian Prining proved to be a good attorney, though, as he readily acknowledged, he was no miracle worker. After intense negotiations, Prining and the district attorney agreed Emily would enter a guilty plea to one count of second-degree murder. The prosecutor's office would ask for the minimum sentence of fifteen years in prison, based on her prior clean record. With good behavior, Emily might make it out in a decade, though the notoriety of the crime lessened the possibility she'd be sprung at the first parole board hearing. "People do forget a lot in ten years," Prining said, "but I'm not sure this one will fade quickly."

"How did Emily take the news?" Scott asked.

"Indifferently. Like everything else. I think she said thank you."

"Where will they send her?"

"Bedford Hills. It's the largest women's prison in the state."

Scott did a quick calculation on Google Maps on his phone. Bedford Hills was about a thirty-minute drive from his house. When he had tried to visit Emily a second time before sentencing, she'd told him not to come. She sent a message through Prining. It was nothing personal, but Emily was adapting to her new world, and intrusions from her past hindered that effort. "This is a true goodbye. I will always remember you fondly."

He winced at the word "fondly." Such a weak word. Like something out of a nineteenth-century novel. And yet he knew deep down he didn't deserve even that, given the major role he had played in putting her behind bars and the terrible secret he had withheld from her. At the final court hearing, the fifteen-year sentence for Emily Skilbahl was officially intoned by the judge, and she was led by a female guard from the courtroom, in her orange prison one-piece, hands cuffed behind her. There were no photos from inside the court. Scott saw artists' renderings online. Emily looked so fragile at the defendant's table. In support of his mother's character, Justin Skilbahl delivered a letter that one of the newspapers excerpted. Scott was impressed. "No finer person walks the earth," Justin wrote. "No one deserves less to be behind bars." Colleagues and friends of Emily chimed in with other testaments to her sterling character, charitable nature, and good-heartedness. News reports took note that no victim impact statements were filed with the court and no one rose when offered the chance to try to influence the judge's sentence by decrying the personal loss brought on by the death of Ed Blaus. There were his writer friends. Certainly, some people were positively influenced by Blaus's debut novel. Maybe some of his aspiring writer students benefited from his half-hearted pedagogy. But in court, when it came time to speak up for Ed Blaus, there was only silence. Fitting, Scott thought, very fitting. Then he wondered whether anyone beyond his daughter would feel compelled to put in a good word for him if ever he wound up in a similar circumstance. His parents and his brother were dead. Friendships were superficial or had lapsed. His wife had cheated on him and was estranged. He could imagine the firm's chairman standing in court to say Scott was a smart, calculating operator always ready to wholeheartedly pursue the interests of his clients. Meaning it, of course, as the highest compliment he could pay.

— 47 —

A few weeks after Emily was sentenced, Scott's heart raced when he saw Detective Delmore Kerbich's name come up as his phone buzzed a few minutes after 8:00 a.m. What? Everything was over. Guilt for the murder of Ed Blaus was established in a court of law. Emily Skilbahl was serving her time. What could this be about?

"You probably didn't expect to hear from me again," Kerbich said.

"Social call?" Scott tried to sound relaxed. "A bit early in the morning for that."

"Not really. We cracked the murder of Mickey Genz. Have the killer in custody. Thought you would want to know about it."

Relief coursed through Scott's body. His legs sagged, and he brought them back up straight. He thought of what he'd read of the great Russian writer Fyodor Dostoevsky, placed before a firing squad, prepared to die, and then reprieved at the last possible moment. Well, this wasn't that. But still.

"I thought if you were free, we could discuss it in person," Kerbich said.

Scott's return to work was still two weeks away. He agreed, and Kerbich suggested an Irish pub a few blocks from the precinct house. "A little early for that, too, isn't it?" Scott asked. "Very funny," the detective said. "They serve good coffee there. Little known fact, except among us cops."

No one else was appreciating the fine coffee at McMurphy's at 10:30 a.m. when Scott entered the bar and found Kerbich nursing a mug at a booth on its far side. The detective convinced Scott to try a cup and Scott acknowledged the coffee's quality.

"So, it seems Mickey Genz was heavily into the bookies," Kerbich said. "Off and on for years, but this latest and last hole he dug was the deepest. What you paid him didn't nearly cover it. Anyway, when Genz didn't come up with what was needed, they sent a leg breaker. If you remember, we did find him with two shattered knees. But it seems the beatdown went further than it should have, and it killed him."

Scott nodded solemnly. "That also explains, I guess, the pretty poor attempt to blackmail me. He was desperate. I might have been his last chance." Scott wondered how he would have reacted if Mickey Genz had been honest with him and described the fix he was in. Maybe not $200,000 worth, as Mickey demanded, but something. For old time's sake? A tribute to some not-believed-in deity for Scott getting out of the old neighborhood, while Mickey Genz never did? A payment to assure good karma? Scott wanted to think he would have been generous if Genz had opened up to him, but he wasn't certain. He liked nothing about the man.

It was as if Kerbich read Scott's thoughts. "I know a few guys like Genz," he said. "Guys I grew up with in Queens. The world changes, but they rarely venture beyond the twenty square blocks from where they were born."

"Does it go higher up than the guy who actually killed Mickey?"

"For sure it was on orders from someone. But the killer's not talking. He'll do his time."

Both men sipped their coffees. "I was looking back at my notes on the Blaus case," Kerbich said. "I got hung up on the thing that I thought was the strangest aspect. Unusual timing." He waited for a response from Scott. None was forthcoming, so the detective continued. "When that roommate of Justin Skilbahl came in to say Justin had confessed the murder to him. So many months after it supposedly happened."

Scott felt he had to say something. "A late attack of conscience?"

"Yeah, he said it was something like that. That his first instinct was to not believe Justin, but when the investigation dragged on without resolution, he felt he had an obligation to come forward."

"I've read stories where someone, not even under suspicion, walks into police headquarters twenty-five years after a crime and confesses to it. Whether or not he was actually guilty."

"Exactly, you read stories. That's what they mostly are, stories."

"It doesn't happen in real life?"

"Not often. People tend to keep their secrets."

Kerbich took another sip of coffee.

"The timing," he continued. "So curious. He came in with his story about Justin soon after we discovered your daughter lied to us about what time she left the office the day of the murder. Which made her, I am sure you realized, the number one suspect. Then, all of a sudden, we have this Justin Skilbahl angle, which we needed to follow up. But it didn't get us anywhere. There was nothing to back up the roommate's story."

"Coincidences do happen," Scott said.

"They do," Kerbich replied. "This one worked out pretty well in your daughter's favor. As did the confession that followed. Is there anything you want to add to my store of knowledge?"

"No," Scott said firmly.

They sat in silence for a time. Then Scott said he needed to get going; he had an appointment. He thanked Kerbich for the coffee.

"Are you back at work?"

"Not yet. Soon."

"Tell me again what consultants do." Kerbich smiled.

"Well, there's a host of things," Scott said, settling back onto the booth bench. "Advising companies about how to reduce costs, or doing research for them when they are considering going into a new line of business, or deciding whether to keep an existing one, or whether to buy another company or be bought themselves. Then there's helping in a crisis. There are a lot of things in between."

"I bet you are particularly good at the things in between."

"I'm not sure you meant that as a compliment, but I'll take it that way."

Kerbich raised his coffee mug as Scott stood to leave. "Here's to your daughter finding better boyfriends in the future."

"Amen to that," Scott said.

− 48 −

Scott and Sarah picked up dinner at a Chinese restaurant, the same one they'd ordered from since Sarah was a child. When she was growing up, Sunday evening meant Chinese food for the Morgans, and young Sarah was always pleased when that came around. On this day, she was quiet. She had been since Scott picked her up at the train station.

"How is your mother?" Scott asked once they were back at the house and seated at the kitchen table, disposable cartons of food and paper plates arrayed around them. When Sarah was younger, Meredith would insist that when Scott was home in time—not that often—they eat dinner in the dining room. After all, she'd say, why have a dining table if you never use it? Scott remembered how the three-person family felt too small for the long table in the large room. That scene always told him they should have had more children. Meredith always said the three of them were enough. They had a healthy child. They didn't need more. He preferred eating at the round table surrounded by four stiff-backed chairs in the kitchen.

"Oh, she's okay," Sarah said softly, using chopsticks to push around the moo shoo pork on her plate. "She's a survivor. That's what she says anyway. Once I agreed to speak with her again, we had weekly calls for a while, met for dinner once, which was really awkward. But for the past few months, it's been a call maybe once every few weeks. Some texting in between."

"She's probably busy setting up her new life," Scott said neutrally. After Emily Skilbahl's guilty plea had settled the murder investigation and lifted the cloud of suspicion that hung over each of the Morgans, Scott decided it was time to close out the gaping issue he hadn't had the desire to tackle while the Blaus murder file was open. Lawyers for Scott and Meredith quickly came to a divorce agreement. Scott's lawyer thought Scott was being overly generous, given the publicly humiliating circumstances in which their long marriage had come crashing down. Scott disagreed. They'd been married, though not always happily, for more than thirty years. Both were closing in on sixty. "I'm not interested in scorched earth," Scott told his attorney. "Enough damage has been done." Once she had money from divided savings in hand, with alimony to continue for many years, Meredith told Sarah she was moving to Los Angeles. She'd reconnected with a close college friend in California whose husband had recently died. The friend had sold her house, and she and Meredith were going to rent a condo together. Meredith said she needed a fresh start.

They ate in silence for a few minutes. "You don't seem very hungry," Scott observed.

"Dad, can we talk? I mean really talk?"

Scott laid down his chopsticks. "Of course. Do you want to go sit in the living room?"

"No, this is fine."

"Okay. Shoot."

"Through everything, you never asked me. Not once."

"Asked you what?" Scott said. Even as he uttered the words, he understood how foolish they sounded. Yes, he'd avoided the question. The careful, always-looking-out-for-danger part of him hadn't wanted the words said out loud. Who really knew who would hear them? But it had been more than Scott's ever-present radar for self-protection that kept him from asking the question. He hadn't asked because he didn't want to know. Didn't want the confirmation that would eradicate the scintilla of doubt he'd managed to nourish. Why ask? What father would want to ever hear the awful answer? Now he knew he had to listen.

Sarah pushed the chair back from the table. She stood behind it. She looked toward her father but not into his face. Instead, she seemed focused on a spot on the wall a couple feet above his head. There sat a drawing of an old-fashioned bicycle in bright colors, rendered somewhat abstractly. Sarah was with her mother when Meredith had bought it at a crafts fair.

"So, even though you never asked, I need to tell you. To tell someone."

"Go ahead," Scott said firmly. "Tell me. Give me all the details. But tell it this once and never speak of it again to anyone. Ever."

Sarah kept looking at the wavy bicycle. "I left work a few minutes after all the others. It was very much a get-out-at-five group. I took the subway down to the apartment..."

"And yet you weren't seen on the video camera from the building next door. But Emily, Emily Skilbahl, she was caught by that camera."

"The subway stop where I get off is below the building, south by a couple blocks on Eighth Avenue. The building with the camera is just north. That's the direction she must have come from. Also, I think you know, my building had a side entrance. You need a key, so only tenants went in and out that way. Visitors had to come through the front door on Seventh Avenue."

But the building just north couldn't have been the only one in the neighborhood with security cameras. Wouldn't the police have checked for security video from points south of the building too, the direction from which Sarah had walked? Maybe she was lost in rush-hour sidewalk crowds. Maybe there weren't as many security cameras as he imagined. Maybe somewhere video of Sarah returning around 5:35 p.m. on the day of the murder had existed, but was wiped clean before the police went looking for it. Maybe the police simply hadn't looked hard enough.

"I did really think Ed would be gone by the time I got there." Sarah took her hands off the chair back and started pacing the kitchen. Scott sat still, waiting for her to continue. "Oh, I don't know. I have gone over this in my head so many times, I don't even know anymore what I actually thought at the time. Ed was always late. For everything. One of his many narcissistic qualities, I guess. Whatever I was thinking, I opened the front door, and he was still there."

"What did he say?"

"Something stupid, like 'Fancy meeting you here.' I said, 'Why are you still here?' I hadn't seen him since the day I told him he had to leave. Then he started in. It was often like that in our relationship. He assumed he was the teacher and I was the hopeless student."

Scott wanted to interject a defense of Sarah, but there was no point in piling on the dead man. *Let her talk,* he told himself. *Just let her talk.*

"'None of this should be necessary,' he said. He pointed to the suitcases, which were lined up outside our bedroom door. It was all because I was such a shallow, affluent, spoiled brat, he said. 'What difference does it make if your mother and I had sex? You know I don't care for her. I care for you.'"

"Where were you during this?"

"In the kitchen. I wanted the harangue to end. So I opened the refrigerator. I don't know why, exactly. To distract things. To stop the tirade. I took out a bottle of Perrier. I took a glass out of the dish drainer. He said he was going back into the bedroom to make sure he hadn't left anything behind. He told me to join him there because he wasn't finished with me.

"That line I remember exactly. Those words. He hadn't said anything quite like that before. It sounded ominous. He was always so superior. He gave orders. 'I'm not finished with you.' Like he was disgusted with such a terrible pupil. My hand was shaking a little. I took another swallow of water. I put down the glass. I picked up one of the steak knives that were also in the dish drainer. Where I'd gotten the glass. They came to my attention, I think, right after he said he wasn't finished with me. Then he went into the bedroom, leaving me there. The knives seemed like they were staring at me. I put one in my shoulder purse. Then I walked into the bedroom.

"He was standing by the bed, looking angry. He clearly wasn't checking to see if any of his stuff was still lying around. He got vulgar . . . " Sarah stopped talking.

Scott looked down at his shoes. "Go ahead, Sarah, tell me what happened. It's okay. It's better if you get it all out, this one time."

"He called me a stupid bitch, a rich cow. A hopeless wannabe writer with no talent. He said the only thing I was good for was . . . you know, in bed. He grabbed me by the shoulders. I tried to push him away. But he was strong. He was enraged. He tried to push me down onto the bed. I was able to hold my own for a moment or two. The backs of my legs were against the bed, but I didn't fall over. He kept trying to get me onto the bed. I freed my right hand and poked him in the eye. He let go of me and cried out and put his hand over his eye. Then he was back at me. He slapped me, hard in the face. I almost fell over onto the bed then, but I didn't. He grabbed me. I kneed him in the groin and he backed up a few steps. Had to catch his breath. Cursed at me. Told me what he was about to do to me. That I had it coming. That's when I saw my purse, which landed on the bed during the scuffle. I pulled out the knife. He came forward anyway, arms outstretched to grab me again. I stabbed him in the chest. My first thought was surprise that the knife went into him. You know, I thought it might not be sharp enough. He gagged and staggered backward. But he didn't fall, so I stabbed him again, closer to the neck this time. I wasn't really aiming; it's just where my hand landed. There might have been one more. I'm not really sure. He made a gurgling noise. That was an awful sound, deep and throaty in a way that didn't seem human, like some wounded creature in the woods. Then he fell backwards."

Scott's heart thumped in his chest. *The bastard*, he thought. Blaus had come on to Emily when she'd pleaded with him about Justin. He tried to trade a last name for sex. Scott believed that part of Emily's confession was true. There couldn't have been much time between that incident and Sarah's arrival. Then he assaults Sarah.

Scott looked at his daughter. He stood and walked the few steps to her. He wrapped his arms around her. She put her head against his chest and began to cry heavily, her upper body heaving.

"It's all right, Sarah," Scott said softly. "You're safe now."

Sarah broke the embrace and sat back down. The crying quieted. "You never told that story to the police," Scott said. "What you did was self-defense. You had a right to keep him from hurting you."

"The first few minutes I was in shock. I just stood there, trembling. I did nothing at all. I knew I should get help. I think Ed was still alive, at least for a short while after he fell, though there was a lot of blood from the stab wound near the neck. He made that horrible gurgling sound a couple more times, then he was quiet. When I came out of whatever trance I was in, I decided I couldn't tell what happened. That I wouldn't be believed."

"But . . ."

Sarah held up her hand. "I didn't say it was the right decision. It was the decision I made. I weighed things. As best I could, standing over a dead man in the bedroom. I thought I wouldn't be believed. I thought when it all came out, I'd be dragged through the mud, forever to be known as the girl who claimed rape. But in the end, there was no rape, and I was the one still alive. They'd say, 'Oh sure, she says she was attacked by the same man she'd lived with.' My word against his silence. Dead silence. 'He's a well-known writer who could no longer defend himself'—that's what I figured people would think. No arrests for sexual assault. No public accusations. That stacked up against my word. Only my word. If I told the true story, I thought I'd still be arrested, go to trial, and even if I was acquitted in the end, the incident, those minutes, would consume the rest of my life."

"So instead?"

"So instead I walked into the kitchen, washed the knife thoroughly and dried it with a paper towel. I put it in the silverware drawer. I left the two other knives in the dish drainer. I inspected my clothes as closely as I could. I took off my blouse and my skirt and examined every inch. Amazingly, there was no blood. None that I could see anyway. I guess Ed backed away from me with the first stab and then afterwards he fell backwards, so no blood got on me. Just to be safe, I threw the clothes into the garbage bag in the kitchen, along with the paper towel I used on the knife. I changed into another work outfit and threw the garbage bag down the chute in the hall, into the compactor. I washed my hands. I looked them over back and front. Checked my wrists. No traces of blood."

Scott thought about Delmore Kerbich. When the police arrived on the scene, should they have made Sarah change her clothes, bag what she was wearing and test it for blood spatter, maybe even spots too tiny for the eye to see? How about testing the knives? It wouldn't have mattered if Sarah had gotten all the blood off the knife she used. The clothes would have been clean, since she had changed. They could have asked her colleagues what she had worn to work that day. It would have been a big problem if someone remembered her in a different outfit from the one she was wearing when she spoke to Kerbich and his NYPD pals.

"The trash," Scott said hesitantly. "Did you think about the police checking it?"

"I knew the compactor would be emptied the next morning. Twice a week. Ed always complained about the noise. 'Why did they have to come so early?'"

Still, Scott thought, the police could have checked that very evening. But they didn't. By the next day, it probably would have been impossible.

"Okay," he said. "How about the knife? Did the police ever check the knives in the drawer?"

"During one of my police interviews, Delmore said Ed's stab wounds could have come from one of the knives in our kitchen drawer. Just said it like that, expecting a response. I didn't say anything. It scared me, but later on, because they never added to that statement, never mentioned it again, I figured it couldn't be anything definitive."

Scott nodded and asked her to continue.

"Then, I waited. I remembered that I was the last one out of the office, so if I said I left much later than I did, who would know? If I said I got home around seven, rather than just after 5:30, it gave me a better story. I tried not to touch anything while I waited. I didn't even sit down. I just stood near the front door. Once the clock hit seven, I called you."

"But you didn't remember about the swipe cards and your company ID, which would say exactly when you really did leave the office."

"I didn't know they were tracked to individuals. Stupid, I guess, looking back, not to have known that. When the police found out about that, I thought that was the end. I thought they had me."

Me too, Scott thought, *me too*. That was the moment Scott was glad he'd gone to DARK DAY, and DARK DAY came through with Justin's supposed confession to his friend. Yes, it meant trying to frame an innocent young man. Yes, it meant watching the woman he cared for sacrifice herself and go to prison. These were terrible, terrible things that he had done. He told himself it was because he had to protect his family. To make sure it ended differently than when he'd failed his brother and his parents. He clung to that idea, like fingers grasping at the edge of a drifting life raft. But if he had known there was a self-defense option? Would he have acted differently? Convinced Sarah to tell the police the truth? He didn't know. Sarah might have been found guilty anyway. Her life might have been ruined even if she wasn't charged with a crime. Now it was too late. He had done what he had done. What was lost was permanently lost.

"When Ms. Skilbahl confessed, I thought it was a dream, a gift from God really," Sarah said. "Utterly undeserved, of course, but a gift. It felt like I'd been holding my breath the whole time, especially once the police found out when I really left work. When she confessed, it was like I got permission to breathe again. To live. My life wasn't over. It was the most incredible feeling. I wondered why she would confess to something she didn't do. I figured it had something to do with her son and Ed, that her son was a suspect.

"You know, Ed never mentioned his son while we were together. I asked him once or twice about Justin, why he never saw him, never seemed to have anything to do with him. Ed said an accident isn't a son."

"The man was wretched," Scott said.

"After the confession, I got the new job and a new place to live, and it looked like everything was going my way," she said. Scott had overseen the sale of the apartment, with the proceeds going to Sarah. "I thought I must be a pretty awful person, extremely shallow, just like Ed always said, to be able to move on so easily. New job, new apartment, no longer under suspicion. The heavens had opened up for me, and I was so happy. I didn't think much about Ms. Skilbahl sitting behind bars. I didn't even think much about Ed, who was dead because of me. Whatever you think of him, or what he did to me, or what I think of him now, he did have his life taken away from him. By me. Still, in the days after the confession and the arrest, I was happy.

"But recently, now that it's all settled and Emily Skilbahl is off in prison and no one thinks or talks or writes about Ed anymore, now just when it should truly be over, now is exactly when it has become unbearable to me. I am obsessed. I can't think of anything else. The details of that afternoon in the apartment. Ed's dying sounds. And this poor woman withering away. Who had nothing to do with it. Once or twice, I wanted to arrange to visit her. I searched for where they have her. How crazy would that be?"

"Don't do that," Scott said softly. "I mean try to visit her. That would be a mistake."

Sarah nodded. "There's no one to talk with about this, of course. I can't talk to my therapist. I can't talk to any friends. I worry about taking too many pills when I'm unable to sleep. I think I'm slipping up at work, which would be really bad, since I'm still new, but I have such a hard time focusing. On anything."

Scott looked at Sarah. He wondered if he had really ever before seen his daughter, now this adult woman standing distraught before him. Truly seen her. Was he always too caught up in himself, in his work, so that Sarah became an abstraction? Before Blaus, he'd rarely seen or even spoken to Sarah outside the company of his wife. He was always the third wheel in the family dynamic. Sure, he knew her personality quirks and what sorts of food she liked, but as she had advanced into adulthood, how well did he actually know her? She'd killed a man who was in the act of sexually assaulting her. Once the deed was done, she didn't panic. Instead, she calculated the best way to proceed and stuck to the plan. She confided in no one. When she was caught in the lie about the time she left work, she didn't melt and confess to the police. It was exactly as Scott would have done: figure out the best path toward self-preservation, make it the one and only goal, and then execute. Truth had no role. Stay the course. Sarah was his daughter.

"I mean how much can a person live with and just go on? How much is too much to bear?"

"Listen to me," Scott said. Sarah looked directly at his face. He stared back unblinking. "This will get better. I promise you. I can't tell you when, but I can tell you it will. Anyone who did what you did, who was capable of saving herself and destroying what wanted to destroy you, that person will survive. I guarantee it."

"You make it sound so simple," she said.

He thought about all the harm he had caused in his life, to Freddie and his parents, in business, and then, most recently, to Justin and Emily Skilbahl. Still, here he was. He was breathing, he was talking. On most evenings, he did not dread the coming morning.

"Not easy, no. But true. Emily Skilbahl had her own reasons for confessing to the murder. She is her own person, an independent actor, and you have no responsibility for her. You have seen this through for so long, you need to stick to your plan. Don't falter. Go to work. Force yourself to concentrate. You can. You are strong. So strong. I see that now. I didn't before."

Scott could tell the last thing he had said pleased Sarah.

"I know this will sound crazy, but it won't later. I wish I knew when later will come, but I don't. After a time, you need to open yourself up to being with another person, a good man this time. Someone to share your life, though not this. This you've got to bury within yourself. You can't speak of it to anyone else. When you meet this man, this good man, you should start a family, because if I know one thing, I know that family is most important. The one I was born into was busted up when my brother died. The one you were born into is also busted up, but it still exists, it is real. You will wake up one day, look around and appreciate your own breathing, your arms and your legs and the walls of the room, everything that you still have. From that point, whenever it happens, you will be able to live, not erasing the past, no, not that, but living alongside it."

Scott was done talking. Sarah lowered her eyes from his face and focused on the hands intertwined in her lap. Scott looked there too, and saw her hands shaking.

–ABOUT THE AUTHOR–

Neal Lipschutz is a former deputy editor-in-chief of *The Wall Street Journal*. He also previously served as the *WSJ*'s standards editor as well as the top editor of Dow Jones Newswires. His short fiction has appeared in a number of publications. This is his first novel and the initial installment in a series of mysteries.

MORE TO READ AT TUCKERDSPRESS.COM

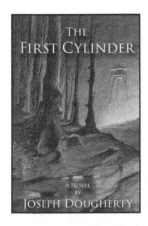

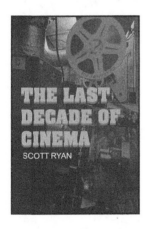